"Murray, a former bist, knows his history e- creating the past ne changing landscape or- ward so that reade ht Western where, ult

—*Rocky Mountain News* on *Gabriella*

"[Isabella's] old-time story, which is still somewhat appropriate for this day and age, has it all—an independent woman, a wealthy British sportsman and investor, a self-proclaimed protector of the Estes Park area, and more."

—*Western Horseman* on *In the Arms of the Sky*

"A poignant love story that will linger in the reader's mind long after the last page is read."

—*Roundup* magazine on *In the Arms of the Sky*

"Based on a real-life story, Murray makes his independent heroine and the man she loves come vividly alive."

—*Booklist* on *In the Arms of the Sky*

"Isabella Bird, an independent English woman of the nineteenth century, is fascinating. Earl Murray's fictional portrayal of the world traveler is enchanting. . . . A must-read for anyone interested in the strong women of the Victorian Age . . . The story doesn't end the way you would like it to; it simply ends the way that it did in the shadows of the Rocky Mountains in the height of the Victorian Age."

—*The Billings Gazette* on *In the Arms of the Sky*

"Murray incorporates period detail and native lore to create an engaging tale of an uncommon heroine. Bittersweet love and adventure combine in a winning way."

—*Greensboro News & Record* (North Carolina) on *In the Arms of the Sky*

GABRIELLA

Earl Murray

A TOM DOHERTY ASSOCIATES BOOK
NEW YORK

GABRIELLA

Maps by Victoria E. Murray

A Forge Book
Published by Tom Doherty Associates, LLC
175 Fifth Avenue
New York, NY 10010

www.tor.com

Forge® is a registered trademark of Tom Doherty Associates, LLC.

ISBN: 0-812-56546-0
Library of Congress Catalog Card Number: 99-21932

First edition: August 1999
First mass market edition: December 2000

Printed in the United States of America

0 9 8 7 6 5 4 3 2 1

Again, to my wonderful wife, Victoria, a lady
with true pioneer spirit.
And to all good dogs everywhere,
especially terriers, and most especially our
terriers, Katie and Pearl.
You are a pair of wonderful* little dogs.

(*Pearl is also known as No, No, Bad Dog,
but we love her anyway.)

ACKNOWLEDGMENTS

I am greatly indebted to the following for their able assistance in the completion of this work:

—Eleanor Gehres and staff, Western History Department, Denver Public Library, for assistance with Bent's Fort information.

—John Newman and his assistant, Pat Van Deventer, Archives, Morgan Library, Colorado State University, for background information on all facets of historical Colorado.

—Rheba Massey, local history librarian, Fort Collins Public Library, for allowing me access to her great map collection.

—Doug Kemp, Missouri Historical Society, St. Louis, for his assistance in researching early St. Louis.

—Nicholas Bennett, The Oregon Trail Foundation, for directions and insight into "behind the scenes" Oregon of 1846.

—Tom Doherty, my publisher and good friend, who has always had an avid interest in Oregon history.

—Stephanie Lane, my editor, whose fine direction helped me strengthen Gabriella's character.

—And my wife, Victoria, for keeping me on track with feminine feelings and frustrations.

GABRIELLA'S JOURNEY

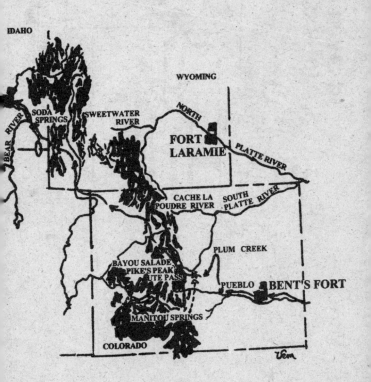

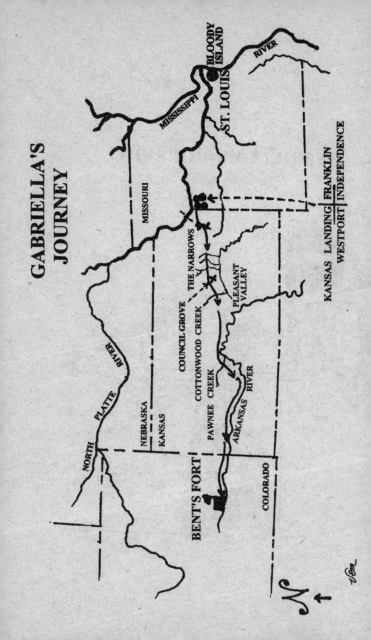

GABRIELLA

St. Louis

Gabriella's Journal

This morning I watched my fiancé kill a French nobleman.

It happened on Bloody Island, a large sandbar of willows and brush in the Mississippi River across from St. Louis, a place where gentlemen settle their differences by dueling with the weapons of their choice. It had been decided that pistols would be used, at a distance of thirty feet, with each man to be allowed one shot towards his adversary.

I held my silken hat down with a gloved hand against an early morning wind, wishing that I might be any place else in the world. Nearby, my fiancé, Sir Edward Albert Waterston-Garr III, second son of the Fifth Earl of Waterston, and late of Lancashire, England, had removed his topcoat and hat and was readying himself. He had bested many men before, fourteen at last count, and appeared to show no fear.

His adversary, a French-Canadian named LaBruneue, had arrived in St. Louis only that spring. He was no stranger to violence himself and it was said he had faced eight men, killing each one.

A large crowd had congregated on the main shore to await the outcome. Many were Mr. LaBruneue's associates but most were employed by Sir Edward, who had come to America a month earlier to plan a hunting expedition into the Rocky Mountains. I joined him from Lancashire just two weeks past, along with my aunt and uncle, Lady

Avis and Sir Walter Dodge, looking for adventure on my own behalf. But in my wildest dreams I never expected to witness the scene that played itself out before me.

Those present on the island had arrived by special invitation only. Duels of this sort are illegal, but deemed necessary by the upper class of St. Louis society in lieu of fighting in the streets or in the alleys along the levee. They are conducted for the satisfaction of both parties, one or both having been insulted during an exchange of conversation.

Present on behalf of both men were three surgeons, including my fiancé's personal physician, Dr. Noel Marking, a stout man of stern countenance who had attended to several of Sir Edward's dueling victims. The Frenchman had brought two of his own physicians, and also a frontiersman dressed in buckskins and a wide-brimmed hat.

The frontiersman stared at me intensely with unsettling dark eyes. He was lithe of figure and movement and, I would judge, nearly six feet tall. He stood out from the others, being much cleaner in appearance, and exuded an air of supreme confidence.

Standing near the frontiersman was a large Indian with roached hair and wolf-teeth earrings. He wore a breech-cloth and buckskin leggings, and a buckskin waistcoat adorned with horsehair and beadwork. I heard the frontiersman refer to him as Lamar, a name that seemed more suited to a tamer-looking man.

Overall, I found Mr. LaBruneue's men to be generally frightening in their dress and appearance. They had all lived in the mountains for many years and had taken on the habits of wild survivalists, being uneasy around civilization in general. I wished that I had remained back at the hotel with my aunt and uncle. But I had felt obligated to come; Edward had insisted that I attend and stand by him.

As he and Mr. LaBrueneue completed their preparations for the duel, I was asked by the gentleman in charge of the event, a circuit judge named Arlan Hathaway, if I didn't wish to reconsider my decision to be present.

"I shall remain at Sir Edward's side as long as he needs me," I told him, displaying more confidence than I felt. "I see it as my duty."

Also present was my fiancé's newly acquired slave, a small, middle-aged man known simply as Bom, said to be the best servant his previous master had ever known. He is a very articulate man with a keen sense of humor, but I know little else about him, as he has yet to speak with me and Edward says little about him. I did learn, however, that the man speaks fluent English, French, Spanish, and German, as well as his own native tongue.

Perhaps he considers it respectful to remain at a distance; I cannot say. But I could see, as we stood close together on Bloody Island, that he had witnessed duels before, and from his concerned expression, that he also worried for my fiancé's safety.

I realized that my heart was pounding as Sir Edward and the Frenchman awaited their firearms. Each was to receive a matched flintlock pistol made by the respected English arms dealer, Joseph Manton. The frontiersman stopped staring at me long enough to load Mr. LaBruneue's weapon, then check his own pistol and step back out of the way. He had come as Mr. LaBruneue's second, a protector of sorts, in case Sir Edward did not follow the prescribed instructions.

Assisting my fiancé was his eighteen-year-old nephew, Barton Strand, whom I watched with despair while he fumbled anxiously with the pistol. Finally, Edward took it from him and loaded it himself. He placed a second pistol in the young man's trembling hands.

"What is the matter with you, Barton?" he asked through pursed lips.

"I'm sorry, Uncle. This is difficult for me."

"Are you capable of proceeding as my second?"

Barton nodded feebly.

Edward gave him a little shove and said, "Then take your position and listen to the instructions."

I then stepped over to Edward. "Are you certain you can't talk Mr. LaBruneue out of this?"

"Why would I want to? It was he who insisted." He waved his hand at me. "Get back."

Judge Hathaway ordered the two men to exact a distance of thirty feet between them. His orders continued: "Upon my command, you may fire. If either of you takes aim or otherwise pursues to discharge his weapon before the appropriate time, you will be fired upon by the second of the opposing party. Is that understood?"

Sir Edward and Mr. LaBruneue nodded, as did the frontiersman and Barton Strand. I noticed Barton shaking uncontrollably and saw that Bom was biting his lip.

Sir Edward positioned himself sideways to the Frenchman, holding the pistol downward at his side.

"It's not too late to call this off, my good man," he said, "if you wish to spare your life."

"*Non, Monsieur!* Never!" Mr. LaBruneue replied. "A man does not call me a liar publicly and live to boast of it."

The judge said, "Gentlemen, cock your weapons."

Unable to watch, I turned and stared across to where St. Louis was bathed in early sunlight. The river sparkled and birdsong filled the air, and I wished that nothing but this chorus of nature could be heard.

Then came Judge Hathaway's gruff command:

"Fire!"

Two blasts sounded in unison. I turned to see Mr.

LaBruneue fall to the ground, writhing in agony, his hand on his throat. Edward was merely frowning, inspecting a neat round hole in the fold of his shirt sleeve.

The frontiersman and the Frenchman's physicians hurried to Mr. LaBruneue's side and inspected his wound. One of the surgeons stood and addressed Judge Hathaway.

"He is seriously injured, Your Honor, but can be saved."

"Very well," the judge said. "Mr. LaBruneue, are you satisfied?"

With the help of his attendants, the Frenchman rose to his feet and stood shakily. A long, scarlet stain trailed down the front of his starched white waistcoat. He spoke in a faint voice.

"I am satisfied."

Edward broke the crowd's silence. "Your Honor, I am not satisfied. I demand that Mr. LaBruneue and I have our pistols reloaded and take position ten feet apart."

There were gasps and murmurs. I heard the judge say, "You can't be serious."

Edward stood firm. "I am, Your Honor. This man insulted me deeply and now considers the matter closed. I do not."

I shook my head in disbelief and looked at Bom. He was no longer chewing his lip, but stood impassively, watching Mr. LaBruneue bleed down his front.

The frontiersman then stepped forward in defense of his friend. "Your Honor, this man is in no condition to fight again today."

The judge asked Sir Edward if he might give the Frenchman time to recover.

"That is not possible," Edward said. "We are scheduled to depart at first light."

"Why not consider the matter settled then?" the frontiersman asked. "Surely there can be no good cause to continue."

"Mr. LaBruneue can continue the fight now, to my satisfaction," Edward said, "or be forever branded a coward and scoundrel."

The Frenchman pushed away from his physicians and ordered that the pistols be reloaded. The frontiersman stared hard at Edward and I knew that had he been able to fight in Mr. LaBruneue's stead, he would have in a split second. But the Frenchman would not allow it, and the frontiersman couldn't approach Sir Edward, as the rules forbade a similar challenge made by another party against one of the duelists on the same day.

Sir Edward, knowing the frontiersman's feelings, smiled and said, "Perhaps you would like your chance soon."

"Perhaps," the frontiersman agreed. "But you haven't finished this morning's duel yet."

A funny expression appeared on Edward's face and I knew that he must be remembering his very first duel. According to my uncle, who had told me numerous stories about my fiancé, he had won the day only because his opponent had been too cocky. Instead of concentrating on the matter at hand, he had winked at one of his friends just as the command to fire had been given, and had taken a ball in the temple from Sir Edward.

I cannot speculate why Edward was so determined to finish the Frenchman off. Their weapons ready, he and the Frenchman faced off once again, this time so near to one another as to almost touch the outstretched barrels of their pistols. Mr. LaBruneue trembled, his eyes wide, his face lined with sweat. All of us watching could plainly see the river of blood that bubbled from the hole in his throat.

At the command, Sir Edward fired. The ball tore into

the Frenchman's right eye, splattering gore and bone fragments everywhere. The crowd gasped and he fell dead without even having lifted his pistol.

Edward flicked at small specks of blood and brain tissue on his waistcoat, then dabbed at them with a kerchief and allowed Bom to help him with his topcoat.

I stared at the fallen Frenchman and realized there had been no honor on Bloody Island. I could see no good reason for one man to kill another over mere words, a senseless conversation that had taken place the previous day in the Planters' Hotel, where we were all staying. During drinks before dinner Mr. LaBruneue had said to Edward that he suspected him to be more than just a hunter on holiday, and that maybe he should stay out of American affairs. Sir Edward had replied, "You are like a small dog whining. You should find a bitch to suckle."

Edward has never made a secret of his dissatisfaction with the flood of American emigrants into Oregon, depriving the established Hudson's Bay Company of trade territory. The region had been under joint ownership for some time and the settlers would soon be the majority of the population.

An argument with Mr. LaBruneue regarding the matter had ensued, resulting in Edward's defaming remark. The Frenchman had immediately called for restitution of his character and my fiancé had eagerly denied it, resulting in the Frenchman's challenge.

I had to ponder Edward's lack of judgment. We are, after all, in a foreign country and not well liked by much of the populace. St. Louis has become a mecca for travelers, and English tourists have become the norm, but local authorities here are tiring of the settlement of differences by the old standards. I knew then and certainly know now that nothing good can possibly come of this.

But it had been done and the frontiersman, along with

the Indian and the two surgeons, lifted Mr. LaBruneue from the ground and carried him to a boat. The judge followed closely behind. Across the way, I could see two women on the shore, now in tears, leaning against escorts who tried in vain to comfort them.

Before leaving, the frontiersman took one last, long look at me. Sir Edward hurried me ahead of him and asked me why I was dallying.

"Who is that man staring at me?" I asked him.

"Why does it matter?"

In the boat, I pressed the issue. "I want to know who the frontiersman is."

"Why must you concern yourself with him?" he snapped. "He's a mountain man named Quincannon, who was affiliated with LaBruneue. As you can readily see, he should have picked better company."

Gabriella's Journal

5 APRIL 1846, 2ND ENTRY

I know Sir Edward to be a man up for a challenge, and somewhat secretive in his manner. He carries two pistols under his belt at all times, along with a large dirk, which he keeps honed to a razor's edge. I realize that he's a hunter and sportsman, but he has a great many weapons at his disposal at all times, whether or not he's in the field.

I worried as we neared the levee from the island. Edward had pulled both pistols and was shouting for his men to take position facing Mr. LaBruneue's men, who were assembling and readying their arms. Bom and Barton Strand rowed and as our boat neared the landing, Edward's riflemen formed a semicircle, effectively keeping the mob from us. I awaited certain conflict, but then the frontiersman began to motion for the Frenchman's followers to disperse—and they soon did.

Barton Strand, looking sick with fear, said, "It could have been very bad, Uncle."

"But it wasn't, Barton, so get yourself together."

"Why are you so inconsiderate of our feelings?" I asked angrily.

"We have no time for feelings, Ella," he said to me. "When will you understand that?"

I turned my attention to the intense activity taking place not far away, on Laclede's Landing, where numerous steamboats and other rivercraft awaited the loading of goods and passengers. Among the craft was a large steamboat named the *White Bull*, newly built to Sir Edward's specifications for our journey upriver into the West. Burly men in head bandanas and soiled cottons loaded provisions as fast as they could, but not fast enough for me. I have never wanted to leave anywhere so badly.

It saddened me to feel that way, as the city offered many beautiful sites and had certainly held my interest. Upon my arrival downriver in New Orleans with my aunt and uncle, a month previous, I had never before witnessed so much activity. My life in Lancashire seemingly never changed, but since coming to America, nothing had remained the same. The steamboat trip upriver to St. Louis had been filled with fascinations and I learned much about America and its mix of cultures. But our stay had turned from a few days into a few weeks, as the *White Bull* had taken much longer than expected to build.

Edward had commissioned construction three months

earlier, but there had been several delays in the delivery of materials, causing problems with the workers. Had the boat been completed on time, perhaps this unfortunate duel would never have taken place.

Edward had insisted I accompany him on his hunt, as he wished me to paint portraits of him beside the big game he brought down. I decided that I would also endeavor to paint the native peoples who live on the plains and in the mountains. I had become familiar with George Catlin's works and his writings of life among the American Indians, arousing my curiosity. I had also looked into the work of other artists and was fortunate enough to accompany Sir Edward and a group of his friends to Murthly Castle in Scotland, as invited guests of Captain William Drumond Stewert, an adventurer who had accompanied fur traders into the wilds of the Rocky Mountains.

While the men and other women sat talking, I roamed the castle, viewing paintings of warriors in full battle regalia, or on horseback, hunting buffalo, all work by an artist named Alfred Jacob Miller, who had journeyed into the American West with Captain Stewert. What I viewed on those castle walls had hopelessly captured my imagination.

After the hunt, Edward and I plan to cross into Oregon and after a stay at Fort Vancouver, return to Lancashire, to be married and live in his castle. I had resisted his attempts, and those of my mother, to have us married before the journey. I have felt somewhat uncomfortable about the union of late and wanted the time to sort my feelings out. Edward was annoyed, but since we hadn't yet declared a wedding date, he agreed to wait.

At the landing, Bom threw a rope from the canoe to a worker who tied it to the dock. Sir Edward stepped out and hurried to the *White Bull*, roaring orders at the men, urging them to work faster. Bom assisted me onto the dock and escorted me, with Barton following, to a waiting carriage.

"Thank you, Bom," I said.

He bowed slightly, without looking me in the eyes. I told him that this would be a good time to begin to get to know one another, since I was to become Sir Edward's bride.

He simply bowed again and turned to greet Edward, who was hurrying to the carriage.

"I cannot come with you," Edward told me. "There is much left to do."

I was sorely disappointed, as he promised to take me to the opera. He told me he would return to the hotel in time for a late dinner.

"We will do a grand meal," he promised, "as this is our last evening in this fair city."

"Aunt Avis and Uncle Walter will be equally disappointed about the opera," I pointed out.

Edward shrugged. "It cannot be helped. When you get back to the hotel, make sure they're ready for departure early tomorrow. I want no more delays."

He abruptly turned and left, Bom right behind him. The driver started the horses in motion. The sleek black carriage had been custom-made to Sir Edward's specifications and brought from England. The doors were scrimshawed and flaked with gold, and the seats were of red velvet. It held four people comfortably and was doubly reinforced for travel over rough terrain. The heavy canvas top, now down, could withstand extreme weather variations, which we were certain to face on the plains.

As I passed along the cobblestoned streets, I tried to shake the vision of the duel from my mind. Beside me, Barton Strand continued to shake as badly as he had on Bloody Island.

"The morning's events are over now," I said. "We can look forward to our journey."

"Yes, the journey." He nodded to me blankly. "We can look forward to it."

I knew he was being facetious. Edward had taken his nephew along as a favor to his sister, Lady Clara Strand, who had married well and was looked upon with favor among her peers. Lady Clara believed her son had not been allowed the life a young man of stature should lead, even though her husband, well respected and from a family of lawyers, wanted Barton to follow in those footsteps. She had told Edward that she wished Barton to become well rounded and that he needed to experience other things besides libraries.

Though he had spoken little to me about it, I knew Edward was a trifle miffed at having to nursemaid his nephew. Barton had no outdoor skills whatsoever and the first time he had fired a rifle, he had fallen backwards. Luckily, Edward had been able to react quickly enough to catch the weapon. Barton had continually balked at firearms after that, so Edward deemed it his duty to make the young man learn, at all costs, what was required of a hunter and a gentleman.

As we rode through the streets, I felt deep concern for him. He was definitely at odds with his fate.

"I have no business on this journey," he told me. "I told Mother at the outset that the trip would do no good for anyone, but she has never listened to my wishes. This is going to be the worst experience of my life."

I stood at the entrance to the cathedral and listened to prayers said by LaBrueue's men, Catholic rites they had learned as children from Jesuit priests. The French nobleman already lay at the foot of the altar, dressed in his finest suit. Though the burial was still two days away, the family wanted him in the presence of the crucified Christ for as long as possible.

Though lost in the shock and sorrow of the occasion, I refused to give up on his goal of reaching Oregon on behalf of the American Fur Company. Owen James Quincannon, whose mother had never given up, even under the most dire of circumstances, would press forward ever harder. I would go on without my newly made friend, leading the once greatly anticipated expedition that would now be without its strongest partner.

I thought back on the morning, wondering at the strangely brutal behavior of the English nobleman. He had wanted LaBrueue dead, of that there could be no question. The reason why remains obscure. I must not linger on it, but put it behind me and move quickly or lose the jump on the numerous emigrant and trading parties that will leave the city for the West.

I had spent many long hours with LaBrueue, planning the journey and deciding on the best of all possible locations to establish our initial trading post. It was to be a large facility, located somewhere near present Fort Vancouver, where the emigrants would be rejoicing after their long ordeal. They would welcome an American to trade with, and not the hated Hudson's Bay Company.

LaBrueneue had worked for the company at Fort Vancouver but had defected in January, after John McLoughlin, the Chief Factor, had announced his departure. "He was a great man and the only good thing about the Company," LaBruneue had said. "When he decided to go, it was time for me, also."

François LaBruneue had come to St. Louis, bringing many Hudson's Bay defectors with him, hoping to sign on with a company of American traders. I once worked for Ramsey Crooks and the American Fur Company, formerly powerful and now, like the others, only a distant memory of the earlier days of glory. When Crooks left the trade, I quit the mountains, resigned to give up the only life I had ever known, until I met LaBruneue and learned of the possibilities in Oregon.

The Frenchman informed me that the settlers who first arrived there had started their own government, in a land initially held under joint ownership. Because of Hudson's Bay holdings, the British now claimed first rights. The Americans, by reason of total land usage, wanted full jurisdiction. Tensions were continuing to mount.

"There are many Americans already there and more going all the time," he told me. "They will need provisions. And there are still the Indians to trade with. We will do very well."

He had sold me on the idea immediately. After a meeting with old Ramsey Crooks, retired but still interested in profits, I knew we could count on backing for the venture.

Then Edward Garr entered the picture. I'm still puzzled over the incident that precipitated the duel. I was looking over a flatboat, deciding if it was fit for purchase and use in moving goods upriver to Kansas Landing, when LaBruneue arrived from the Planters' House and announced that he was to duel a British nobleman named Sir Edward Garr.

LaBruneue, who had always been an intense man, had fire in his eyes. He informed me that he knew Garr to be a spy for the British. When I asked if he accused the nobleman, he said, "No, it was Garr who provoked me, so much so that I couldn't let it pass."

"You should have let it pass," I said. "We haven't got time for this."

Of course there was no way to talk him out of the duel and the result was his death and the deep anger of all his men.

At the cathedral, I left them to pray and walked slowly down the steps. It was a beautiful afternoon and I couldn't believe all that had happened since sunrise.

I continued down the street to where Lamar, my friend and longtime associate, stood waiting for me. A Delaware Indian, large and powerful, with two decades of experience on the frontier, he would not go near a church, nor any symbol of the white man's religion. "Wherever you see the Blackrobes, you find death," he always said. "The Blackrobes carry bad medicine."

When I approached him, he was quiet for a time, then asked me how the men were doing. I told him they were grieving hard.

"It seems the Britisher has won," he said. "He has taken LaBruneue's life and now many of the men are talking about quitting. Latour has told me this."

Jean-Claude Latour, LaBruneue's close friend from the days with Hudson's Bay, was volatile and unpredictable. I knew that had LaBruneue chosen him as his second, he would have shot Garr without hesitation. Anyone who met Latour, especially when he was angry, invariably took a step back. His hair hung long and loose, and seashells dangled from both ears. A scar traced the

left side of his unshaven face and a gold ring hung free
from a stud that pierced his lower lip. Many said he
looked more like a river pirate than a fur trader.

"Maybe Latour can talk some of them into coming
back," I suggested.

Lamar said Latour had told him that anyone who quit
was a coward, and that he didn't want them. "He wants
only men who aren't afraid to fight. He cares about
nothing now but fighting the British."

"Has he given up on our plans for a trading company
in Oregon?"

"I think he wants to go to Oregon," Lamar said, "but
not for trading. Only to drive Hudson's Bay out. He says
the Britisher knew about our plans and deliberately
called LaBruneue a coward, so that he would fight. It
might be true."

"Garr can't reach Oregon on his dueling skills," I said.
"Who's guiding him?"

"Devon Machele," Lamar replied. Known as the "Big
Frenchie," a large man with dark red hair, Machele was
widely known in the trade business. He had seemingly
disappeared two years previously and the rumor was he
had joined the Hudson's Bay Company.

As Lamar said his name, we heard yelling and turned
to see the men descending the steps of the cathedral.

"There is going to be a lot of trouble now," Lamar
said.

I've always cared for my uncle Walter a great deal. It was he, more than my father, who looked after me as a child and saw to it that I didn't get myself into more trouble than I could handle. He owned the finest horses in Lancashire and taught me to appreciate them, not just for riding but for their noble character as well.

He and Aunt Avis took a room next to mine on the third floor of the Planters' Hotel. He finds St. Louis far too busy for his liking, but has deemed it necessary to be on the trip when he would much rather be back in Lancashire, resting his sore leg.

As a young man he made lieutenant in the British army, receiving a ball in the knee at Waterloo. The wound never healed properly and being on the go so much has taken its toll on his physical well-being as well as his sanity.

I've always known that Aunt Avis, thirty-one years his junior, adds to his mental discomfort. I find it unfortunate that they have so much trouble with their marriage, as she is but five years my senior and has been my closest friend from childhood on.

We rode horseback together many times in our youth, before we both became sophisticated ladies of elite society with more important matters consuming our time. Now we often talk about our early days in the Lancashire countryside, where we ranged far and wide, riding the windy seacoast, without rule or constraint. We took those days for granted and I believe Avis now sees this trip with me into the American West as her chance to relive lost memories, and gather many new ones.

She insisted on accompanying Walter as my chaperone, as she deems it not proper to allow me to travel with Sir Edward on my own. Walter tried to persuade her to remain in England, but she would not hear of it. Disease and inclement weather and warring Indians notwithstanding, she wanted to be part of the adventure.

Uncle Walter has just passed his sixtieth birthday. He knows that even in good health, the journey will present him with a severe challenge. He has never wanted to show his lack of enthusiasm to Avis and says that he has always wanted to visit the American Rocky Mountains and see what everyone is so enamored with. He also wants to be there when I begin my portraits of the wild Indians, something that seems very exciting in itself.

Earlier in the week I set up an easel in one corner of the room and insisted on painting a portrait of him and Aunt Avis. He couldn't get over how quickly I had completed the watercolor and said that I had captured their essence perfectly, complimenting me as a very gifted artist.

While in St. Louis, I wanted to pursue some extraordinary subjects, so I sketched various inhabitants of the city, from the French aristocracy sipping cherry liquor on their balconies to drunken rivermen lying senseless in the streets. Avis continuously worried for my safety and warned me against excursions into the infamous Battle Row, near the levee, where the worst of the rowdies and ruffians congregated.

"You need not worry," I told her repeatedly. "If ever they come for me, I'll throw paint in their eye."

She saw no humor in my lack of concern and was even more appalled by my interest in the ladies of the evening and their gaudy poses. On the occasions when I pursued safer sojourns, she would accompany me and J. T. Landers, a botanist from London. We visited the many and magnificent Creole gardens of the city, while Mr. Landers, who had been commissioned by Edward to study the flora of the mountains and plains, marveled at the multitudes of roses, touch-me-nots, poppies, and hollyhocks, among others, that graced the courtyards and terraces of the luxurious homes.

I occasionally sketched Mr. Landers, a small man with a shrill voice, as he excitedly examined a specimen, detailing its taxonomy and botanical name, placing it in a plant press for drying and future reference. Many of the flowers had originated in Europe, the seeds having been brought over on the boats of the early settlers. He knew the history of each and every species, and spoke at length about wanting to compare these varieties to their wild cousins of the American West.

Uncle Walter never questioned my trips throughout St. Louis and environs, but I think he still worried about me in his own way. The city was not the open country of my childhood, where the hills and seashore were my friends. In fact, I believe he hated to see me grow up, wishing instead that I remain forever the young girl with light freckles and deep red hair.

My freckles have now departed and my hair has turned a mature auburn. I have gone from Gabby, my childhood name, to Ella or in the case of my mother, Gabriella, my full name. Uncle Walter still calls me Gabby at times, but more often Ella, and in more somber moods will say, "Gabriella Hall will someday be a name associated with masterpieces of art."

He has always maintained that I needn't marry again until I'm ready, and then to think about it a very long time. I must admit, the thought scares me since I was literally abandoned after three years of marriage by one

Sir Richard Mann, who disappeared, never to reappear. I've never learned the reason why, though I suspected he had not been killed, as some said, but had simply moved to another part of England. I cared not to pursue him, for I hated the thought of him. And though I suspected that Mother knew the reason he had left, she wouldn't think of admitting it. After that, no other suitors arrived until Sir Edward came calling.

Uncle Walter once asked openly why I had so hastily agreed to accept Sir Edward's proposal. His being fifteen years my senior was nothing exceptional; but according to Uncle, he didn't seem at all my sort of man. I will admit I had to agree with him on some counts, as I believe horses are for showing affection to while he cares little for them except to ride and draw carriages. I've always enjoyed hours spent in the open country, listening to birds and watching the animals, while he believes such activities a total waste of time. In fact, he often seems to have little patience with any form of life: he has specifically forbade the accompaniment of dogs on the trip, thinking them a bother, even though he realizes that greyhounds could offer valuable capabilities and locate game for him at long distances.

I will confess that I've tried to overlook all of those traits, including some new ones that have left me wondering of late if he even cares to have me with him anymore. Walter, in his impish way, told me not long ago that he had no idea why there would even be need of a chaperone. He told me that it appeared that Sir Edward always had better things to do than spend time with me and that I was more gracious than I ought to be at his behavior. He made the point that I would never tolerate rudeness from strangers and had little patience for people of lower class, but that I seemed all too eager to accept whatever lack of courtesy my fiancé offered me.

During my first meeting with Edward, he seemed an entirely different person, walking and talking with me, sitting atop the hills overlooking the ocean. There were evenings when we got back quite late, having made love in the grassy woods. Perhaps I believe that he'll return to that earlier man of adventure who swayed me to his affections. Until then I will have to content myself with believing, as he says, that he loves me, whether he shows it or not.

In all truthfulness, I had decided never to marry again. I had at times wanted to prove myself worthy of someone, but in the end had decided that I had value, whether or not I was married. Then, upon meeting Sir Edward, something within me changed. I had been alone long enough to think again of marriage, and he said and did so many gracious things that I believed I had met someone who loved and understood me.

Mother advised me against rushing into anything. She pointed out that we had no financial concerns of any kind, as Father had left us very well off, with two estates in Lancashire and property in Liverpool. She is now living with her sister and has no plans for ever marrying again. "Of course I wish for your happiness," she told me, "but be very certain of your feelings."

I know that she would never say it to me, but her feelings towards Edward's father run to disdain. I once overheard a conversation in which Father told her that the Earl of Waterston had ruined his chances for high rank in the British army. I have brought the subject up with Edward and he assures me that his feelings towards me have nothing to do with anything but love.

The main reason I agreed to marry him was his assurance that I could pursue my own career. It has been my intention from the beginning to make myself well known and garnish a fortune of my own. I feel I can achieve that through my art.

I owe much to Uncle Walter, who took it upon himself to look after Mother and me after Father's death. He insisted that I pursue my interest in painting by attending the École des Beaux-Arts in Paris, at his expense, where I studied portraits and landscapes, and developed a unique style of my own that, should the right opportunities present themselves, will surely bring me fame and fortune.

I have long been planning on that success and have told Uncle often that one day I will pay him back in full. "Nonsense!" he always says. "Your talent was well worth the investment." He has asked only that I not hastily marry Sir Edward and ruin any chances of making my own fortune. Uncle says he knows Edward well enough to understand that he will not accept being "upstaged" by anyone.

He once wondered aloud why Sir Edward chose me. "You are far too independent for his tastes, it would seem," he said. "And there were a number of us who wagered he would never marry anyone."

Edward supposedly had never approached a woman for marriage before me, though he might have taken any one of his choosing. There will never be a shortage of women awaiting a wealthy man's hand.

Though Uncle might believe that Edward is not the right man for me, the two share the same ideals. As military men both are dedicated to the Crown and both see the burgeoning American boundaries as a threat not only to England but Spain as well. Though I'm not a student of war, I do know that they both believe it would be of great benefit to all of Europe if Britain and Spain could somehow hold their claims within the North American continent.

Word of intense American expansion into New Mexico and California to the southwest and Oregon to the northwest fills the St. Louis papers. Imminent war with Mexico looms on the horizon, and along the northern boundary of Oregon, the cry of "Fifty-four, Forty, or Fight!" has aroused ire in the settlers there.

Uncle Walter realizes that the Mexican conflict will never concern him, but he told me that he thinks constantly about the Oregon trouble. He and Edward, both, have holdings in the powerful Hudson's Bay Company and perceive the American expansion as a dire threat. The Company has over many decades successfully competed for furs and trade goods from the Indians, and now their stronghold is weakening.

Another of my uncles, Walter's younger brother, Reginald, holds a position at Fort Vancouver, on the Columbia River, right in the heart of the contested territory. It bothers me not just a little that our ultimate destination is that very location. Should war between England and the United States break out, it will certainly prove troublesome.

Gabriella's Journal

5 APRIL 1846, 4TH ENTRY

I disembarked from the carriage in front of the Planters' Hotel and looked up towards the third floor. Uncle Walter was peering down, puffing on his ever present cigar. I knew what he was thinking: He was trying to read my mood from the manner of my gait, which I must admit was rather stiff. He could no doubt see that I didn't appear shaken, which meant Sir Edward had prevailed in the duel. But he was aware that Edward had likely ordered me back to the hotel while he remained at the boat.

Barton escorted me to the third floor and departed for his room down the hallway. I asked him if he didn't wish to visit Walter and Avis with me, but he begged off, saying all he desired was rest and a chance to be alone.

I didn't even have to knock, for Uncle was holding the door open for me, bidding me inside.

"You didn't see your aunt, did you?" he asked.

"I assumed she was here."

"I fell asleep and she left a note saying she was going shopping with another lady from the hotel and would try to meet you at the boat."

"I didn't see her."

Walter puffed on his cigar. He turned to the window and after spotting a carriage with Avis in it, turned back to me.

"She's becoming more adventurous than you."

Soon she came into the room and asked about Edward.

"I thought you went to the boat," Walter said.

She took off her wrap. "I decided to come straight back. So, what about the duel?"

"He prevailed," I said.

Walter added, "Certainly you couldn't believe he'd get the worst of the morning."

"I should doubt it," she said. "He never has before."

"Perhaps you worry too much about him, my dear," Walter said.

"He should be here," I said. "He remains on the levee. His work is much more important than me."

Uncle took a seat in a nearby rocker and puffed his cigar while Avis put her hand on my arm.

"You must understand, Ella, he has a lot to do before we can leave."

"I wish you wouldn't defend him all the time," I said.

"I'm merely stating a fact. He must see to it that the workers do their job. Tell me, did he have trouble besting the Frenchman?"

"No, and I'm afraid he's made some bitter enemies in the process."

"Surely it was a fair fight?"

"It was fair, but he insisted on killing the man from point-blank range. That puzzles me."

I related how Mr. LaBruneue had announced his satisfaction in the dispute after having been wounded and how Edward had then demanded his own satisfaction.

Walter turned in his chair. "Are you saying that he insisted on dueling again?"

"Yes. First he shot him in the throat, and then he blew his brains out."

I watched Uncle puff hard on his cigar.

"That Frenchman should never have made accusations against Edward," Avis said.

"Edward could have let the remark pass," I said. "It would have saved time and, I fear, trouble."

Walter rocked in his chair, smoking his cigar.

"Oh, well, we'll be well on our way by tomorrow this time," Avis said. "It should be lovely traveling upriver."

She took a seat and began writing in her diary. I walked to the easel in the corner of the room and studied my latest watercolor. I shouldn't have worked so fast. There were many details that glared out at me. Perhaps not to Avis and Walter—they thought the work a masterpiece—but certainly to me.

The two sat for a good period of time, making it easy for me, never complaining. I've often thought what it would be like to complete a portrait of a true wild tribesman of the plains and what kind of subjects they would be. The European establishment is very interested in the American Indians and I am counting on a strong market for my work.

The European frontier has been gone for many years and everyone is curious what it must be like traveling untamed wilderness peopled by untamed savages. I use the term "savages" because that is the term most often heard. I was once told by a fellow student in Paris, though, that the warriors are seldom as uncivilized as the artists who pursue them.

I intend to finish many pieces both in watercolor and oil. The oils will have to be completed after my return to Lancashire, as working in the field and protecting the canvasses would be next to impossible. Having the work jostle about in a wagon would only be inviting irreparable damage.

I will complete the new paintings in oil from sketches and watercolors made in the field, and hope to have many hundreds of pieces to work from. The prospect excites me and I grow ever more anxious to leave.

I don't know at this point if I can agree with Uncle about Edward's concern over my art. Though he has never commented on my work, I believe he cares, for he's very eager to have himself painted with a trophy white buffalo he has promised himself he will locate and shoot. He has found and commissioned a taxidermist to travel with us for the sole purpose of preserving the heads and hides of various game animals for mounting later.

Uncle Walter says that the task will be immense. Our initial destination is Fort Union, somewhere along the upper Missouri, where Edward intends to procure enough horses and mules to haul at least one specimen of every large animal he can find. He intends to sell the steamboat to Alexander Culbertson of the American Fur

Company, and we will travel on from there over the trails and to the distant boundaries of Oregon, where, at Fort Vancouver, we will board a ship and return to Lancashire.

Edward will never be deterred from his plans, be they oftentimes far-fetched. I wonder if he considers my desire to make my own fortune painting portraits unattainable, or if he even thinks about it at all. I see no reason to dwell on it one way or the other, as I shall be successful some-day, whatever it takes.

Avis eventually put her diary away and said to me, "Why don't we do some shopping?" I told her that would be fun and she added, "You can choose a new dress and I'll buy it for you."

"Oh, Avis, you don't have to do that," I said.

"I want to, and I'll get something new myself. We'll dine on the plains in style." She turned to Walter. "Can you do without me for a short while?"

Walter lit another cigar. "Of course, my dear. Take your time."

Gabriella's Journal

7 APRIL 1846

Avis and I had a grand time shopping. Though she has never concerned herself about spending money, I found her to be overly generous. She almost tried too hard in her efforts to see me smile.

Back at the hotel, Uncle Walter informed us that Edward had finally returned, but just long enough to an-nounce that he must go back to the boat and oversee the last of the loading. He told Uncle that he would join us all for dinner well before sundown. Since the sun was falling and he still hadn't arrived, I insisted we go and look for him.

We reached the *White Bull*, which lay at anchor along the levee. The boat rested gently in the current and as twilight settled in over the city, it appeared that the work had been finished. But there was still no sign of Edward.

I left Walter and Avis in the carriage while I went to look for him. Uncle puffed anxiously on a cigar while Avis concerned herself over the dangers of a lady exploring a riverboat on her own. I assured her that at this point, I would be the one who was dangerous to anyone who crossed me.

I lifted the hem of my new gown and strolled along the upper deck, calling for Edward. I worked my way down a stairway and stopped again to call out for him. A slight breeze had arisen and with it a hint of moisture.

I stopped at the furthest point forward on the bow and leaned over the railing, looking towards the carriage. Perhaps he had left the boat and I had missed him somehow. But he was nowhere below, and I continued my search, passing what appeared to be two guards who stood watch, their flintlocks resting over their shoulders. I asked if either had seen Edward.

"Not for some time, m'lady," one said.

The other one added, in a heavy French accent, "*Oui*, not for some time."

I stared at the Frenchman and he regarded me with an odd expression. I had seen neither of them before and felt certain they were not among the guards Edward ordinarily kept on watch.

"Don't worry," the Frenchman said. "We will find him."

"Are you saying he's lost?" I asked.

The other one spoke up quickly. "No, ma'am, he's not saying that."

"Then what exactly are you saying? Where is he?"

"He's on the boat," the Frenchman said. "Somewhere on the boat."

I was certain now that I had never seen either of them before. The other man, tall and thin, would not look at me, but the Frenchman now glared with defiance. He had dirty long hair and large seashells in his ears, making his appearance appalling. When I asked him his name, he handed his rifle to the tall man and grabbed me roughly around the waist, pinning my arms at my sides. I shrieked and fought but still could not break his hold.

A large man in buckskins, who had come out of a nearby warehouse, looked up and asked what was happening. I recognized his voice and knew him to be Devon Machele, our guide. I continued to struggle, losing my hat, but could not break free. The Frenchman had clamped his hand over my mouth, making it impossible to cry out. Devon Machele hurried up the stairs, still demanding to know what was going on.

The tall one had hidden himself from view and when Mr. Machele approached, he showed himself and shot the guide through the breast. Mr. Machele toppled backwards and over the railing, into the river below.

More men burst from the warehouse and suddenly rifle fire broke out everywhere. The *White Bull* began to drift away from the levee and I clawed at the Frenchman, my fingernails digging into his face. He cursed and dragged me to the deck's edge, and threw me overboard.

I hit the water hard, losing my breath. I could feel myself sinking and struggled to swim upward, my water-soaked clothes holding me back. When I broke the surface and gasped for air, I discovered the Frenchman beside me in the water.

"Do not struggle against me," he warned as he grabbed me, dragging me to a canoe that hugged the levee. Another man pulled me up, while the Frenchman, spitting water, climbed in after me.

"Hurry!" he told the other man. "We must get away."

I demanded to know what was happening, but the Frenchman again covered my mouth with his dirty hand.

"Don't talk. You hear me?" he hissed. "I won't tell you again."

The two men worked feverishly to paddle the canoe. Soon we were a hundred yards from the *White Bull*. I sat silently between them, still stunned from my fall into the river. I stared back to see the large riverboat drifting out into the current. Men jumped from the deck into the water, and the darkness was filled with flashes of fire from the rifle barrels.

Suddenly a series of explosions hurled fire into the night. Flames quickly engulfed the boat and more men jumped overboard as the sides blew out. The yelling grew fainter as my captors paddled the canoe steadily upriver.

I felt weak-kneed, worrying that Edward had been caught in the blast.

"Why would you do such a thing?" I asked.

The men rowed silently.

"I demand to know the meaning of this."

"I told you not to speak," the Frenchman said. "Do you want me to gag you with a filthy cloth?"

I sat silently while they paddled through the darkness. Behind, the flames danced against the city's outline and finally disappeared as we rounded a bend.

I realized we had entered the mouth of the Missouri River. The two men kept the canoe near the bank, as the river was swollen from spring rainfall. The water roiled and boiled in the channel and in the darkness, it roared in my ears.

A distance upriver, we were forced to put ashore and walk along a trail steeped in shadows, the two men carrying the canoe over their heads. In no time my dress was torn by wild roses and thornapple, my skin scratched and irritated. Clouds rolled in overhead and covered the moon. Soon the air filled with mist.

I thought about running away but the Frenchman said, "If you don't want to drown in the river, you'll stay close."

We came to a calmer stretch of water and put in, angling out into the current. The clouds parted briefly and I could see the moon, milky white in a strange and distant sky.

We put ashore again, and after more thrashing through the undergrowth, I grew completely exhausted. I told the men I had to stop and rest. The Frenchman took me by the arm and pulled me close to him.

"Maybe you want me to lay with you, is that it?"

Angered, I pushed away from him, but he grabbed me again.

"Leave her alone," said the taller man. "We have no time for that."

I was fighting with all I had. The taller man took a length of tree limb and threatened to club the Frenchman.

"I said, leave her alone!" he yelled. "Jean-Claude Latour! If you must have her, then wait until we get back to camp. I'm not getting myself into any bind over the likes of you."

The Frenchman pulled his knife, then sheathed it, saying, "We have lost too many as it is. But don't ever threaten me again."

Latour looked at me as if he would take any opportunity to rape me.

Back in the canoe, I told myself that I had to try to

escape. In the darkness it was impossible to tell how far we had come or how many little settlements we had passed.

They steered the canoe to a large island, where Latour ushered me roughly through a dense stand of willows and into a small clearing where a dozen white tents stood in a circle. Lanterns glowed within each of them and soon a half-dozen coarse-looking men encircled me, staring.

Lamar, the large Indian on Bloody Island with the frontiersman, stepped forward and addressed the Frenchman.

"What is this? Where are the others?"

"We fired the boat," Latour said. "This woman is insurance that Edward Garr will not go ahead with his plans."

"What a fool you are," Lamar said. "You say you go in to recruit others for the journey, but instead you lie and make a lot of trouble for us."

"You talk as if you don't care about LaBruneue's death," the Frenchman said.

"I cared a great deal for, him," the Indian said. "That does not mean I believe in doing crazy things."

"Then you must believe it is good to have the Britisher building an army against us."

I had wondered if the attack on the boat might not be in retaliation for Edward's killing of Mr. LaBruneue, but now it seemed as if they had other motives as well.

"What are you talking about?" I asked the men. "What is this talk about Sir Edward leading an army?"

Latour walked up and glared at me. "He is a Hudson's Bay man. Don't you know that?"

Lamar pulled him back. "She's not part of this."

Latour said, "But of course she is! What is wrong with you? Are you all mad?"

I looked to all of them, wondering what Edward had kept from me.

Lamar spoke to Latour again. "Did you know Quincannon followed you into the city?"

"I don't care what Owen Quincannon did or whether he is angry with me. I am my own man."

A form emerged from the shadows and the men began to murmur. The frontiersman who had stared at me for so long on the island walked straight up to Latour, his strong features hard with anger.

Latour stepped back. "You stay away from me, Quincannon. I did what I thought best."

"No. You cost us time and a lot of men. That's not what's best. I'm taking the woman back."

Latour protested and argued that Mr. LaBruneue was his commander and he needn't take orders from anyone else. The frontiersman told him that Mr. LaBruneue was no longer with them. "He and I were equal partners," he said, "and now everything belongs to me. If you want to stay employed, you will obey my commands. Understood?"

Latour shuffled his feet. "Maybe I will lead these men. Not you."

Quincannon looked at me and turned to the men. "How many of you agree with kidnapping this woman?" No one spoke and he added, "How many of you want to leave my employ for Latour's?"

Again, no one spoke and no one stepped forward. Latour shouted that they were all cowards.

"You decide right now," Mr. Quincannon told Latour. "Obey my rules or leave."

"I will stay with you," Latour said, "but I'm right in taking the woman. We need a way to make the Britisher go back to England."

"He won't go back, no matter what," Mr. Quincannon said. "He hasn't even sent men out to find her."

I felt embarrassed at hearing that, but believed that

Edward hadn't yet been able to and would certainly do so before long.

The men continued to argue, and finally Latour left for one of the tents, pulling the flap closed behind him. One of them told Mr. Quincannon that the Frenchman might be looking for a weapon. He responded that Latour wasn't foolish enough to do that. "He doesn't fight from the front," he said.

"What happened on the boat?" Lamar asked.

"They sank it, but they're gone—dead, badly wounded, or ran away."

"What are we going to do now?" one of the men asked.

"Maybe we can find some others who will join us," Mr. Quincannon said. "We'll go to Oregon, one way or the other."

The men retired for the night and the frontiersman led me to a tent at the edge of camp. Inside, a lantern burned brightly, casting flickering shadows against the canvas. I shivered in the chill air and he threw me a Mackinaw blanket.

"What about my fiancé?" I asked.

"He was wounded in the explosion, but not seriously. I pulled him from the water."

"Were they holding him somewhere on the boat?"

"Yes. They were going to hang him when it got dark, but then you showed up."

He told me that he had taken Edward back to the hotel, where his personal physician, Dr. Noel Marking, attended to him.

"What happens now?" I asked.

He retired to the opposite side of the tent and fixed his bed. "We'll leave at first light, which isn't far off," he said.

"This is a fine mess your men have caused," I said.

"Be thankful you're alive," he said, and blew out the lantern.

I crawled under the blanket, shivering, and removed my wet dress in the darkness. I didn't have the strength to protest sleeping in the same tent with him. He was right about my being ungrateful and I considered myself lucky to have been rescued by this man, who had been kind enough to allow me shelter and a blanket. My only other alternative would have been to sleep outside, and that held no attraction to me, for it had started raining once again.

Gabriella's Journal

8 APRIL 1846, 1ST ENTRY

The canoe ride back downriver took little time compared to my ordeal of the night before. Though still fatigued, I enjoyed the bright morning and the thought of reuniting with Sir Edward, as well as Walter and Avis. Most of all I felt very fortunate that I had come to no relative harm.

Owen Quincannon seemed a man given to introspection, alone within his own thoughts most of the time and not prone to discussion for discussion's sake. He answered questions politely but asked none of his own. He had given me a heavy woolen shirt to wear over my dress, which was still damp, and had allowed me to share his breakfast of bacon and cornmeal.

I didn't feel at all comfortable until we had left camp. Though none of the others concerned me at all, I worried about Latour. He kept pestering Quincannon about what he was going to do with me, saying I could testify against them in court and spoil their plans. The frontiersman reminded the Frenchman in no uncertain terms that it was he who had already spoiled their plans.

Once underway, I asked Mr. Quincannon why he had rescued me.

"It would seem that you would desire the same revenge as Mr. Latour," I said. "In fact, I might have thought you were behind it."

"My business is to reach Oregon," he said. "Not burn boats and kidnap women."

"Mr. Latour is right, my fiancé is bound to demand restitution. He may want to pursue a legal course."

"He can pursue all he wants, but he won't get any-where."

I knew he was right. Alleged complaints by British aristocracy against Americans were not a priority in the court systems. A hearing might possibly be held, but there was no guarantee.

"How will you make it right?" I asked.

"Bringing you back will have to do."

"It seems to me," I said, "that you could have avoided all this by stopping Mr. Latour from carrying out his plans."

"We could have avoided all this if Sir Edward Garr hadn't insisted on killing François LaBruneue," he said.

I watched a pair of ducks fly past the canoe, their wing-tips skimming the water. Quincannon said they were teal and that every spring nesting pairs filled the bottoms along the river. He pointed out a small wildcat peering at us from the brush, only its face visible in the dense foliage.

Though uncomfortable with the situation, I wasn't concerned about my safety any longer. He studied me on occasion, but made no untoward remarks and asked more than once if I was comfortable. He was strong and defiant and in many ways just as wild as the others, but he seemed more educated, with higher goals in mind.

"Have you always been a mountain man?" I asked.

"I came back from the mountains four years ago," he said. "I thought it was time to change. But I can't, so I'm going back."

That was how he answered my question. He said nothing more, but worked the paddle effortlessly, maneuvering the canoe through floating debris and around downed trees.

He may have thought I was prying, which I was, so I stuck to pertinent questions.

"What are you going to say to Edward?" I asked.

"I'm going to wish him good luck on the trail."

"We might not be going on the trail. Our guide was shot through the breast last night, right in front of me."

"Devon Machele is dead?"

"Did you know him?"

"Very well, but I thought the rumor that he was to lead you to Oregon was untrue."

He said nothing for a long time. Finally, he turned the canoe towards shore, suggesting we stop for a meal. He jumped into the shallows and after helping me out, pulled a bundle of dry wood from the canoe and started a small fire next to a cold-running spring that fed the river. There was evidence of past fires and he told me that he often camped there when traveling the river.

He pulled a small bag from the water and skewered two squirrels on small willow branches. While they roasted, he asked me, "How many times have you traveled into the wilderness?"

"This will be my first journey."

"How about your fiancé?"

"He's been on expeditions to Africa, but never to this country."

"Do you know what to expect?"

"We were well prepared," I said. "I assume that Edward will reoutfit us and find another guide."

He tested one of the squirrels with his knife and, finding the meat fully cooked, carved off pieces for me.

"This is no dining-room atmosphere and our utensils are primitive," he said, "but you'll gain some strength back."

I took a small bite, finding it very tasty. "I take it that you've experienced fine dining," I said.

He laughed. "You're very curious about me, aren't you?"

"You don't seem anything like the others."

"I go to the mountains to make money for the fine dining," he said. "I did well at one time, before the bottom fell out of the price of beaver."

"I don't know much about that commerce," I said, "but I do know that English gentlemen now prefer silk hats to those of beaver fur."

"There weren't a lot of beaver left to trap anyway, but there's a growing trade with the settlers moving west, and those already in Oregon."

"And that is what's causing all the friction with the British government. Is that right?"

"That's right. The British want everyone under their control, and the settlers want them out."

"That hardly seems fair," I said. "From what I understand, the British settled the country."

"No, they didn't settle it, and they've said they don't want it. But the Hudson's Bay Company is not ready to give up."

"Do you think there will be war?"

"It looks like it."

"What might stop it?"

"If the Hudson's Bay Company moves out."

I finished my meat and Mr. Quincannon offered me

more, saying it would do no good to decline, as he knew that I must still be hungry. I accepted another cut and ate it with relish.

"How will your fiancé find another guide at this late date?" he asked.

"Surely there must be some left."

"The good ones have already left."

"I'm sure Edward has thought of something," I said. "He's not a man to give up."

He doused the fire, then rose and helped me into the canoe. He shoved off and began rowing methodically while I sat quietly, looking at the river. We spoke no more and suddenly St. Louis appeared, a beehive of activity. When we landed, I could hear everyone on the levee as they talked about the *White Bull*, now reduced to a few floating, blackened timbers that workers were pulling to shore with flatboats. Everyone stared at me, with my torn dress and disheveled and dirty hair.

I offered to get myself to the hotel and he insisted on escorting me. He hailed a carriage, and at the Planters' Hotel, the doorman helped me down. He stared at Mr. Quincannon with contempt and said, "Are you a guest here, sir?"

"I soon will be," he said, and tipped the man with a twenty-dollar gold piece.

On the way up the stairs, Mr. Quincannon apologized for his appearance, saying that he had intended on getting new buckskins. In Uncle's room, I hugged Walter and Avis tightly, explaining to them how I had been abducted and then rescued by Mr. Owen Quincannon. Avis said, "We feared the worst for you, dear."

Uncle Walter shook his hand. "We are deeply indebted to you, sir. How much for your trouble?"

"I'll not take your money, but would appreciate an in-

troduction to Sir Edward Garr. I have a business proposition. I'm sure you can relate to that."

Walter's eyebrows raised, as did mine. My uncle led us
to the next room and knocked. Bom opened the door.
Edward lay tossing fitfully on a bed against the wall, his
head and back propped up by pillows, still dressed in his
clothes from the night before, which were soiled and still
damp. His right arm was supported by a sling. He held a
glass of brandy with his good hand, his speech showing
evidence that he had been drinking for some time.

"Here's a salute to strange fortune and impeccable bad
luck," he said to me.

"Thank God you weren't killed, or seriously injured,"
I said. I started to hug him but noticed a look in his eye
that kept me back.

"Ah, yes," he said. "My physician says it's but a sprain."

"Mr. Quincannon says that he helped you from the
water," I said.

Walter turned to Edward. "Is that true?"

"I suppose you could call it help," Edward said. "I don't
ever remember being treated so roughly."

"You were drowning, sir," Mr. Quincannon said. "Men
in that condition are difficult to help."

Edward drained his glass and Bom refilled it. I had
never seen him so anxious before.

"So, am I to understand that you've some part in Gabriella's return?" he asked Mr. Quincannon.

"I told you last night that I would find her."

"Yes, I suppose you did. How did you know where to
look?"

"I know the river well."

"I'm sure you do. What do you want in compensation?"

"A position as your new guide."

I must admit I hadn't expected that. Edward pointed

out how odd his request appeared, as he was a friend of
LaBruneue.

"Yes, but the circumstances of my travel plans haven't
changed," he said. "And I can't believe that you've made
other arrangements."

"You are a curious sort, Mr. Quincannon," Edward
said. "I kill your friend and you offer your services to me
as if we had much in common."

"We do, and I believe that we can serve each other very
well. After all, a man who drinks Droulliard brandy is
certainly able to make the best of unusual circumstances."

Edward rearranged himself on the bed, grimacing in
pain. "If we were to even consider an arrangement," he
said, "then I would want it understood that you'll be serv-
ing me. There'll be nothing mutual about it."

"I would hope that you would respect my knowledge
of the trails and conditions."

"I said that I will make the decisions."

"Very well. It doesn't appear that you even need my
services. Have a good journey." Mr. Quincannon turned
for the door.

Uncle Walter stopped him. "Please, do not be hasty,
sir. I believe what Sir Edward was trying to say is that he
requires any decisions, even about the trail, be made mutually. Isn't that correct, Sir Edward?"

Edward sipped his brandy. "I know more about wilderness trails than one might think, but I will concede
that Mr. Quincannon, having spent time out there, should
surely know his way around."

"Very well, then," Walter said. "I say we toast our arrangement."

Edward ordered Bom to get three glasses and open a
new bottle for the toast.

"Make that five glasses," I said. "Aunt Avis and I would like to join the toast." Avis declined and I said that four would do. Bom filled the glasses and Uncle Walter said, "Here's to good health and the mountains."

INDEPENDENCE

Quincannon's Journal

7 APRIL 1846

I keep seeing Indians in my dreams. They ride at me, screaming and spitting blood, their lances and their bows raised high above their heads. I raise my rifle to fire but they ride right through me and onward to who knows where, night after night, ever since I made the decision to go to Oregon.

I've fought them and lived among them, loved them and hated them. I realized within the first year in the settlements that their style of life had become my own and their values my values, and that sooner or later I would be back riding the plains and mountains.

I have fond memories of sharing days on horseback with them. I believe in their ceremonies still and know they have a connection to the divine that is to be envied. Some of them accepted me; some of them didn't, and I'm certain a few would have loved to have cut my heart out.

I'll be going to Oregon and if I have to fight them again, so be it. Yet they are certainly less the enemy than Edward Garr. I never thought I'd be breaking trail for a man who killed a good friend, but it's the best way I know to keep an eye on him.

There will be nothing easy now. Before the duel, I could see making the trip rather handily and reaching the Columbia in late summer. If the show was to be war with the British, we'd already have front-row seats. I'd never heard of Sir Edward Garr and I certainly had no idea I would be traveling to Oregon with a spy.

Lamar will accompany me and Latour will go on ahead and wait for us. I can see no reason to worry for my life, since Garr needs me to guide him. In addition, I don't think he would kill someone who rescued his fiancée. So far she seems quite a woman. He did well in securing her hand, though I don't know why she gave it to him.

So, we'll all be facing Indians together. I told them what to expect over drinks and I don't know how much they believed. We'll see if they heard me as time goes on.

Gabriella's Journal

8 APRIL 1846, 2ND ENTRY

Avis and I spent nearly the entire day in front of the mirror, giggling and laughing while we tried on additional new clothes, more of the latest apparel from the shops. Dresses and hats and shoes laid scattered about while we refitted ourselves over and over, and told Walter not to turn around.

Three days have passed and Edward says it will be just

a few more until we depart. His arm appears to have healed nicely and he has arranged for another steamboat, this one leased, with the services of a captain. Uncle Walter, now sitting in the corner, puffing on a cigar, is looking out the window and scowling. I know he believes Edward is either daft or incredibly stubborn to be tempting fate that way. But Edward has tripled the guard on the new boat and has even stationed men on the levee to watch in all directions.

His intent is to haul the newly acquired provisions up to a place called Kansas Landing, where it will all be transferred to the backs of mules and into small carts designed by Mr. Quincannon and made by craftsmen to order. The mountain man has insisted on mules instead of oxen, and carts instead of wagons, for the expressed reason of an easier haul over rough trails, saving both time and trouble. Many provisions will be secured at either Independence or Westport, two jumping-off points no longer used as much as in the past.

Even though everything seems in order and Edward is using all precaution to forestall another disaster, I know Uncle Walter still worries. There have been several who have met death on Bloody Island over the years, but they have all been local businessmen or lawyers or judges, usually with high political aspirations, settling power grudges within the confines of their own system. Walter says that Edward has introduced a foreign element into the already controversial mix and that the locals feel threatened.

Uncle Walter had warned Edward before that any kind of serious trouble could cost them dearly; but as usual, Edward didn't listen. "As much as he desires many of the same things as me," Uncle told me, "I can't for the life of me understand the man's behavior. He will affront anyone who might question his authority."

As an added worry, Uncle Walter doesn't know what

to make of Mr. Quincannon, whom he agrees is surprisingly well educated for a mountain man. He had once thought the two terms mutually exclusive, but is beholden to him for having rescued me from a dire situation that might have ended very badly. He also said that anyone who knows good brandy like Mr. Quincannon can't be all bad.

They had drunk together the night before, discussing the upcoming journey and what supplies needed replacing. Edward would not stay at the table, but retired early, and I had a chance to listen to some very interesting stories, some of them bad enough to make one reconsider crossing the plains.

I asked Mr. Quincannon if that was his point, to talk us out of our journey. He assured me that it wasn't, but he was merely describing the way it is. "You can't get halfway out," he said, "and decide to turn back."

I reminded him that we were committed to reaching Oregon, Fort Vancouver in particular, no matter the odds against us. We had already come through a great ordeal, I told him, and would press on. He did not seem impressed, reminding me that Edward's wealth is the only thing allowing for our reoutfitting for the trip. I could not argue with him on that point. We had a great many items that had to be replaced.

Though some of our belongings had remained at the hotel, the great majority of our clothes, and all of our trail gear, furniture, food supplies, and dinnerware, had been loaded onto the *White Bull* and lost, including a case of fine china Edward had brought over from England that once belonged to his mother.

Aunt Avis quickly picked out a new set from a shop near the hotel and assured Edward that it was so similar in design to the original that he would barely be able to tell the difference. Whether he agreed with her or not, none of us had been able to determine. He merely stated that the china would do for our purposes.

I breathed a huge sigh of relief at having kept my sketchpads and other art supplies in my room. I had wanted to touch up the portrait of Walter and Avis before putting everything into boxes. Should I have lost that piece, plus all the sketches of St. Louis and its people, I would have been devastated.

I have just shipped the completed work back home. Certainly it won't suffer any worse fate en route than possible destruction on the trail. From what Mr. Quincannon says, all manner of disaster lurks behind every tree and bush. It seems almost laughable. But considering the destruction of the steamboat, I have decided to believe him—but only to a point.

I cannot bring myself to swallow everything he says, especially regarding the Indians. If reports are to be believed, they have to be extremely dangerous and warlike. But, according to Mr. Quincannon, they are not savage. He avoids that word, maintaining that the native people have their own values, and even though they are different from those of the settlers, it doesn't mean they are an inferior race.

He told me that, in fact, the Indians believe themselves superior to the whites. "They can't understand many of our customs and think them barbaric," he said. "And they have no tolerance for farming the land."

I found the reference to agriculture interesting and perplexing. He explained that many tribes, especially the ones nearest the rivers, grow vegetable gardens to envy, but that the nomadic horse tribes, with the especially volatile warrior societies, find cutting down trees and disturbing the virgin sod a sacrilegious practice. The pursuit and consumption of buffalo, and the gathering of wild roots and herbs and berries, is the only respectable use of the natural resource.

All this information makes me that much more eager to meet these people and see them in the flesh. I look forward to the test of capturing their essence on canvas. The challenge is beginning to dominate my thoughts night and day.

The warriors Mr. Quincannon speaks of are not those seen loitering in the streets and back alleys of St. Louis, barefoot and wrapped in ragged blankets. These people were once members of proud nations but are now reduced to begging for food and liquor. According to Mr. Quincannon, those still living free will fight to the death rather than end up in a life of squalor.

Mr. Quincannon made other valid points, including the fact that I will see a change in my life the likes of which I cannot begin to imagine. He says that I cannot hope to always sleep in a bed, to which I responded that I've never desired that form of rest exclusively. I've slept out-of-doors often, mainly during my formative years, but I can certainly adjust.

I will have to admit that going without a regular bath will be very trying. Mr. Quincannon has said that there will be stretches where the only water available will come from holes in otherwise dry creekbeds, or by digging beneath the sand with our bare hands. "You'll have to drink fast," he said, "before the horses and mules stomp it to mud." I cannot imagine taking a sponge bath under those circumstances.

So here I am, ready to conquer the unknown, yet unwilling in part to leave my comfortable civilization behind. There are some habits I cannot and refuse to shake. I study myself in the mirror and admire my newest and most favorite apparel—a fine blue dress with matching hat and slippers.

It is a wide-brimmed white hat with black velvet ribbons tied in bows, both front and back. The tails from the black ribbon flow halfway down my back. My dress also has black lace along the shoulders, and the bustline and a black velvet sash fit nicely, making me feel sleek and trim.

I love both the hat and the dress, and all of their particular features, but it's the matching pair of blue satin slippers that I truly adore. I admire the style and fit, the ribbon-bound topline with a larger, braided blue ribbon sewn into the lining near the arch, for use as a tie around the ankle, complete with a pleated satin ribbon rosette edged with a lace oval buckle and a velvet bow in the center.

I could wear them all day, every day. I can't get over their light but sturdy structure, and the curious way they caress my toes and make me want to dance. Nothing I have ever worn before has made me feel so good. And now I shall take them on the trail and perhaps we will discover a settlement somewhere with a hotel and a ballroom. There I will certainly move awkwardly with Edward as he struggles to feel the rhythm of the music, holding me in his stiff way until he tires of it, which won't take long. Then I will see what Mr. Quincannon knows about waltzing, and if he can step as nimbly as he walks and talks.

We left St. Louis early yesterday morning and reached Independence by late this afternoon. The little log town rings with the sounds of blacksmiths' hammers mixed with the yells of men hitching unruly mules and oxen to harness. The streets are filled with wagons and carriages, with children and dogs circling around and under them, and mothers shaking their fingers. The smell of leather and manure, mixed with fine dust, hangs like thick fog.

According to Mr. Quincannon, the settlement was once the main jumping-off point for the westward movement, and before that a little burg named Franklin. Times changed and travelers wanted a location farther upriver from which to start. Westport and Kansas Landing have both grown quickly to suit that need.

However, many still depart from Independence, as a hotel owned and operated by Smallwood Noland, affectionately referred to as Uncle Wood, can comfortably house four hundred guests at a time. I now sit in my room, wonderfully accommodating for a facility near the frontier. I don't know if I will get the opportunity to have Uncle Wood sit for me, but will draw a resemblance of him nevertheless. I am lucky to have the gift of remembering a subject's every feature in my mind.

This afternoon at the landing, Edward greeted Mr. Quincannon rather curtly. I don't believe the two will ever be friends. Our new scout looked sharp in a new set of buckskins, lightweight and fringed along the arms and shoulders, and a new wide-brimmed hat. Edward wore a similar hat with a pair of stout corduroy breeches with buckskin leggings, and a cherry-red velveteen shooting jacket, complete with enormous pockets for carrying ammunition.

In addition, he wore crossed bandoliers filled with bullets for his Purdey double-barreled rifle. His ever present dirk rested inside his belt, along with a brace of Joseph Manton pistols.

It is nearly dark and the workers are still unloading the provisions from the boat. They are to have everything ready for packing the mules and filling the carts so that the journey might begin soon after dawn. I will have my own tent and will sleep in style and comfort, having a brass bed and feather tick, and a shag Persian carpet underneath. Edward is outfitted similarly in his own personal tent, as are Uncle Walter and Aunt Avis.

Just prior to leaving St. Louis, Edward purchased for me a young mulatto woman named Jessie, barely fourteen years of age, who is separated from her mother for the first time. She held up remarkably well at our first meeting on the banks of the river near the boat, but I could see that she was devastated at her situation.

She told me that she had been taught by her mother and would serve me well. I then said that I wouldn't mind if she wanted to return to her mother, as I didn't need a personal aide.

"She was taken away by her new owners two nights ago," she said, "and I don't know where she's gone."

Bom then spoke to me for the first time. I asked him if he wouldn't look after Jessie and make her feel at home, as much as that was possible. "Yes, ma'am, I would be happy to," he said. "I thank you for your kindness."

Jessie is to aid Uncle Walter and Aunt Avis as well, since another young woman whom Edward had acquired at the same time disappeared into the night. I have decided that I will allow Jessie to help Avis most of the time.

Sir Edward has brought along his two French cooks, Jon and Pierre Rivet, inseparable brothers, to select the majority of the foodstuffs for the journey, including many spices and fine wines, as they are expected to provide cuisine up to the same exacting standards as at home. Edward believes there to be no finer chefs anywhere and will not tolerate for any reason a meal that is anything less than superb.

The two Frenchmen scurry about, yelling at the workers to handle the goods carefully, as they will be held accountable by my fiancé for any loss or ruination of foodstuffs. I am fortunate to share a friendship with both of them. They are fine and talented men whom Edward takes for granted.

Edward's palate takes second place behind his attachment to firearms. He acquired the Purdey rifle and the ammunition in St. Louis, along with numerous shotguns and pistols, to supplant the collection lost on the *White Bull*. His mood has remained somewhat tolerable only because he kept his favorite piece in his room at the Planters' Hotel, a Westley Richards pill-lock rifle, model 1821, made in Birmingham.

His nephew confided in me that helping procure the new collection was both exhausting and boring in the extreme. Though not eager for the instruction, Barton accompanied Edward the entire time, quickly tiring at the endless flow of information that he is expected to remember. Edward told him, "I hope to see you shoot as well as I do someday, though I realize you have an almost hopelessly long way to go."

When able to escape Edward's tutoring, Barton takes the opportunity to converse with Bom. I understand that the new servant is a fascinating individual. Though just a young man when he and his family were captured in northern Ghana and transported in a crowded ship to Louisiana, he had already learned the culture of his people inside and out, and it would always be a part of him.

"He talks about things spiritual and difficult to understand," Barton told me, "as if everybody lived that way."

When I questioned Barton as to what he meant, he told me that I would have to hear it all from Bom himself, as he didn't feel comfortable telling me about things he could not relate to.

Mr. Quincannon frowns upon the use of servants. He refrains from the political aspects, alluding to the supposition that he might have taken a life freeing some slaves from a compound not far from the city. Ethics notwithstanding, he maintains that too much luxury will slow the expedition down and cause serious setbacks at some point along the trail. He and Edward had a heated argument regarding the subject just before we left St. Louis and neither would back down. I believe it to be the first of many.

Edward has, however, listened to some of Mr. Quincannon's advice. We have procured a number of mosquito nets and Mackinaw blankets, to ensure comfort during the night and during grazing and watering stops along the way. We also purchased a large quantity of German-made Osnaburg canvas, a waterproof fabric of coarse linen that protects goods from driving rains.

I cannot say if I will have dinner this evening or not. It makes no difference to me, for I'm not interested in dining with people who intend to run my every affair.

Soon after reaching Independence, Edward dragged Barton out with him to hunt passenger pigeons. Bom accompanied them, as did Edward's personal taxidermist, Norman Stiles, who will accompany us also. Early this afternoon J. T. Landers told me that he had entered heaven, as there are hundreds of spring wildflowers in bloom. He left with a load of plant presses and is still out, likely working by lantern light.

While all this occurred, Mr. Quincannon took the liberty of talking to me as I sketched a scene of the river. He had been having a discussion with Lamar, who was alarmed at having to travel with Edward and his men.

"He's fought the British and doesn't want to do it again," Mr. Quincannon told me.

"I don't believe Edward wishes him harm," I said.

"After what happened on Bloody Island, you can see his concern," Mr. Quincannon pointed out. He had a small red and white pinto with him and I stood up to pet its nose.

"You have a pretty horse there," I said. "What's his name?"

"Whistler. He's noisy when he runs. But you can rename him if you want."

"Why would I want to rename your horse?"

"He's not mine. He's yours."

Astonished, I said, "Are you serious? But why?"

"He's an Indian pony and has been on a lot of buffalo hunts. If you want to paint warriors, you'd better get to know their horses."

"He doesn't seem so wild."

"He's well trained. I got him from an old friend of mine near Franklin. He said there was no place for the horse to run and sold him to me for a good price."

"But surely you want to keep him. He's so very pretty."

"I'm afraid Parker would get jealous."

I laughed. Parker is Mr. Quincannon's buckskin gelding, a pony he has ridden for nearly five years. He invited me to ride the pinto and I couldn't resist. I rode through town, as happy as I had been in a good while. Walter and Avis, sitting on the hotel balcony, stood up to watch.

Sir Edward took that opportunity to arrive back from

hunting. Mr. Quincannon saw him coming and left to avoid trouble. Edward gave the pigeons they had bagged to Barton for delivery to the cooks and rode over to the creek, where I was watering the pony.

"He's a present from Mr. Quincannon," I said.

Edward frowned. "Well, you can give him back."

"I don't have a horse. I intend to keep him."

Edward then informed me that he insisted I have no interactions with Mr. Quincannon whatsoever. "I have reason to believe that in addition to becoming a trader, he is also organizing an army of frontiersmen to drive the Hudson's Bay Company out of Oregon," he said. "I intend to see that he fails."

"What makes you so sure?" I asked.

"I have means of learning things."

"You believe this, yet you are allowing him to guide us?" I said.

"Certainly," Edward replied with a smile. "What better way to keep track of him."

I insisted that he was merely jealous and had made it up.

"Absolutely not!" he said quickly. "I knew about La-Bruneue's involvement but did not know that Mr. Quincannon had become his partner."

"So you killed Mr. LaBruneue because you believed he was going to fight the Hudson's Bay Company?" I said. "Is it true that you're a spy for Great Britain?"

"You mustn't get upset," Edward said. "I forbid it."

"You *forbid* it? I came along thinking this was a holiday. Now I learn it's a military expedition. I can't believe it!"

I left him, and after giving my pony over to one of the herdsmen, retired to my room, where I have been ever since. Though Edward and Walter, both, have knocked on the door, I have refused to come out. Avis has yet to try the door, though, which I find interesting. She's usually the one most able to reach me in times like this.

But I can't remember ever having a time like this, far away from home, trapped in a circumstance not of my choosing. Perhaps I'm making too much of it, but I don't think so. I believe the situation to be very serious. If we are on a path for Oregon, and war might come at any time, there can be no other way to see it but as a very dangerous proposition.

ROUND GROVE

Gabriella's Journal

10 APRIL 1846, 1ST ENTRY

We left in the cool dawn, the mules grabbing clumps of grass as their drivers urged them into motion. Mr. Quincannon and Lamar led the column, followed by a man named Robert Colville, whom I understand Edward refers to as his "lieutenant." I had never met any of these men and presume they arrived in St. Louis just prior to our departure. They arranged themselves at order in double lines and followed Colville at a march. But for the absence of a drum and fife, it seemed to me like a regiment of ragtag soldiers headed to war.

I had breakfasted with Edward and Uncle Walter and Aunt Avis, a somber meal at best. I wonder if they all don't believe I will eventually come to my senses and stop worrying about the situation. I think not. Mr. Quincannon must feel odd, traveling with a group who so outwardly displays honor to the British throne. His friend, Lamar, is right to feel uneasy.

Sir Edward insisted that I ride in the front seat of his carriage with him, with Walter and Avis in the back. Directly behind, workers led the mules in pack strings and herders kept the horses together, allowing them to graze at intervals along the trail.

Edward had picked a special handler to care for his stallion and the chestnut mare he had bought for me. Whistler was turned out with the other horses. I didn't mind having my pinto given a second-rate showing, as I knew all too well that I would be riding him when I wished, and not the red mare.

Ten miles out, Mr. Quincannon greeted a trader and his caravan coming towards St. Louis. He stopped to talk. Edward became upset with the delay and urged him to complete his discussion. Mr. Quincannon said that he needed to learn details of the trail ahead and that if he was in such a hurry to move forward, Lamar could take us onward.

"How can I trust your Indian to lead us?" Edward asked.

"Anyone could follow the wagon tracks," he said.

Edward left it at that and waited for Mr. Quincannon to finish his discussion. We soon reached Round Grove, a large stand of various hardwood trees with an abundance of grass and water. Three separate wagon trains were camped there, all headed to Oregon. The area could have been Independence without the hotel and other buildings, with men working on wagons and tending stock, while women cooked over large fires and watched over their children.

We camped nearby, but kept our mules and horses separate from the emigrants'. Mr. Quincannon knows all too well that mingling stock could cost a lot of time and

possibly hard feelings, if there were arguments over un-
branded mules and horses. He told Edward that most
usually there was trouble over animals and it often resulted in bloodshed.

Mr. Quincannon and his men set to cutting hardwood,
for use as axles and wagon spokes should one of the carts
break down. He told Edward that there was no wood to
be found on the open plains and many a traveler, upon
studying his broken-down wagon, had wished he had cut
extra spokes and axles when he had the chance.

I was sitting at the table with Edward, having tea and
awaiting our meal, when a lost pony wandered into our
camp, followed quickly by a girl of eleven or twelve. The
little horse jumped through the fire where the Rivet
brothers were cooking, spilling everything.

I quickly stood up and addressed the girl before Edward could display his anger. The girl apologized for her
pony's behavior and I told her not to worry about it.

"You have a beautiful pony," I said. "Would you like
to pose for me?"

"What do you mean?" she asked.

I took out my easel and set it up. "Just stand over
there," I said, "and hold your pony as still as possible."

Her eyes lit up. "You're an artist?"

"Yes," I told her, "and I think you and your pony would
make wonderful subjects."

The girl, her long blond hair shining in the late sun,
smiled broadly while I worked. Edward came and stood
looking over my shoulder.

"Why are you wasting your time and your supplies
drawing this wagon girl?" he asked.

"She's an interesting study, Edward."

"Just be certain you have plenty of pads left to draw
me when we reach buffalo country."

Edward mounted his stallion and rode away by himself, his rifle in a buckskin sheath and a shotgun in hand, leaving Bom staring after him at the tent, wondering what to do. Barton, also beside the tent, shrugged and the two began a game of checkers.

I continued with the girl and her pony, deciding to do a watercolor. I finished a small piece quickly and gave it to her. She beamed and hurried back to her camp, leading the pony behind.

After she left, I began a larger watercolor of the girl and the pony. Mr. Quincannon walked over to where I was working and stood to one side. He held the reins to my pinto and his buckskin.

"That amazes me, how you can paint from memory like that."

"I'm lucky to have the gift," I said. "What are you going to do with Whistler?"

"I thought you might be interested in going for a ride."

"Quite presumptuous of you, isn't it?"

"It doesn't seem to me like Edward cares for Whistler like you do. Take advantage while he's gone."

"I don't make a habit of riding alone with people I don't know, Mr. Quincannon."

"That's understandable," he said. "Maybe Bom would like to ride along, or even Barton."

"The point is," I said, "I'm not interested in riding right now, thank you."

"Sorry to have bothered you," he said, turning away.

"One thing before you go," I said. "Would you answer a question for me?"

He stood holding the horses, waiting for the question. I couldn't read him at all, to tell if he was angry or didn't care. He simply stood there waiting, as if my rejecting him didn't matter one way or the other.

"Why didn't you insist that I go riding?" I asked.

"I don't care to ride with someone who doesn't want

to ride with me. And I don't value tests to see how far I'll
go."

"You had no business asking me in the first place," I
said. "I'm engaged to be married."

"Then why aren't you riding with Edward?"

"As you can see," I retorted, "I'm practicing my art. I
want to be sharp when Edward downs his game."

"I'm afraid Edward doesn't really appreciate your talent," he said.

"Don't be so harsh, Mr. Quincannon. After all, my portraits of him will be far more valuable than those of any
wagon people."

"What makes you so sure?"

"Don't you know the value of subject matter?"

"That, as you should well know, is in the eye of the
beholder."

"I believe Edward will make a fine subject," I said. "And
I know for certain that many of my countrymen are eager
to gain an image of a true hunter on the American plains."

"Are you saying that portraits of Edward Garr standing
beside a dead buffalo will be more sought after than the
image of a Comanche or an Arapaho war leader in full
regalia?" he asked.

I persisted. "Of course! Edward will certainly make his
mark in history. You can be sure of that."

"You are truly dedicated to him, I'll say that."

A rider suddenly appeared in camp, calling for a doctor. Noel Marking emerged from his tent with his bag and
climbed onto a borrowed horse. Mr. Quincannon handed
me the reins to my pony and mounted his buckskin.

We followed the rider to a group of ten wagons that
had just arrived from the Platte River Trail. A bearded
man in late middle age was sitting slumped against a
wagon wheel. Women of various ages surrounded him,
offering solace. One woman in particular, with graying

red hair, held the man's hand, tears streaming down her face. Others from the nearby camps crowded around.

Dr. Marking dismounted and tied his horse to a nearby wagon. He examined the injured man's right shoulder, where an arrow had entered from the back, driving the head deep into the socket. The shaft, broken off three or four inches out, protruded from a wound dark and swollen. Smears of old blood had clotted around the tattered hole.

The redheaded woman, whom I guessed rightly to be his wife, asked Dr. Marking if he could save her husband.

"I won't lie to you," the doctor said. "It looks bad."

The lady dabbed at tears. "I don't want to lose him. I've lost two husbands before, and three sons, all to fighting of some sort."

"Was there no one with you who might have extracted the arrow?" Dr. Marking asked.

"They were all afraid to," she said. "Even the wagon-master."

"It would have been much better," the doctor said, "if the arrowhead had been removed right away."

A woman whom I learned later was her daughter turned to the crowd. "The McConnell family will not give up, no matter how many arrows we take."

The daughter's husband, also standing nearby, said, "The Sioux won't stop us, they won't. We'll carry on."

Mr. Quincannon asked him where they ran into the Indians and the young husband stated, "We weren't but a week out."

The onlookers gasped. During his stories at the hotel, Mr. Quincannon had talked about the Sioux, explaining that they were a large tribe who lived and hunted in the very territory we were headed into. He had talked about an additional two tribes, the Cheyenne and the Arapaho, and had stated that they and the Sioux were allied, and comprised a very large number of native people who were not happy with the American movement across their lands.

This incident seemed to alarm him. He announced that to have the Sioux marauding emigrants so far east was a bad sign.

"It means they've decided to try and stop the wagons even before they get into their country," he said.

Mr. Quincannon began to mingle among the emigrant men, asking them about the attack and exactly where it had taken place. Dr. Marking continued to treat his patient. He asked him, "Can you stand me probing for the arrowhead?"

"Just give me a long drink of whiskey and a stick to bite down on," the man said, "and do what you must."

The doctor began his work. The man held up well, but his wife and daughter were so worried that I took it upon myself to console them, stating repeatedly that this very surgeon was among the best England had to offer.

Sir Edward arrived and stepped down from his horse, visibly upset, and asked me what was going on. I told him about the Indian attack on the emigrants and he turned his attention to Dr. Marking.

"Does that man intend to pay me for your services?" he asked.

The doctor looked up from his work. "Take it out of my wages, if you must."

Edward told Dr. Marking that it would be a costly night for him, but the doctor ignored him and continued.

"Are you returning to your tent?" Edward asked me.

I stepped away to speak to him. "When Dr. Marking is finished and the ladies are settled, I'll be along," I said.

He grabbed me by the arm and jerked me a short distance before I kicked him and broke away.

"I'll not be made a laughingstock of here," he said.

"Don't ever do that again," I said, rubbing my arm where he'd grabbed me.

He stared at me coldly. "Think about this: It's not too late to send you back."

I couldn't believe he had said such a thing. It made me determined to resist him even more.

"You won't send me back, Edward," I said finally. "After all, who would there be to immortalize your all-important hunt? You can't just find an artist anywhere you look."

"That might be all you're good for," he snarled.

He mounted his stallion and rode off. Still in shock from the incident, I returned to the younger woman and began again to console her.

"I'm sorry to be this way," she said, "but I don't want to see my father die."

Annie Malone was three years my junior, and eight months pregnant. She had married Sean Malone in Ireland a year before and together with her father, Martin McConnell, and his new wife, Millie, had decided to come to America for a better life. Millie said often that her flaming red hair had turned gray early, but would become natural again along the Oregon seacoast.

Being from farming families, they had not adjusted to the East Coast and after moving to Illinois, had not found it to their liking, either. They hoped Oregon would offer them the new start they so badly desired.

Annie told me all this and thanked me for my help. "You don't seem like a stranger," she said, "but a sister, maybe." Sean, now assisting the doctor, was a strapping man who never seemed to give up on anything.

"I told you we'd find a doctor and that you'd get fixed," he told his father-in-law. "We'll find our dream yet."

Martin McConnell nodded feebly. Millie, who had pulled a rosary from her apron pocket, smiled for the first time. She told me later that she and Martin had married together with Sean and Annie, in the same ceremony. Both had been too long widowed and had decided to commit to one another and reach out for the shores of America. When she had seen the arrow strike Martin's shoulder, she had wished they were still back in Ireland.

I could see her spirits improving rapidly. Having found Dr. Marking, and gaining hope that her husband was going to mend, she believed that their lives would surely go forward now as they had planned. Dr. Marking didn't have the same confidence, though he said nothing to the family. I didn't know how she would react if Martin passed on, as she had told me that all her family had died in the old country and she believed this new road to Oregon would bring them the comfort she had prayed so hard for. If they could just get past the Indians, the fighting would be over at last.

I didn't want to bring up the notion that Indians were only part of the problem, that war with my native England might break out in her promised land. I said nothing and watched her kiss the crucifix of her rosary and place it back in her apron pocket. She smiled and gave me a hug. She said that she had to get to work, as it was time to bake bread for the evening meal, so they could prepare for a renewed journey again.

Quincannon's Journal

10 APRIL 1846, 1ST ENTRY

With the sun falling fast, I joined Lamar atop a nearby hill to sing an evening song. I kept seeing the vision of LaBruneue's death and the strange turns my planned journey to Oregon have taken. I listened to Lamar, but my mind wandered. His low chants and drumming against the small, handheld drum made me feel close to creation, yet I couldn't release myself enough to make that all-important connection.

I have a hard time praying under difficult circumstances; ironic, because that's usually the time a person needs the most help. It's always easier for me to pray during the good times, when everything's going well. I always pray for those times to last, though I realize that they won't, that they can't. That's just not how life is.

Lamar's small pipe—filled with his own blend of tobacco, as handed down through his family—felt heavy in my hands as I accepted it and smoked, acknowledging the earth and sky, and the four directions. Praying with a pipe was a good means of reaching the Creator, but there needed to be some stress placed on the body before prayers really brought benefit.

Even more than I, Lamar has become distraught of late, wishing there was a means for us to take a sweat bath. He does not have the right to conduct a sweat himself and is worried that we won't have the chance to sweat with anyone before reaching Oregon. I told him that with a good amount of luck, we might locate the band of Arapaho I once lived with. He reminded me that the Arapaho had gone to war against the whites crossing their lands and that their old feelings toward me might not apply any longer.

I have been a part of many sweat ceremonies and since coming back to St. Louis, have missed not participating. I had to think that what he said about the nation of people I once called my own might be true.

As darkness fell, we left the hill and returned to camp. Lamar went to his tent while I became curious about a group of pioneer men who had just finished laying boards tightly across the grass. Nearby, another group began playing fiddles, banjos, and guitars, while everyone gathered to dance.

Sean Malone stood with Annie, he holding a mandolin and she a fiddle, resting it against her very large stomach.

"Good evening, Mr. Quincannon," she said. "Have you heard? Father is improving."

"Already?" I said. "He's hardly had time, has he?"

"He's ready to turn right back around for Oregon," Sean said. "The Sioux be damned."

"What about the Sioux?" I asked.

"Nothing can stop us now," Sean said. "We've joined up with a big caravan."

"We'll get there," Annie said, "God willing and the creeks don't rise."

"Believe me, the creeks will rise," I told them. "Teach your baby to swim."

"He's going to learn to do a lot of things," Sean said.

Annie whacked him on the arm. "He? I won't tolerate another man in the house." Then she turned to me and asked, "What's it like out there, so wild and open?"

"You'll have to see it for yourself," I said.

"Folks say you're the real thing," Sean said. "That you've done it all—fought Indians and near starved and chased buffalo. However did you stay alive?"

"A day at a time," I said.

Annie studied him. "And that English lady, she's a painter, she is. I watched her earlier this evening. Is she going to paint you? I'll bet she does."

"Now, Annie," Sean said. "She's with that British lord, you know."

"Maybe," Annie said, smiling at me. "Maybe not. Here she comes."

I turned to see Miss Hall approach. Her hair hung in

ringlets and she wore the new blue dress she'd spoken of, with the little slippers that matched.

"Good evening, Mr. Quincannon," she said.

She looked magnificent to me and I couldn't help but smile.

Gabriella's Journal

10 APRIL 1846, 2ND ENTRY

Before coming to the dance, I had spent a lot of time in front of the mirror and knew that it had paid off when I saw the light in Mr. Quincannon's eyes. Sean and Annie took their places with the other musicians and Annie winked at me as they broke into a rendition of "The Irish Washerwoman."

"Can you step to that?" I asked Mr. Quincannon.

Without waiting for an answer, I pulled him onto the dance floor and, to my amazement, he was adept at the Irish reel, moving with grace while I followed his lead. When the song ended, we both clapped and moved to one side to catch our breath.

"How do you like my new dress?" I asked.

"It's very nice," he said. "But where is Sir Edward?"

"Asleep in his tent. He doesn't appreciate a good time."

"You've suddenly become less committed."

"Please, Mr. Quincannon, don't misunderstand. I just enjoy dancing, that's all."

"I would think your fiancé would oblige you," he said.

"Edward is under a lot of pressure," I told him. "He'll be back to his old self soon."

Mr. Quincannon smiled slightly. "Are you sure you really know his 'old self'?"

The players began another tune and we watched the dancers as they weaved their way around atop the creaking boards, laughing and clapping their hands to the music.

"Even if he didn't want to dance," Mr. Quincannon said, "I would think he would be standing here with you."

I told him that Edward didn't like mingling with a lower class of people.

"I must say that these folks are polite, for the most part," I said, "but they definitely lack social graces."

Mr. Quincannon frowned. "Their lives have been hard," he said. "They weren't born with the proverbial silver spoon hanging from their lips."

"Do I detect a hint of sarcasm?"

"Perhaps."

"But why be upset with the facts? You seem an educated man."

"There's a number of ways to become educated."

"I mean classroom study."

"I've studied history and some law," he said.

"Then why aren't you making good use of it?" I asked.

"Who says I'm not?"

"Come, Mr. Quincannon. Tell me why you're not a wealthy St. Louis lawyer with a wife and family, and high political aspirations."

"I intend to utilize my expertise in Oregon. I will file on the land I choose for my trading venture and in the end there will be no question as to who owns it."

"I hear a bitter note."

"My father left my mother to go west before he had finished the legal work on his claim. She discovered his error when a group of land grabbers took it away from her. I was ten. My mother and I nearly starved to death."

"What did she do to make ends meet?"

"Took in washing, mainly. In the end, she worked herself to death."

I noticed the lean muscles in his face, the smooth lines knotting like twisted rope.

"Did your father ever come back?"

"Never."

"Do you know where he went?"

"Into the mountains. I never sought to find him and I don't care to."

"Perhaps it would be better for both of you . . ."

"Perhaps it would be better if we ended the discussion."

"You're right," I said. "It is getting late. Perhaps there will be another dance, another place."

"Perhaps," he said. "I'll see you to your tent."

Bom was waiting for us. He opened the flap for me, and before entering, I said to Mr. Quincannon, "You will be a success at whatever you want to do, I can tell. Thank you for escorting me and good night."

ROUND GROVE

Quincannon's Journal

10 APRIL 1846, 2ND ENTRY

I walked with Bom away from Ella's tent and toward Garr's, asking him whether I had to worry about the nobleman charging out with his rifle.

In response, Bom edged the flap open and peered inside. "You don't have to worry about Master Sir Edward.

He is very much asleep, as are Walter and Avis in their tent. I can assure you, I won't discuss your time with Miss Hall." He motioned toward the dancing. "I would like to go watch for a while."

Bom seemed comfortable, almost content, with his role as servant. I concluded that, like other slaves I had known, he had grown accustomed to his condition on some level. I don't mean to say he was beaten down— there was too much sparkle in his eyes for that—but he held no rage, as I had so often seen.

While we walked, I asked him how he had come to be with Garr.

"Master Sir Edward bought me off the block the first day he came to St. Louis," he said. "I guess Mr. Lawson had no more need for me."

"I don't know why you haven't found a means of escape long ago," I said.

His expression changed. "Do you know what they do to runaways?"

"If I'd been you, I would have taken the chance."

"You don't understand," he said. "They take you when you're young and show you what they do to those who don't please them. And I don't mean just to our folks. I mean to anyone they own—black, white, or otherwise. When I first got off the boat, they made us all watch somebody butcher a white man who tried to help some slaves get away. When they got done with him, and they took their sweet time, he was in a lot of pieces, and they put his head on a pole for us to see. I can still hear his screams at night."

I watched the dancing, remembering screams I had once heard. As Bom continued, I knew what he was going to tell me.

"Small kids were made to watch that, some as young as five years old, both black and white. Men with knives walked around and said that anyone who turned away would get their eyelids slit off. They wanted everyone to know what could happen." He paused. "You say I should have run. I might have got away, but couldn't have fallen asleep from then on and I would have had to do a lot of killing to stay free."

Bom's story left me hollow. I was reminded of the afternoon I had killed for the first time. Father had been gone for three or four years and my mother was having difficulty feeding me. I ran the streets of St. Louis with my friends, seeing things we couldn't forget. The worst of it all was the capturing of street children for slavery.

Thugs would roam the alleys day and night looking for stray kids. I learned later that these men were paid well for them by merchants who dealt in child exploitation. I had found a flintlock pistol laying beside a drunken riverman and was toying with it when a greasy man in tattered clothes grabbed my best friend's sister. She struggled free and ran for my friend and me, with the man close behind. I stepped in front of him, stuffed the barrel of the pistol into his stomach, and pulled the trigger.

I can still hear that sound plainly, a muffled explosion that doubled him over and burned my hand. The ignited powder clung to his filthy clothes and he rolled to the ground, his stomach ablaze and his pants soaked with blood and urine.

My friend tried to pull me away, but I waited to be certain that man never got up. I clung to the pistol in my trembling hand, even though my skin was scorched and swelling rapidly. I was ready to club him when two men came to rob him. When he tried to rise, one of them stabbed him about a dozen times. My friend pulled the pistol from my grip and flung it away, and we ran.

That day I decided that I would leave the city as soon

as possible. I didn't care about finding my father; I just wanted to get away. I never told my mother what had happened and she believed me when I said I had stuck my hand in a burning barrel trying to retrieve a scrap of meat.

After that I stayed clear of the alleys. My friend kept going back there, as if he knew no different, and I never saw him again.

"In some ways, you seem a slave yourself," Bom said. "Your feelings are trapping you."

Bom's gift for seeing into me made me nervous and I stopped talking. We got to the dance floor and he watched with interest, saying that in his homeland, they celebrated all the time. "We dance and dance and dance, and we sing all the day long." I remarked that he sounded as if he was still there. He pointed to his heart. "I've never left. I'll always be there."

"What about your family?"

"I'll never see them again, I know that. It's the same with you, isn't it?"

"What makes you think you know so much about me?" I asked.

"A man without a family knows another like man," he said. "But I know that for you, it's hard to talk about."

"So why do you think Edward Garr is any different from the others who've owned you?" I asked.

"When you get bought by someone who don't crack the whip," he said, "there's just about nothing bad he can do to you."

We watched the emigrants dancing and I thought about Miss Hall. When I turned and looked toward the tents, I noticed her flap was slightly parted.

"Yes, she's watching you," Bom said with a laugh. "I suppose she's trying to understand her feelings."

"They seem an odd couple, her and Edward Garr," I said.

He smiled. "It's natural that you would say that. It's you that's making her wonder about things."

"She need not wonder," I said. "I've got a lot to do and I don't think a genteel English lady would fit in."

"She's some genteel and some not," he said. "She's a little of everything and can't decide what she wants to keep and what she wants to throw away."

"I don't think Sir Edward is going to dictate terms to her."

"He will have a difficult time." We started back and Bom said, "I saw you on the hill with Lamar. You seem to know that kind of religion very well."

"As well as any other."

"That's good. I've heard that you frontiersmen know the soul of the land like the natives. That's what my people know, the soul of the land. I believe Miss Ella feels it, but cannot live it like she wants."

"What do you think about Sir Edward?"

"He doesn't want to take the time. Maybe he will get better, if he ever stops pacing."

"You must see something in him that I don't," I said.

"Perhaps," he agreed.

I returned to the tent and found Lamar sitting up, waiting for me.

"We have some things to take care of," he said, leading me out of the tent.

11 APRIL 1846

The morning was as beautiful as any this entire spring. After breakfast, I told the men to make more axles and cart tongues from whatever hardwood they could find. We haven't made near as many as we'll need, owing to the fact that so many merchants and emigrants have the same idea in mind and have used up a great deal of the right-sized wood.

The mules and horses are grazing peacefully. They'll need the extra fat when we get farther south along the Arkansas. I've heard the buffalo have trimmed off what grass the emigrant oxen and mules haven't gotten to. And being this early in the year, the grass won't be that high to begin with.

I find it interesting to discuss the vegetation with J. T. Landers. He's collected a number of specimens already and checks his presses daily to be sure the plants are drying properly. He says he'll be very interested to learn the various plants that we'll run into as we travel, as he's always wanted to do a study of Rocky Mountain plants and their uses, especially by the Indian tribes.

I combed dust from my buckskin's coat and mane, getting him ready to turn out. I couldn't stop thinking of the previous night and my dance with Miss Hall. It made me want to dance with her again, and soon. She had a sparkle to her eyes that reached deep into me. Maybe I shouldn't have put her off when she asked me about my past.

It bothers me that she feels so committed to Garr; but she's told him that she will be his wife and I have to respect her for standing by him. I don't believe Garr feels the same closeness. His desire to control her is evident, but beyond that there's little to show that he cares at all for her.

I worry now about how this trip is going to end. If there's war with England, I'll have to kill Edward Garr. It will be him or me.

Miss Hall would hate me for that. I know she doesn't think the way Garr does, but she's still British aristocracy and inclined toward their views.

It would be better if she ignored everything she's been told and just concentrated on her artwork. She has alluded to her many dreams and how she's going to accomplish them, which is good. A person has to have goals and the belief that he—or she—can reach them. What bothers me is how easy she believes it will be.

She seems more naive than even the young settlers, Sean and Annie Malone, chock-full of their own dreams and determination. Despite Martin McConnell's arrow wound, they appear unafraid of warring Indians and whatever else lies in front of them, convinced that Oregon will change their lives. I'll admit that I have a bit of that feeling myself. In fact, it's what drives me. But I have no doubts about the sacrifices I'll face in reaching that promise.

For a short time I entertained the idea of our traveling with the McConnells and the Malones, but quickly realized that it wouldn't work. Heavily laden wagons drawn by oxen move a lot slower than mule-pulled carts. We would outdistance them by a good ten miles the first day. We couldn't travel with anyone, so I've begun to consider an alternative route from the Platte Road.

When Lamar was waiting up for me last night, he said that Garr's men were nervous about the Sioux and that Colville, the "lieutenant," had approached him to suggest that they reconsider new travel plans. They wondered about another way of reaching Oregon.

I found it odd that one of Garr's top men couldn't even reveal his feelings to the nobleman himself, but had instead sought out someone he barely knew.

We went to Colville's tent and after a short discussion, agreed to bring the matter to Garr's attention at the first opportunity. I was thinking about that opportunity when Bom suddenly appeared and bowed.

"Master Sir Edward wishes to see you. Says it's urgent."

"Tell him I'll be right over," I said.

"He says it's very urgent and that I bring you back with me."

I stopped combing my pony and made it clear to him that I would be over when I was finished.

"Make some tea for him," I said. "Keep him occupied until I'm through."

Bom smiled. "Will you drink, also? I would like to see that, a mountain man with a teacup." I agreed to have a cup and he said, "Good. That will go a long way in making you two friends."

"Friends?" I said.

"It is important for all of us, every one, that you and Master Sir Edward become friends," he told me. "If you do not, the journey will be fraught with bad omen."

"My friendship with Sir Edward, or lack of it, won't change the problems we'll face on the trail," I said.

"Oh, but you're wrong, Master Quincannon. You see, where no animosity exists, there is a smoothness to everything."

Bom hurried back to Garr and I led my buckskin out to graze. When I arrived at the tent, Sir Edward was pacing and puffing on the stub of a cigar.

Bom brought the tea. "Sit down, both of you, please.

You can talk better that way." He poured the cups full and stood back.

I sipped at the mixture of a black India blend and wild mint, finding it more than tolerable.

"I didn't know your kind took tea," Garr said. "Don't mountain men drink liquor?"

"Among other things."

Garr called Bom to him. "I want you to have Pierre Rivet sauté me some wild vegetables in butter," he said. "Perhaps Mr. Quincannon would like a plate as well."

"Yes, I will join you. Thanks," I said.

Bom bowed and hurried toward the cook tent. Garr threw the small cigar away and pulled a fresh one from his pocket.

"Regarding our journey to Oregon," he said. "I hear you're spreading the word that we're taking a different trail."

"I was discussing it with some of the men."

"You were discussing it with *my* men. Robert Colville, to be exact. He said you told him we shouldn't go the Oregon route."

"That's true."

"Why didn't you discuss it with me first?"

"I'm the guide," I said. "I know what's best for us."

"Our agreement is that we make decisions together," Garr said. "I expect you to honor that."

"Are you interested in risking your life and those of your men fighting Indians?"

"Isn't it inevitable?"

"Not necessarily. Not if we avoid Sioux territory."

"I didn't know there was a trail that avoided the Sioux."

"How much do you know about the Santa Fe Trail?"

"I certainly know it doesn't lead to Oregon. Why should we veer off our intended course?"

"If you had been listening to the settlers the other night, you would know," I said. "But you had domestic matters concerning you."

The nobleman leaned toward me across the table and shook his cigar in my face.

"Gabriella is none of your concern. The sooner you understand that, the better."

"If you're continually angry with her," I said, "then there's little time left to discuss important matters with me."

Garr sat back in his chair. "You're right. Perhaps it is of greatest importance that I keep track of what you're doing. Who knows what decisions you'll make if left on your own."

Bom refilled our cups, smiling at me. "You're doing very well with the tea," he said.

"Don't expect me to do this every day."

Garr lit another cigar. "If we take the Santa Fe route, how will we reach Oregon?"

"We'll head toward the mountains from Bent's Fort, then cross over and work our way up toward Fort Hall and hit the main trail again."

"Are there no hostile Indians in any of that region?"

"A few Cheyennes and Arapahoes. And Utes in the mountains. They should be on their spring hunts. They won't bother us if we don't bother them."

Garr chewed his cigar to shreds and I asked him why the rationale for changing routes was so hard to understand.

"I understand perfectly! I simply don't like the diversion. You see, I have my reasons for wanting to travel the northern route, Mr. Quincannon, reasons I wouldn't expect you to understand. However, I will concede to your plan, just as long as I reach Fort Vancouver before winter."

He stood up and spat out the remains of his cigar, then ordered Bom and the other servants to gather around him. He barked orders, gestering wildly with his hands. Bom climbed into the carriage and began circling through camp, announcing immediate departure, while others began packing and taking the tents down.

I watched for a short time, very amused. Ella was out riding and Garr yelled wildly for her to come in. I don't think she heard him. If she did, she didn't pay any attention.

Her aunt and uncle had to move quickly to avoid the workers. Barton Strand, who had just returned from target practice, hurried to find J.T. Landers and help him with his botanical specimens.

Peter Rivet stood holding the plate of freshly cooked vegetables, which Garr promptly knocked from his hand. "Can't you see that we're leaving?" he said. "I'll expect you to clean those dishes and then carry them along with you until we stop again. Is that understood?"

Rivet appeared crestfallen, and then frightened. He nodded and picked up the dinnerware, realizing he had to wash and box the dishes before he was left too far behind. He would then have to catch up as best he could, for Garr would expect to eat off the same plates at the next meal.

Garr turned to me. "What are you waiting for? Lead the way."

"We're not going anywhere until tomorrow," I said. "My men are working."

Garr began pacing. "I want to leave now!"

"Leave if you want," I told him. "We'll catch up tomorrow."

Garr threw up his hands and ordered the servants to

erect the tents again, and for his chefs to prepare another
meal. Everyone stared at him in disbelief. He ordered
his stallion saddled and, taking his Whestley Richards
rifle, rode off into the distance alone.

Gabriella's Journal

11 APRIL 1846

We discovered three head of stray cattle,
one a milch cow. Mr. Quincannon tells me
she is a Brown Swiss and has recently lost her calf. He
named her June and Mr. Quincannon is teaching the
Rivet brothers how to milk her, as Edward now wants
cream for making sauces.

I spent the entire day and much of the evening riding
Whistler and getting to know the little horse. He's as rugged and sturdy as they come, and can turn on a dime.
Mr. Quincannon had mentioned that the pony had once
been used exclusively for running buffalo, and I can see
that he must have been highly prized.

After setting up logs and other obstacles, Mr. Quincannon had me ride the pony toward each one and turn him
at the last second with my knee. I'm learning quickly to
stay atop a swift-moving pony that can move in any direction with the slightest command.

Edward has said nothing to me about riding Whistler
or consorting with Mr. Quincannon. It seems to me that
his mind is elsewhere. Perhaps he is overly concerned
about not taking the regular route along the Platte River.

He has no doubt made secret plans that have been disrupted by the change.

I don't much care about his secret plans and, frankly, I'm beginning to care less about him as time goes on. I'm beginning to believe that he's the most selfish man I've ever met, which makes me think again of Mr. Quincannon's remark about knowing the "true" Edward.

I must admit that I've been sheltered from most of the world and what goes on outside the higher classes of Europe. I have known no other people besides aristocrats and have been to no other lands. I've tended to believe what I've been told, that the British and their homelands are beyond compare. Now I'm beginning to think differently.

Europe is an old land and little fresh and new exists there. This journey has yet to really begin and I'm seeing that a different world exists here, one of a wild and free nature that I could never have dreamed of. Perhaps my belief in this fact has come about in part or in whole because of Owen Quincannon.

THE NARROWS

Gabriella's Journal

13 APRIL 1846, 1ST ENTRY

We're now two days out since we made our camp at Round Grove and what an unusual time it's been. I've been riding a great deal, getting more used to Whistler and gaining confidence that I'll ride him well once we reach the open plains. The little horse lives to burst forth across the grasslands, stretching his legs out and surging ahead, never stopping until I rein him in.

I've grown used to turning him with my knees, a very simple means that leaves me astounded every time I do it. I've never ridden a horse so well trained. It will be an educational experience to see how the Indians accomplish such a feat.

I ride and come back to camp without concern about arguing with Edward. He and I haven't spoken a dozen words between us since leaving Round Grove. He hasn't given any indication of anger towards me, but there is no indication of anything else, either. He acts as if I simply do not exist.

Last night I did an unusual thing. I asked Mr. Quincannon if I might join him and Lamar for their evening prayers. I walked with them to the top of a rise bare of trees and listened to Lamar pray in a low chant. I had never heard anything like it and it seemed so natural and peaceful within the setting. A soft breeze whispered through the grass and the sounds of crickets mixed with the low pounding of the Indian's small drum.

Mr. Quincannon later told me the song's wording:

Hear me, Great Father.
I come to talk.
I come to talk.
I live with the earth and the sky,
and all the beings that are,
and I wish to know their truth,
for I want to be in harmony with all.
Hear me, Great Father.
I come to talk.
I come to talk.

After the ceremony we sat quietly, watching the sky change colors. The clouds turned pink overhead, and in the west, a streak of crimson colored the horizon. Mr. Quincannon kept his eye on a nighthawk, watching it soar and swoop far above us. Sitting there, I felt a bond unite the three of us—he and I and Lamar—a unity that can't readily be explained until you rest in the twilight and listen to the low prayers of a native person.

Mr. Quincannon told me that Lamar prays every morning and evening, in clear or rainy skies, in cold or heat, without fail. Once he had to cover Lamar with a buffalo robe to keep him from frostbite. It angered the Delaware, but it was better that he live to pray another day than perish for the sake of a few hours of sacrifice.

I believe I will ask to accompany them again, though Mr. Quincannon says that there are certain ceremonies reserved for men only, as there are ceremonies only for women. Many prayers are for both sexes together and Lamar indicated that he would be happy to include me anytime I so desired.

Before we went to pray, we had a slight scare. Mr. Quincannon had to stop Edward from positioning his men for battle. A group of Osage Indians had appeared and were waiting for a signal to enter camp. They are a harmless tribe at this juncture in time, I learned, and only wanted to talk and trade for cloth.

Their heads were shaved except for a roach along the top from the forehead nearly to the neck. This ridge of hair stood straight up, plastered with animal oils and filled with hawk or turkey feathers. Many had painted their heads and faces in various combinations of red and black, but Mr. Quincannon assured everyone that the symbols were not those of war.

They came dressed in breechcloths and wrapped in trade blankets. Lamar and Mr. Quincannon smoked a pipe with them, and after a period of talking and sharing bowls of stew, they left. I wanted to inquire into painting a portrait of one or more of them, but decided I would do the work later and not interfere in their meeting. Edward had told me not to go anywhere near them and I suppose that entered significantly into my decision.

This morning we found ourselves facing bad weather. The dawn broke to a misty sky and clouds blanketed the land. The distance appeared to be without dimension, except for the hazy outlines of trees along the creeks. Mr. Quincannon advised Edward's servants that they wrap all the spices and expensive foodstuffs in canvas and seal everything tightly, leaving just enough out for a midday meal. At first they protested, but when he suggested that all the provisions could be spoiled, they set to work immediately.

As we broke camp, a chill wind began to blow. I decided not to ride my pony but instead sat in the front seat of the carriage with Edward, while Walter and Avis huddled in the back. Edward began a discussion about firearms and the weapons he would choose once we reached buffalo country. He talked about finding a giant bull buffalo, so white in color as to stun the onlooker.

"Perhaps I shall find two," he said.

I paid no attention to his conversation, simply nodding in acknowledgment whenever he looked my way. Just before noon we stopped for a meal, and by the time we had resumed travel, it was pouring with rain. The skies seemed to have broken apart, never to close again, and the wind grew to gale force. Sir Edward ordered his stallion caught and saddled, and charged into the weather, while I squeezed into the back seat of the carriage with Walter and Avis and wrapped myself in a Mackinaw blanket.

Even with the carriage cover up, the wind blew torrents

of water in on us and Avis squealed constantly, crying out that before long, we would all be washed away.

Bom braved the ordeal without a word, urging the horses forward when all they wanted to do was turn around. In the caravan of carts, the mules also resisted pulling into the storm and the drivers' loud cursing could be heard over the rain.

Mr. Quincannon and Lamar led the column. I don't see how they were capable of finding the road ahead of them. Waiting the storm out was not possible, as the longer and harder it rained, the worse trail conditions became.

Nightfall arrived, changing the gray bleakness of the day into black. As we made camp along a small creek, the rain momentarily ended, but soon the skies were filled with lightning, and thunder echoed through the darkness. The servants laid canvas upon the ground and erected the tents as best they could. Edward complained continually, infuriated at the conditions.

Mr. Quincannon provided dried beef, while the expensive foodstuffs and spices remained wrapped and watersealed. The shriveled meal was laid out on Aunt Avis's fine china.

Jon and Pierre Rivet, having changed into new white cooking clothes, worked in their small tent. They told me later of their ordeal, trying to make the jerky suitable for Edward's taste. They had a great deal of discussion regarding their situation, making a lot of faces and talking rapidly in French.

With Pierre's help, Jon struggled to make a sauce, hoping to soothe Edward's irritation. They had been working by lantern light and Pierre removed the chimney while Jon swirled butter in a small pan over the flame. He added cream and a pinch of flour and dried herbs, and stuck his finger in to taste it.

"We knew we had made something that, even under

these conditions, would please Sir Edward," Jon told me later.

Pierre jumped suddenly as thunder cracked overhead, dropping the lantern into the side of the tent. Flames rolled up the wall and he began frantically slapping puddled water with his shoes, coating his starched white trouser leg with mud.

Jon stood and watched, coaching Pierre to kick more water and to kick it faster. Finally the flames hissed away and the two stood coughing in the smoky darkness.

Jon then said, "To hell with it all," and flung the sauce out into the rain.

All this time we sat in Edward's tent, waiting, while he kept a cigar going and peered out into the storm, wondering where his cooks might be. I remained huddled in the blanket, sitting between Uncle Walter and Aunt Avis.

"A wonderful evening, indeed," Walter said, rubbing his knee. "I'm having fun much sooner than I expected."

"Will you stop complaining?" Avis said.

"I'll shoot you in the knee," Walter said, "and then we'll see how you tolerate the damp."

The Rivets finally arrived with a tray of beef jerky and set out the china. Edward stared at the bleak-looking meat and Avis began to moan.

The Rivets quickly hurried back into the rain before Edward could yell at them. I doubt they had any concerns about being fired on such a bleak night. After all, where would Edward find replacements?

I selected a chunk of meat and began to gnaw on it. Aunt Avis scowled.

"Isn't it a bit dry?" she asked.

"More than a bit," I said. "But we have no choice."

"I can't wait for breakfast," Edward said.

Walter chewed methodically, encouraging Aunt Avis

to eat. "Never mind the taste and texture, dear," he said. "You need your strength."

"Ah! It's so horrible."

Edward set his plate down after but a few bites and lit a cigar. Outside, the rain began easing up and soon stopped entirely, at which time he stood up and left without a word.

"It seems he doesn't like our company," Walter commented.

"Speak for yourself," Avis said.

I left the tent, eager to avoid witnessing another conflict between my aunt and uncle. Clouds were swimming before a nearly full moon and shadows moved like flitting ghosts across the wet ground.

I held my dress up and found my way to a log near the stream, where I sat for a time listening to the thousands of frogs voicing their mating calls into the night and watching the stars glow in the vast heavens overhead. The scene was perfectly wonderful. The air was cool, the clarity of sight and sound heavenly.

Earlier, I had thought about my decision to come to America and the pursuit of wealth and fame, wishing I could bypass all this inconvenience and just get to the Indian lands and begin my work. Upon sitting on the log, feeling the serenity after the storm, I realized that the tempest had created the quiet and I couldn't have truly enjoyed one without the other.

My thoughts were interrupted by Mr. Quincannon, who was suddenly sitting on the log beside me.

"I didn't mean to frighten you," he said. "I thought you might be hungry." He pulled a small parfleche from his pocket and opened it up to show me the contents inside.

I asked him what it was and he told me it was pemmican, a mixture of buffalo meat and berries that the Indians make for winter food.

"I'd just as soon not," I said.

"You won't even try it?"

"No, thank you."

Mr. Quincannon placed the bag on the log beside me and stood up. "I'll leave it here. You'll need to eat something, as we'll be leaving at first light and travel day and night until we get out of this rain."

"That could be weeks, couldn't it?"

"Not where we're headed. Soon you'll be praying for clouds to block the sun." He pointed to the pemmican. "Consider my offer," he said, and quickly disappeared into the night.

I picked up the bag and smelled its contents, then dipped my fingers in and found the mixture more than tolerable. At that moment Edward appeared, Bom beside him, holding a closed umbrella in case the rain resumed. I swallowed quickly.

"What are you doing out here?" Edward asked.

"I went for a walk," I said.

"Why didn't you tell me? I was worried."

"I planned to return shortly."

He noticed the bag in my hand. I had regretfully forgotten to hide it.

"What have you got there?" he asked.

"It's called pemmican."

"Did Quincannon give it to you?" He didn't wait for an answer, but snatched it from me and threw it as far as he could across the creek. "I told you I don't want you taking anything from him. Do you understand?"

"Edward, you had no right to do that."

"Did you meet him out here secretly?"

"You know better than that."

"I don't know you anymore," he said. "I thought I did once, but no longer."

He wheeled around and with Bom struggling to keep

pace, made his way back to his tent. I wondered what he meant by having once known me, but no longer. I can't remember that we have ever actually known one another at all. Even when we were intimate, conversation was always superficial at best, and never lasted long.

Suddenly, Mr. Quincannon was beside me again. I wonder at times if he isn't more Indian in nature than he is white, but his sophistication leaves no doubt that he lives in two worlds.

He handed me another bag of pemmican and asked me what I thought of it.

"I'll have to admit, it was rather good," I said.

He got up and started again for the shadows, turning quickly to say, "This time, take better care of it."

Quincannon's Journal

13 APRIL 1846

The dream has come again, twice in the past three days. The warriors get bigger and bigger with each recurring vision, their weapons crisper in image and more foreboding. Everything about the dream now seems massive. Either that or I'm diminishing in size.

If I'm worried about shrinking, I would like to know why. I'm feeling as well as I ever have physically and I don't believe my mental makeup is defective. There may be some who would argue that, but I've yet to hear anyone say it.

So I have to conclude that my innermost thoughts

themselves form the basis for my nighttime quandaries. Maybe I should think back on a few things that the Arapaho holy man, Elk Heart, told me some years back. He was ancient when he counseled me and now I wonder where he is, or if he's crossed over to the Other Side Camp.

I think a lot about his grandson, Antelope, my best friend at one time. I wonder if Elk Heart passed the medicine on to him. There would be a lot of responsibility in taking over that kind of duty. I have forgotten much of the old man's wisdom, or perhaps pushed it away from me because I chose to. The things he told me forced me to think about subjects I had long forgotten.

"To reach the realm of Calm you must pass through the land of Truth," he once told me. "There is no other road to take."

He made it clear that no man can grow old in peace until he makes the decision to purify himself.

"There are many ways to make offerings to the Creator," he said. "Each must find his own means. You are having trouble choosing and it will cost you in the end."

He told me something I already knew, but having it confirmed scared me all the more. After that I took part in numerous ceremonies and even fasted on a hill for four days and nights. It opened a world up to me that resulted in many more questions than answers.

Gabriella Hall is also a puzzlement to me. She brings up feelings I haven't felt for a long time. Some, I believe, I've never experienced before. The thought of letting these feelings have their way with me is terrifying. I remember telling Bom that I had no room for a genteel English lady, but I continue to think about her.

All Edward Garr thinks about is Oregon. He must be headed to a very important rendezvous at Fort Vancouver. Certainly that would be the place where the British will convene should war break out. His traveling overland through the heart of America to hunt along the way suggests that his reasoning cannot be completely sound. Either that or he thinks himself totally invincible.

I try not to be obsessed by the man, for there are far too many other concerns that take priority. We haven't even reached Bent's Fort yet. One day at a time. I learned that with my Indian friends, but have put it past me since going back to civilization and then deciding that I need to reach Oregon. I won't get there but one day at a time.

So far my journey toward Truth has been a desperate one. Certainly, as we travel ever closer to the mountains, I'll think more about Elk Heart and his wisdom, and the treacherous journey through my fears to learn what he was saying to me. But there's a lot I don't care to know, and for that reason I fear I'll be seeing huge Indians bearing down on me for some time to come.

Gabriella's Journal

13 APRIL 1846, 2ND ENTRY

Much has happened of late and I believe it's only the beginning of an experience I'll look back on with wonder all the rest of my life. Owen Quincannon treads the edge of danger in his pursuit of me. Had Edward discovered us together it would have been a dire situation.

Mr. Quincannon might think he's just assisting me in getting used to the trail, but I believe it's much more. It flatters me to consider that. But it also creates a predicament for me. I fear the test of who will live and who will die between him and Edward will come before long if I cannot pursuade Mr. Quincannon to remain at a distance.

In order to take my mind off him, I have decided to concentrate entirely on my work. Upon returning from the creek, I discovered J. T. Landers pacing in front of his tent. He informed me that he is worried about the condition of some plant specimens that got wet in the storm. Apparently a mule dislodged them from its back during the storm, and in the fall, the presses burst open.

He took me inside his tent and there, lying on a table in the light of a lantern, were a number of small plants he referred to as *Nemastylis geminiflora*. I asked him to speak English and he said they were prairie irises. Even in their rain-soaked condition they were beautiful, thin-leaved with light blue flowers that emerged from the stalks in clusters of two.

"It is not really an iris as such," he said, fingering them as if they would disintegrate. "I can't go back and collect more, and I sincerely doubt if I will find more specimens ahead."

He explained that a botanist named Thomas Nuttall had journeyed through the West over thirty years earlier and had suggested in his notes that the prairie iris was not found anywhere west of Kansas City.

"This proves new distribution," he said. "If only I could preserve the specimens."

I suggested that he describe them in detail on paper, as I had often seen him do, and allow me to draw them in watercolor. Thus he would have a record of his findings no matter if the collection deteriorated.

"I shall accept your kind offer," he said, "even though I wish there was a way to save the plants themselves."

As I drew and he wrote, he asked if I might be inter-

ested in learning botany from him. I told him that I would
enjoy short lessons from time to time, but nothing too
intensive. He seemed disappointed. The poor man is a
lonely sort who cannot share his passions with anyone
other than another botanist.

He perked up when I suggested that Mr. Quincannon
had told me that he wished to exchange botanical information along the way, as he had learned a great deal from
the Indians about dietary and medicinal plants.

"I would enjoy that very much," he said, "if he remains
alive, that is."

"Do you know something that I don't?" I asked.

"I doubt it," he said. "Edward has said nothing to me
about the matter, but anyone can read his face. He is
aiming his rifle at your suitor every time he looks at him."

"Do you really see that much danger?" I asked.

Mr. Landers had a thick magnifying glass with which
he was studying the plants. He looked up at me and said
that he feared the worst.

"I have no right to say this, but perhaps you should
approach your fiancé and make amends as much as possible."

"Make amends for what?"

"What he perceives as your lack of concern for him."

I will never understand how it is that should a lady
and a gentleman disagree about a matter, it is the lady
who is always in the wrong. I had thought Mr. Landers
to have a bit more perception about my situation with
Edward.

"You have been talking to him, haven't you?" I said.

"We've had but a few discussions," he said. "He seems
certain that one morning he will arise and find you and
Mr. Quincannon gone."

"What nonsense!"

"I'm only relating what he said, Miss Hall, and I would beg you not to repeat it."

"Of course not," I said. "But if he's that concerned, why doesn't he attempt to show me his feelings?"

"His feelings come from the barrel of a gun," he replied. "I believe that to be the only expression he knows."

PLEASANT VALLEY

Gabriella's Journal

15 APRIL 1846, 1ST ENTRY

It has been a trying two days that I won't soon forget. It makes me wonder what other trials lie ahead.

Two mornings past, Mr. Quincannon rousted everyone well before dawn and his men fought the mules to get them into their traces. He told us that we had to be rolling by daylight, for the trail ahead passed through a marshy area called the Narrows and should the rain come too quickly, we could be deterred indefinitely.

As the sky gradually lightened, Mr. Quincannon made his way through camp, hurrying everyone with breakfast and helping with the packing and loading. Edward laughed at him; in his mind, no respectable leader would be assisting servants. I told him that maybe he should take a lesson from our guide and thus gain the respect of his own men. He wasn't pleased with my remark.

Earlier, I had taken Mr. Landers's advice regarding Edward's jealousy over Mr. Quincannon. I told my fiancé that I would be willing to make an effort at communication if he would. He told me that there was nothing to communicate about until I made up my mind to agree with him on all points. "There's no give-and-take in that solution," I said, to which he replied, "I don't expect there to be any give-and-take."

The incident made me wonder just how much the man really cares for me. Our situation does not seem to bother him in the least. I cannot see marriage under such conditions.

Just prior to departure, everyone gathered in a circle to observe the Sabbath. Mr. Quincannon told me later that many of the emigrant wagon trains wouldn't travel on Sunday, but that he felt a round of prayers would suffice and that the Good Lord held no grudges against those who sought to cross dangerous lands as quickly as possible. He said that he had promised his mother he would never forget the Lord's day.

While the sun rose we all stood in a group, the men holding their hats and caps, heads bowed. Edward was dressed in his corduroys, his broad hat, and his red hunting waistcoat. Frowning deeply, he and his soldiers waited impatiently for the service to begin. Bom stood beside him with his eyes closed, his lips moving.

Lamar stood with his head bowed in reverence. Mr. Quincannon had told me before that his friend had no concerns about respecting the white man's ceremonies, that he believed the Creator was the same to one and all, and however one chose to give thanks for life was good.

When everyone was settled, J. T. Landers said a prayer for continued guidance and protection during the journey. The botanist has taken it upon himself to serve as clergyman for the group, stating that they needed one and that his father had been a minister.

I wore the new clothes that Avis had purchased for me

in St. Louis. I wiggled my toes in the beautiful blue slippers, remembering my dance with Mr. Quincannon, who watched me from nearby. Aunt Avis and Uncle Walter stood with me, both dressed in their finest as well.

As the service ended, clouds rolled in, and within an hour of our departure the skies opened again, turning the morning into a blur of falling water. The trail through the Narrows proved to be nearly impassable. The ground turned to a quagmire and the carts, sinking to the axles, had to be pulled out of bogs with double teams of mules, with as many as six men pushing.

I sat in the carriage and held my breath while the horses lurched through the muck. Avis gripped the support bars, nearly shaking them loose, while Walter tried to calm her.

Mr. Quincannon rode up alongside and announced that we must get out and either ride horseback or walk.

"The horses are tearing your carriage apart," he said.

Bom stopped the team and Avis protested. "You can't possibly be serious."

Edward rode up and demanded to know Mr. Quincannon's motive. When he saw that the spokes of the wheels were loosening and the tongue was pulling away from the frame, he insisted we get out. I did my best to comfort Avis, who didn't want to ride but thought it preferable to walking.

"You can get on behind me," I said.

Edward brought up the red mare he had purchased for me. She was giddy and began sidestepping. When I requested my pinto, he broke into a rage.

"If you as much as mention that animal again, I will shoot it myself," he said.

"Surely you're joking," I said.

"I am not. I'm tired of your persistence. You will not ride that horse, and that's final."

He tried to help me up on the chestnut, but I pushed

him away. After mounting, I pulled Avis on behind. Walter struggled onto an older roan and grimaced in pain as he rode through the downpour.

The mare proved hard to handle and I fought continually to keep her under control. She jerked first one way and then the other, disturbed at the weather and having to carry not one, but two people through the mud.

All the while Avis yelled and wailed, making the horse more frantic. I felt the sleeves and neckline of my new dress ripping away as my aunt clutched at me in desperation.

Finally, with a loud scream, she fell off the side, splatting in the mud. The mare jerked and tried to buck, but I held the horse's head up and succeeded in calming her. Walter, sore knee and all, dismounted and tried to help Avis to her feet, but she dragged him down beside her.

I jumped off the mare and she ran away into the storm. I plowed through mud up to my knees, and upon reaching Avis and Walter, helped them both up in turn. Edward watched from atop his horse.

"Ella, why didn't you handle that mare properly?" he asked.

I scooped up a handful of mud and flung it at him, splattering his face and red waistcoat. When he saw me reaching for more, he quickly spurred his stallion out of range.

In my rage, I had not noticed that I was missing both of my brand-new slippers. Not until I began raking the muck from my legs and clothing did I realize that they were lost somewhere deep in the ooze. I searched and scooped and dug with persistence, then discovered Mr. Quincannon standing alongside, holding them out to me.

"If there was music, I'd ask for a dance," he said.

"How did you find them?"

"I saw them slip off when you ran toward Sir Edward."

I thanked him and hoped he couldn't tell the tears from the rain that washed down my face.

Gabriella's Journal

15 APRIL 1846, 2ND ENTRY

Early this afternoon the skies turned blue and the sun shone brightly. We reached an area called Pleasant Valley and Mr. Quincannon stopped the column to rest and locate lost stock. I retired to the creek to rinse the mud from myself and what was left of my new dress. I refused to throw it away, as Avis suggested, but committed myself to either fixing it myself or finding someone who could.

Edward kept himself at a safe distance from me. Uncle Walter told me that in conversing with him, he said he had no idea I was capable of such rage. He had come to complain to me that I had nearly ruined his favorite hunting waistcoat and I had told him that had I a rock, I would have ruined his head.

Edward received little sympathy from Uncle Walter, who simply told him, "You're lucky that she didn't have a rock. Pray she cools off before we reach rocky country."

What bothered Edward the most, though, was my statement to him that henceforth, if I wanted to ride my pinto, I would. "If you have an inclination to shoot the pony, you had better shoot me as well," I told him, "for your life will be worthless after that."

Avis was the only one who sided with him. She told me not to be so hard on the poor man and even suggested that I might be slipping mentally.

"I worry that you're putting too much pressure on yourself regarding your art," she said. "You can't let yourself go mad over the fact that your paintings of savages might not sell."

I asked her what my paintings had to do with Edward's behavior and she told me that he was merely trying to account for my outbursts.

"You must act more as though you want to be his wife," she said. "Can't you see that?"

"Must a wife be the same as a servant?"

"If that's his desire."

I decided that discussing the matter was futile. In fact, I've concluded that it's not a good idea to discuss much of anything with her. I told her that I preferred to limit our conversations to any topic other than Edward. "And if that's not possible," I said, "then we have nothing to talk about."

She didn't seem at all shocked and acted as if estrangement would not bother her. Her reaction caused me some grief, but I have to admit I've felt lately that Aunt Avis is not the friend I once knew as a child.

I diverted my thoughts elsewhere, discovering Mr. Quincannon's mood to be even more foul than mine. He ranted and raved over lost supplies and damage due to poor packing. Everyone under his command busied themselves catching wayward mules or cleaning mud from tarps and guns and food supplies. The storm had caused more delays and difficulties than anyone had time for.

The meals I had with Edward and my aunt and uncle

were strained. I didn't come to tea. Bom and Uncle Walter
both tried to ease the tension, but nothing could be done.

As Pleasant Valley had turned out to be less than pleasant, I welcomed the opportunity to travel on. Yesterday
proved to be every bit as open and sunny as the previous
day had been stormy. We reached the fabled Council
Grove in late afternoon and set up camp along the creek.

It is a beautiful area, with thick stands of hardwood
trees bordering the stream and also growing in dense
patches in low-lying regions. Mr. Quincannon dispatched
his men to cut more limbs and shape them as axles and
braces for the carts. Repairs were in order, as the gummy
mud of the Narrows had popped more than one wheel
spoke and cracked the axles and bodies of a few carts.

It is said that the area got its name from a historic
meeting between road surveyors and Osage Indians in the
year 1825, at which time a treaty was drawn up to allow
the passage of travelers going to and from the Sante Fe
region. The pact is said to have been sealed by the receipt
of eight hundred dollars worth of merchandise to the Indians. Mr. Quincannon told Walter that the amount of
goods freighted by the first caravan could have easily sur-
passed double that amount.

I am beginning to see that the rightful ownership of
lands will forever be in question here. I heard many times
in St. Louis that the Indian doesn't make the best use of
the resource and that settlers should have priority in stak-
ing their claims. I don't know what the best use of the
resource might be, but the thought of right by might can
only lead to a long line of fatalities.

I wished to see what lay before us and rode Whistler
to a hilltop. The trees diminished greatly toward the west,
leaving open grassland ahead of us. The view gave me the
chance to understand some of the defensive traveling
strategies used by travelers, facts I learned from Mr. Quin-

cannon back in St. Louis. There were a number of trade caravans in the vicinity and they were camped with their wagons in large circles, with their livestock corraled inside. We had reached the edge of hostile Indian country and raids could happen anytime.

These caravans were all headed toward the Mexican settlements of Taos and Sante Fe, carrying supplies for trade to the Mexicans. Their journeys might be interrupted at any time should war with Mexico commence.

After leaving the hill, I spent part of the day sketching various travelers, including a young Spanish couple and their family, returning home to their land grant in the Guadalupe Mountains. They were a joyous group who laughed and sang and danced in their festive style, giving me a great deal of grist for sketches and paintings. Had the rumors of war not been so strong, I might well have entertained the thought of going south as opposed to west.

Such is my mood at this time. I feel like going anywhere that Edward isn't going. I can only say that I would miss the company of Mr. Quincannon. But to keep matters from going further, I have decided to avoid direct contact with him. Instead, I have called upon Uncle Walter to act in my behalf and explain the reason I am remaining distant.

Uncle Walter agreed wholeheartedly with my idea and discussed the matter with Mr. Quincannon. He reported back to me that Mr. Quincannon understood my alarm and would make no more contact with me, either, until such time as I thought it prudent. It's going to be difficult, but it's for the best.

18 APRIL 1846

Early this afternoon we reached Cottonwood Creek, a small stream similar to
Council Grove Creek that is an oasis of trees and flow-
ering shrubs. Along the water's edge grow quantities of
gooseberry, raspberry, and wild plum, all blooming in
profusion. J. T. Landers believes he has reached heaven,
as the warm sunshine of the past few days has produced
a number of wildflowers as well.

A small herd of antelope grazed just out from camp
and Edward delighted in the discovery. They were fleet
creatures with tawny coats and curved black horns, and
a large patch of white hair on their rump that flared out
at the first sign of danger. A truer test of skill did not exist
on the plains.

He decided it was time to sharpen his shooting eye,
but knew better than to pursue them on horseback. He
had learned his lesson on that score with the antelope of
Kenya, and Mr. Quincannon had assured him that these
creatures were as fleet as any hooved animals God had
created, no matter the continent. This made Edward certain that it would be an unequaled feat to approach one
on foot and bring it down.

Bom and Barton accompanied him, as well as Mr.
Stiles, his taxidermist. I knew that Edward would subject
them to endless stories of his African expeditions and the
game he had stalked there. Mr. Stiles, who hunted with
him in Africa, would certainly testify to the accuracy of
the accounts.

I watched from my pony for a short time. The antelope

could not be persuaded to remain within rifle range, and even when a shot could be taken, the animals were running so fast that Edward's spent ball came nowhere near its mark.

His frustration grew, and with it, his determination not to be bested. I could see him in the far distance, walking towards another herd, waving for everyone to follow him.

Barton's mood had been foul, even before leaving. He had grown tired of Edward's persistent nagging and had acquired a very sore shoulder from constant target practice.

He asked me to intervene and persuade my fiancé not to take him.

"I believe you should just tell him yourself that you don't want to go," I said.

His concern was that he was being forced to prove himself. "I know we'll be out chasing those creatures for a week," he said.

"Edward will eventually bag one," I said, "and you as well. Then think of the esteem you'll gain in his eyes."

"I am not a hunter, nor do I ever care to become one," Barton said. "I'll simply learn how to handle firearms to the best of my ability and hope to please him any way I can."

I suggested that perhaps Edward thought learning hunting skills to be in his best interest. Barton argued that he had purely selfish motives in mind.

"If he teaches me to shoot, then he can take me to all the contests back home and have me brag on him, and how his prowess as a hunter and teacher has allowed me the skills of a gentleman," he said. "I can assure you that I'll never brag on him and he'll never make a hunter out of me."

I took the rest of the afternoon for myself. After finding Walter and Avis napping in their tent, I left for the creek.

Mr. Landers was but a speck in the distance, busily collecting plants, and the men were lounging in their tents, many of them asleep.

I made my way downstream, enjoying the clear day. The creekbed was alive with birdsong. Small birds flitted among the trees and shrubs, singing nesting songs. A slight wind touched the treetops and against the pale blue overhead a hawk drifted in lazy circles.

Nearly a mile from camp I discovered Mr. Quincannon standing in the creek with his back to me, wearing not a single stitch of clothing. His lean body glistened in the sunlight as he splashed water over his back and shoulders and generally enjoyed himself in the refreshing current.

I settled behind a berry bush and watched him. In England, I had hinted to Edward that we might bathe together, knowing full well it was improper for a woman to suggest such a thing, but believing my need and his to be the same. He had told me it might be a good idea, but not on that particular day. He never brought it up again.

After his initial courtship and following my commitment to marry him, he had been sexual with me sparingly, usually on a whim, and never in a romantic way. I cannot understand his apparent lack of interest in holding me or showing any affection. I don't see how it can become any worse.

I worry that perhaps he has heard that I bore no children for my first husband and has decided, as that man had, that I am no good. I must dismiss that as I long ago decided that Richard Mann wasn't worth the trouble of concerning myself over and now begin to wonder if Edward doesn't fit into the same category.

I watched Mr. Quincannon in the stream, waiting for him to turn around, which he almost did a number of times but never quite got to it. I remembered our dance back at Round Grove and how his eyes had showed his interest in me, and how his strong arms had drawn me close to him. I delighted in wondering how it would be for us to dance once again, without any garments of any kind, in a field of soft grass with the wind blowing at our backs.

My thoughts were interrupted by the sounds of men talking.

Sir Edward had returned.

I watched Mr. Quincannon leave the stream and grab his buckskins. I turned away and began to alternately walk and run back towards camp, hiding in brush and groves of trees as best I could. Luckily, Edward had stopped to talk with Mr. Quincannon or he and the others surely would have caught up with me along the trail.

Back at camp, I collapsed in my bed. My heart beat frantically and I wondered if it was at almost being discovered by Edward, or the picture of Mr. Quincannon in the stream. After a while I drifted off to sleep and later sat up as Bom spoke from outside the tent.

"Miss Hall, Master Sir Edward would like to see you."

I straightened my hair and brushed bits of leaf and twig from my clothes before leaving the tent. Bom nodded and led the way to where Edward sat at his table, sipping tea.

Bom held a chair for me and I sat down. Before I could get settled, Edward stood up and suggested we go for a walk.

I struggled to keep pace with him until he finally slowed down and lit a cigar. We walked along the creek, in the direction where I had come upon Mr. Quincannon bathing.

"I realize that things aren't going well," he said. "I decided to take up your request that we converse over the matter."

"I hope it will make things easier," I said.

He stared at me. "You don't look well."

"It's been a difficult week."

"I trust that's part of the reason for your behavior," he said, "and I certainly hope you have come to your senses."

"I should think that you would agree that you haven't been exactly civil," I replied.

"Come now. It hasn't been me flinging mud and raising my voice."

"None of it would have happened had you not forbade me to ride my pony."

"You would be better off giving that horse away."

"Nonsense! And I won't."

"Why do you want that pony so badly? It's little better than a mule."

"You know better than that, Edward."

"What do you hope to accomplish? Do you want to become an Indian? Promise me, once we get back to England, that I will hear no more of that animal."

"Then I suppose you'll be leaving your stallion behind as well."

"Most certainly. I can get a better horse than that anytime I please."

"Then why not get rid of him up ahead at Bent's Fort, since you think so little of him?"

"This bickering is foolish," he said. "We are soon to be married, and as such, should be civil to one another. I know it's difficult for you out here, but think of it as a mere test, a small speck in time, a speck you must endure until we reach Fort Vancouver and catch a ship back home."

"I don't mind it out here, Edward. Strangely enough, I believe it's you who is encountering problems."

"I have no problems, my dear. I have an irritation, and his name is Quincannon. But we've been over that."

"Mr. Quincannon and I have had no discussions for a number of days now."

"Not any that I'm privy to, I'm sure."

"Are you saying that I've been meeting him secretly?"

"I'm not able to watch your every move," he said.

I found the discussion exasperating and told him I wished to rest before dinner. As I turned, he stopped me and said, "You must consider my position, Ella. I have a great responsibility here and I want a measure of respect from you."

"Respect works both ways, Edward," I said.

He began chewing on his cigar. "I want you to understand that I care deeply for you. It's hard for me to say, granted, and perhaps I cannot show it the way you would like, but nevertheless the feeling is there."

I found it interesting that he never touched me at all, nor did he look into my eyes as he spoke.

"It would be of great pleasure to me," he continued, "if you would henceforth obey my commands without objection of any kind. Is that too much to expect?"

"Why do you want me for a wife if all you care about is ordering me around like one of your soldiers?"

"I wish you wouldn't look at it like that, Ella. After all, it won't be long until I'll be managing your business affairs."

"You want to oversee my art career?"

He puffed on his cigar. "Not so much that as the holdings we will share."

I began to think. He could only mean the land that my father had left to me upon his death.

"Are the holdings those that my father owned?"

"You own them now, don't you?"

"Is that why you want to marry me?" I demanded. "You think you'll get the land I inherited?"

"I'm in a position to make better decisions than you," he said coolly. "It would benefit us both."

"I don't see how it would benefit us both."

"I don't think you understood what I meant," he said.

"I believe I did." I turned away from him and started back towards camp.

PAWNEE CREEK

Quincannon's Journal

22 APRIL 1846, 1ST ENTRY

We reached the Arkansas River early yesterday and are moving along well. The water is not yet bank-full, as snow is still falling in the high mountains. I took a while to look at the river, having missed seeing a good flow of mountain water. It's not as strong as the Yellowstone or the Missouri way north, but respectable in its own right.

We stopped to celebrate by jumping into the water, all except Garr and his men, and Walter and Avis Dodge, of course. I think Miss Hall wanted to join us. I could see it on her face. She told me that I looked good in the water and started giggling. I don't know what that was about, but I felt like pulling her in with me.

We'll make Pawnee Creek before nightfall and Bent's Fort in another week, if the carts hold up and the mules stay strong. The grass has been excellent, owing to the lack of buffalo. Lamar has been scouting out from the column and brings back news that the Pawnees have made a large hunt to the northeast, driving the herds ahead of them, and that a mixed band of Cheyenne and

Arapaho are hunting to the northwest. If the two factions meet, look for a pitched battle.

I worry about Comanches, but guess they're hunting to the south. Lamar won't scout that direction and I don't blame him. There's not much a man can do if caught out in the open.

Two days ago we found a skeleton in the sandy bank along the river. It looked to be a woman with long hair and a patch missing from the top of her skull, her bones dug up by the wolves. She was likely scalped and certainly took a hatchet blow to the side of the head. It's hard to know how she got off by herself and why they didn't just abduct her. Maybe she was already dying and they didn't want to bother with her. Someone found her and dug a hole in the sand, but not good enough to keep the wolves from their work. It couldn't have happened this spring, though. The bones are too bleached.

Though dusty and matted, the woman's hair was red. A real trophy, I guess. I noticed Miss Hall staring and wondered what was going through her head. She didn't seem afraid, but saddened. There seems to be a lot on her mind these days.

Lamar and I gathered the woman's bones, with help from my men. Garr and his "soldiers" stood at a distance and watched. They seem totally unaffected, but then they really haven't witnessed anything yet.

Another bunch that sat at a distance and watched was a pack of wolves that showed up for the first time. Avis Dodge told Walter that she believed them to be the same pack that ate the woman. She must have a keener sense of knowledge than most.

Who knows, though? They could well be the same pack. We've gotten into their territory and they'll be a common sight from here on. They're not nearly the size of the big mountain wolves farther west, but smaller and light gray, and range clear into Mexico.

They've been following us since Walnut Creek and Lamar says that buffalo can't be far off. I've seen that before: A pack shows up and a hunt follows in a few days. The wolves know it's far easier to take the leavings from a caravan than work to bring one down themselves.

It will be a nice diversion from prairie dog. There are thousands of them along the river but it takes too long to get enough to feed a large group. Garr had kept Robert Colville busy hunting them for his chefs to prepare, as he now considers antelope much too gamey for his tastes.

Colville has had his problems hunting them. A pack of coyotes, much slyer than wolves, have decided that they are interested in obtaining easy meals. Colville will shoot a prairie dog and one of the pack will quickly lope in and grab it.

Garr won't allow ammunition wasted on coyotes, so Colville spends a lot of time pulling out his hair.

The coyotes make considerable noise after dark, yapping and singing to the moon, but it's the wolves that give their depth to the night. Avis Dodge—I guess I should refer to her as Lady Avis—is more concerned with them than the mosquitoes. Since the hard rains, the air is thick with whiny buzzing, and the nets can hardly hold them back. Still, she worries every night that she'll be eaten by a wolf and jabs Walter every time one howls.

I don't know how he holds up, what with his crazy wife and that bad knee. I get a chance to talk to him once in a while, whenever he takes a walk alone. He's said more than once that he wishes we weren't on opposite sides of the Oregon issue. I have to agree; he doesn't seem like such a bad sort.

The other night he confided that he and Avis were

growing farther and farther apart, and that he didn't
know how to handle it. He said that Avis had told him
she wanted to take this trip not only to act as chaperone
to their niece, but also to see if a change of air would
help their marriage. I couldn't offer any suggestions. All
I can say is that he must care a great deal for his niece
to suffer as much as he does for her sake.

I'm not content being in the same camp with her and
not conversing. I feel I know her well enough to call her
Gabriella, or Ella—whatever she prefers. But I'll stick to
Miss Hall for everyone's sake.

I still think about the dance with the settlers. In fact,
whenever the raging warrior dream comes to me, I remember how she looked in that blue dress and slippers
and feel a whole lot better. I often think there's no good
reason to allow Edward Garr to cause such a strain on
everyone, but then I know that pushing the issue would
bring certain confrontation. Though I'd never back
down, I'm not used to dueling.

And speaking of those with a short fuse, I can't believe
what recently happened with J. T. Landers. I didn't
know he had it in him, but the little man turned a scowl
into a loud yowl yesterday when we stopped for the noon
meal. I mentioned that the grass looked good and he tore
into me.

"What do you really know about grass?" he asked me.

"It's green and good for mules," I said.

He informed me there was a lot more to it than that.
He borrowed a horse and we went for a ride. He began
to show me things I hadn't thought about.

A distance from camp we rode through forage that
touched our stirrups, tall grasses of various kinds waving
in the breeze, interspersed with wildflowers, a few
shrubs, and an occasional cactus plant.

"This is good grass," he said.

I couldn't argue. It was much taller and more lush than that growing along the river.

"You're seeing a natural system in pristine condition," he said. "This is how nature intended these plains to look."

He explained the various varieties of grass and showed me how to tell them apart, putting them in categories from the best to the least desirable from a grazing standpoint. After listening to him, I could understand his reasoning, and learned how to make the most of our grazing stops as we journey ahead.

"Your mules can graze half the time on some grasses and get twice the nourishment," he said. "That way we move faster and the stock stays healthy."

We rode back toward camp and just like he said, within a mile of the camp, the vegetation changed remarkably.

"Do you see how the major grass species near the river have been grazed out and that different plant species have come in to replace them?" he asked.

He explained that the taller, more robust grasses that we had seen a distance away should also be found close to the river, but that they had been grazed out, allowing smaller grasses to gain a foothold, along with a lot more brush and cactus.

"This has happened since the caravans started coming through," he said. "The mules and oxen have ravaged the river bottoms continuously for the last twenty years and everything has changed."

He pointed out that the buffalo migrate through and after grazing everything off, move on to other locales, allowing the grass to recover.

"But the mules and oxen never stop coming and never stop eating and the grass never recovers, killing their roots. Nature won't allow productive ground to lay barren, so smaller grasses and plants not suitable for grazing come in to cover the soil."

I looked again at the brush and cactus that dotted the landscape. In some places, especially the sandy knobs, the cactus had gotten too thick to ride through. Landers said he could see from reading earlier botany journals that it wouldn't be long before a lot of the grasslands were changed forever.

"I predict that in just another twenty years travelers will come this way and won't ever know what they've missed," he said. "If I was God, I would stop your westward movement."

Quincannon's Journal

22 APRIL 1846, 2ND ENTRY

Pawnee Creek is flowing brimful and our earlier crossing wasn't nearly as easy as I'd hoped. There was still plenty of light left, and after letting the mules rest a short while, we plunged in. The banks were steep and we had to take an hour to dig them back a ways to allow for easier entry for the carts. I have seen wagons and carts, both, tip over by not preparing correctly.

We got the carts across without mishap, but Barton Strand slipped from his horse. Luckily, I was close to help him out. He thanked me and coughed up water, then asked how hard it would be to catch a caravan going back to St. Louis.

"You can make arrangements with somebody at Bent's

Fort," I said. "Are you sure you want to do that?"

"I'm not willing to die out here," he said.

Garr said nothing to him, visibly embarrassed at seeing his nephew in trouble. I wonder how he would react if the tables were turned.

Gabriella did her best to revive Barton's spirits, but it was plain that the young man felt distinctly out of place and wanted nothing more than to be home in England.

We were pitching camp when Lamar came riding in and announced that he had discovered a herd of buffalo moving steadily in our direction from the southwest. It wasn't long until the word spread through camp and the excitement began to build. Garr was ready to leave immediately but I pointed out that the sun was falling and only fools hunted buffalo in the dark.

As my men prepared cuts of antelope for the fire, I got ready for the hunt. Since going to the mountains I've carried a 52-caliber percussion rifle made by Jacob Hawken of St. Louis. I doubt I will ever find a gun I like better. A lot of the trappers and traders prefer flintlocks of the Kentucky and Lancaster styles. They have longer barrels and may shoot farther, but I like the heft of my piece.

I can't hit anything at long distances anyway. I'll leave that to Lamar and those like him, men who can shoot the eye out of a bird at nearly three hundred yards. I've seen it happen—not often, but often enough. In turn, they'll depend on me to drop a bear coming at us. I'll stick with Lucy. She's been my bodyguard for nearly ten years, and I won't go back on her now.

I had finished cleaning and oiling Lucy, and was preparing to take a cut of meat, when Bom appeared and bowed.

"Master Sir Edward would like to see you. He says that maybe you are tired of eating antelope."

"I'm tired of prairie dog as well," I said.

"If you will come," he said, "Master Sir Edward promises a delicacy."

I followed Bom over to Garr's tent and saw that he was offering chairs to Walter and Avis, as well as Miss Hall.

"Please," he said to me, "will you join us?"

He had been out that evening with his fowling piece and had dispatched a number of large grouse. The Rivet brothers had roasted them underground, a trick they had learned from Bom, and had made a red wine sauce and a side dish of roasted Indian breadroots that Lamar had pointed out to J. T. Landers.

The little botanist was delighted, digging up a number of specimens and carving into the large white roots. He told me the plant was a member of the pea family, and from its appearance, had just starting blooming. They were moist enough that we ate some of them raw. I had learned the French name, *pomme-blanche*, during my early years in the mountains. Wild white potatoes is what the trappers called them.

The servants had laid a carpet and fitted three tables together, covering it with fine linen. Poles had been erected back from the tables three feet apart, with lanterns secured to each one, providing nearly as much light as midday.

I took a seat across from Gabriella. She wore her charming blue dress and slippers, all having been cleaned to immaculate condition by her servant, Jessie. Her hair was drawn up in ringlets and a bow fastened on one side. She caught my eye and smiled slightly while Peter Rivet filled her wineglass.

"I propose a toast to the morn," Garr said. "At last we have reached the buffalo and they are mine."

I sipped from my glass, noticing all at the table cared

as little for the toast as me. All but Avis, who giggled after swallowing.

"You've been toasting already for some time, haven't you, dear?" Walter said.

"Now, Walter. Would you fault me for enjoying the evening?"

"Just don't enjoy it too much," he said.

The servants offered a first course of deviled grouse eggs and wild mushrooms. The chefs had learned how to fry bread in a deep skillet from Lamar. But the flour had gotten slightly sandy and Garr threw the offering over the tent into the darkness. He said nothing, but snapped his fingers and ordered the main course.

"I'm delighted that you could join us, Mr. Quincannon," he said. "Are you ready for the hunt?"

"Yes," I said. "We should have a good feast this time tomorrow."

"I will be taking the first shot," he said. "I shall select a trophy bull and then the real hunt can commence. Is that understood?"

"You do what you want," I said. "Far be it from me to give you instructions."

Gabriella's Journal

22 APRIL 1846

I believe our dinner tonight was one of the most interesting I can remember. It might have ended badly but for the calm manner of Owen Quincannon, who continues to surprise and interest me more with each passing day.

I'll never know what struck Edward to bring us all together, except perhaps some quirk in his character that drives him to try to humiliate others in front of a crowd. Had Mr. Quincannon had any idea what was coming, I'm certain he would have declined the invitation. As it was, he listened to Edward and never once even squirmed in his chair.

I would say he is a man who stays detached until something needs to be done, to save lives or somehow survive, and then springs into action. I would also say that whoever stands in his way during those times had better think twice.

He wouldn't allow himself to be disturbed, but ate his grouse with a gentleman's manners. He told Edward more than once that he didn't intend to interfere with his hunting methods, but advised him to be very careful. Edward thinks that just because he's hunted African big game, he has nothing to fear on the American plains.

Barton has suggested to me that his uncle will likely meet a grim fate at the hands of some animal that wishes not to be taken for granted. Bears came to mind and Barton related a story to me that Mr. Quincannon had told him about a hunter who believed his rifle could drop anything to be found in the mountains without difficulty.

It seems they were setting traps in a stream in late fall when a bear charged from a nearby patch of berries. The hunter boasted that he could bring the animal down with one shot. But the bear ran him over, a huge brown and yellow monster called a grizzly, and tore the hunter open from throat to groin and began devouring him in front of Mr. Quincannon and two others, who all fired upon the bear until it fell dead.

"I learned from that story," Barton said, "that nothing is to be taken for granted."

Barton had come to my tent to present me with flowers, a bouquet of bright yellow sweetpeas that I immediately placed in a vase of river water. I thanked him and asked why the courtesy.

"I believe that my uncle takes you for granted," he said. "Perhaps he doesn't mean to, but he does nevertheless. I just wanted you to know that you're admired."

The flowers have remained fresh and I decided to place them upon the table for the evening. I fingered their lovely blossoms while Edward continued to test Mr. Quincannon.

"Have you ever shot a white buffalo?" he asked.

"No," Mr. Quincannon answered.

"Have you ever seen one?"

"I've seen two, and a robe that belonged to an Arapaho medicine man."

"What kept you from shooting the buffalo, or taking the robe from the Indian?"

"I don't want to have anything to do with a white buffalo," Mr. Quincannon said.

"I suppose it has something to do with superstition," Edward said.

"Call it what you want."

"Are you afraid of Indians, Mr. Quincannon?"

"If you show them respect, there's no reason to worry about them."

"It seems that your men have been mixing with mine far too much. I've heard that we'll all be dead if we don't give banquets to every Indian passerby we meet."

"It's only courteous to share a meal," Mr. Quincannon said. "Should we go into a village to visit, they would be offended if we didn't eat with them."

"I choose when and with whom I eat," Edward said.

Mr. Quincannon thought for a moment, then said, "Maybe it would be better if you didn't do any visiting, then."

When it finally became obvious that Mr. Quincannon would not be detoured from enjoying his meal, Edward began talking about hunting Indians. I noticed Mr. Quincannon's face darken slightly and he stated that if what had been said wasn't a joke, then we should all turn around and go back to St. Louis.

"You told me that you weren't afraid of them," Edward said. "I would never have thought you a coward."

"You can talk cowards if you want," Mr. Quincannon said. "I'll talk fools."

"Are you calling me a fool?"

"Didn't you just say that anyone who was afraid to hunt Indians was a coward?"

"I said that."

"Have you ever hunted Indians?"

"That's a foolish question, Mr. Quincannon. I've never been to this country before."

"Then how can you know whether or not you should be afraid of them?"

"I'm not disposed to be fearful of anything, Mr. Quincannon."

"If you're not a fool," Mr. Quincannon said, "then you're a very unusual man."

Edward cut a bite of meat and stared at him.

"How many men have you killed?" he asked.

"One is too many."

"Really," Edward said. "Maybe we should have had this discussion back in St. Louis, before I agreed to take you on."

"You would still have had to cross Indian country."

"Are you certain it's Indian country, Mr. Quincannon? Isn't it now American soil being unjustly occupied by native tribes? Isn't that what your Manifest Destiny is all about?"

"I suppose you would rather it be British settlers occupying those lands."

"Perhaps it will be."

"You've already failed," Mr. Quincannon said.

Edward got up from the table and threw his napkin into his plate. He paced back and forth and asked Mr. Quincannon what to expect at Bent's Fort, whom we might meet there and if, as he had learned, it was a haven for frontiersmen who knew the mountains.

"There might certainly be any number of mountain men there," Mr. Quincannon said.

"That is interesting to hear," Edward said. "I've decided that should I make the right arrangements with the right individual, you and I will no longer be partners."

THE ARKANSAS

Gabriella's Journal

23 APRIL 1846, 1ST ENTRY

I awakened before dawn to the sounds of men yelling and running for their horses. The buffalo had reached the river nearby and there was concern that the herd might stampede across and through camp.

They made a tremendous bellowing sound, and as the light crept into the sky, I mounted Whistler and rode to the top of a hill. They were a rolling black ocean sweeping through the scarlet sunrise, their heads down and their tails flying high. They crossed the river and scrambled up the banks.

Mr. Quincannon and his men had taken position in a line between the herd and our camp. They held their rifles raised in the air, hoping the leading animals would see them and veer away. He told me later that he didn't want to fire even a single shot, for fear of sending them off. They weren't like the wild Spanish cattle to the south and couldn't be turned by shooting in front of their faces.

Edward chose not to heed any such warnings and leveled his rifle at a large bull crossing close to the tents. The ball did nothing appreciable to the animal. It shook its head and began to run—luckily, away from camp.

The bellowing grew to a deafening roar as the herd broke across the open, thousands of them in a steady stream, pounding the ground to a fine powder that rose into the air and clouded the skies above camp. When finally they ceased to stampede, only half the herd had passed and it took fully the entire morning before the remainder had left.

Edward seemed embarrassed but said nothing. Had Providence not been with us, we might all have been trampled to pieces. He deferred to Mr. Quincannon, who suggested we move farther upriver to a new camp and save the hunt for late afternoon.

As it stood, the men had to gather lost mules and horses that had broken from camp in terror. They were all found grazing peacefully along the hills below the herd. But time had been lost in rounding them up.

I find it curious that Edward complains so often regarding our movement, exclaiming that we aren't traveling fast enough, and then makes a silly decision to shoot a buffalo less than a stone's throw from us all. Had he thought for an instant, he would have realized that even

if we had not all been killed, there would be other con-
sequences from buffalo stampeding in the vicinity of the
stock.

Walter was clearly put out. Had there been reason to
scramble for his life, he would have had little chance of
surviving. He and Avis had tried to make for higher
ground and he had fallen twice. He told me later that in
a world where smart decisions are imperative, Edward
should sit back and leave it all to just about anyone else.

I asked him how Edward had managed to rise in the
military ranks so swiftly and become a leader with a lot
of responsibility.

"Family ties," he said. "Nothing more."

After cleaning dust from our tents and beds, everything
was packed and we began our journey anew. The south
end of the herd remained well within view while we traveled. Calves trotted beside their mothers and I wondered
how they had kept pace during the running. Edward
talked incessantly about a white bull, but the sea of black
held no spots of any other color except occasional grays
and reds.

I now ride Whistler much more often than I sit in the
carriage. Jessie has proven a grand seamstress and has
modified two of my dresses so that I might change from
sidesaddle to riding astride my pony at will. Avis is hor-
rified to see me sitting on the horse like a man, but I can
see nothing wrong with it. I'm not athlete enough to ride
with both legs on one side while a sea of buffalo trample
nearby.

Avis asked me before we left if I was getting good use
out of the young slave. Aside from her altering my
dresses, I hadn't desired her services as much as I had
early in the journey, so I wondered what my aunt was
talking about.

"As of late, Jessie hasn't been around for me all that

much," she said. "I thought perhaps you required her services more now, since she was meant mainly for you in the first place."

I realized then why I hadn't seen Bom as often as before, either. When I questioned him about it, he just grinned.

"She needs help adjusting to the frontier," he said.

In midafternoon Mr. Quincannon stopped us where a small stream of good, fresh water emptied into the Arkansas. Edward was so desperate to hunt that even before camp was complete, he mounted his black stallion, rifle in hand, and charged towards the herd. A number of his men followed, and before long, they had scattered buffalo in every direction.

Walter and Avis watched from in front of their tent. Avis was not looking forward to dinner, but Walter had told me earlier that he was looking forward to the taste of buffalo and to telling stories to his friends upon our return to England.

I'll admit, I had tired of sketching antelope and landscapes. The thought of seeing and painting the same wild scenes as those famous artists before me created an intense excitement. Mr. Quincannon said that the herd was large, but not nearly so as in years past. Their numbers were suffering terribly, he said, from all the hunting. He was not happy that Edward was already shooting.

I rode with him and Lamar atop a small rise and saw Edward repeatedly dismount and fire, stamping his feet in frustration, as no buffalo were falling. Mr. Quincannon stated that the animals must be shot in a certain spot behind the shoulder to fall. Otherwise they might never go down, or wander off and die some distance away.

I asked him why neither he nor Lamar were joining in the chase and he informed me that there would be plenty of meat for the evening cookfires and that wasting ammunition was foolish.

I noticed Barton standing by himself at the edge of camp. He had convinced Edward not to insist that he hunt, so was content to just watch.

Robert Colville had stated often that he would show his prowess at hunting when the time was right. He rode between two large bulls and lowered his rifle to fire. Both animals swung their heads into his horse at the same time, goring it terribly on both sides.

The horse rose as if blasted off its feet, twisting in midair, then tumbling to the ground. With the initial thrust, Mr. Colville flew from the saddle and landed awkwardly in the dust. He tried to rise but fell back, while his horse screamed and stumbled in circles, its intestines dragging on the ground. The animal finally sank to its knees and rolled over, groaning out its final breaths of life.

"I certainly didn't come for this," I said.

"If your fiancé continues to conduct his hunts this way," Mr. Quincannon said, "you'll see a lot worse."

The buffalo had left and there was no cause to believe they would return. Edward and his men were still out and shots could be heard in the distance. While Lamar rode to find Dr. Marking, I went with Mr. Quincannon to Robert Colville's aid. He had risen to his hands and knees and was vomiting violently.

We helped him lie down and he didn't seem to know who or where he was. And he kept touching his eyes.

"I can't see," he said.

He began to panic and Mr. Quincannon assured him that if he laid still and waited for the doctor, his sight would likely return. He gained some memory back and then began to worry what Edward would say to him.

Lamar appeared with Dr. Marking. They had brought a cart lined with blankets. As they loaded him, I noted

with astonishment that Mr. Colville's head had begun to
swell terribly. Dr. Marking told us that his scalp and the
skin around his temples had ballooned full of water, not
uncommon for a serious head wound.

I rode out with Lamar and Mr. Quincannon on their
way to dispatch wounded buffalo. In the near distance,
the wolf pack was tearing at the hamstrings of a badly
wounded bull, working to pull him down. He fought
them by kicking and tossing his head, but his strength
was waning.

Other buffalo were down and some of Mr. Quincannon's men were already butchering a fallen cow. They
turned the carcass up on its belly, splaying the legs out
to the sides for support. They cut the hide from the back
of the neck down to the tail and peeled the skin down,
using it to stack choice cuts from the hump and along
the back.

Soon Edward had the Rivet brothers touring the field
with him, cutting tongues and sirloins from fallen buffalo.
Bom rode beside him, holding out a flask of drink whenever Edward called for it.

They rode over to where I sat on Whistler.

"What did you think of the hunt, my dear?" Edward
asked.

"I don't see your taxidermist at work anywhere," I said.

"There were no bulls suitable for my collection." He
called to Mr. Quincannon, who was helping with the
butchering. "I thought you were a hunter," he said. "You
haven't made one single kill."

Mr. Quincannon smiled back at him. "You seem to
have shot more than enough meat for everyone and most
of the wolves for fifty miles around."

"There are plenty of buffalo here for the taking."

"How many do you need?"

"As many as I wish."

"Are you going to have your men butcher them?" Mr. Quincannon asked.

"You know fully well that my men are not adept at such things," Edward said.

Mr. Quincannon smiled. "They had better learn. If you're getting rid of me, you'll lose my men as well."

Edward rode towards camp, not bothering to ask if I was coming or not. I have come to believe that he doesn't care anymore, or is playing a coy game of some sort. Since his attempt to tell me that he loved me and, at the same time, wanted to take control of my inherited land, he's made no overtures of any kind. Our "celebration" dinner upon having discovered the herd was the first time in well over a week that I had seen him in a festive mood.

At another location I noticed a group of Mr. Quincannon's men had built a fire and were preparing for what he termed "a contest that you may not want to witness." Of course his saying that made me all the more curious.

A strip of hide cut from one of the buffalo was placed on the ground. Two men seated themselves cross-legged next to the hide, opposite one another. Another man who held the position as judge of the contest drew a long length of small intestine from the coals and placed it upon the hide between the two men. At the judge's command, the event began.

The two men began pushing lengths of intestine down their throats as fast as they could. Mr. Quincannon explained that the cooked entrails required no chewing and that it was common for a contestant to swallow several yards very quickly. He emphasized that it was all in fun, and I saw that the two men often yanked at each other's coil, pulling it back out nearly as fast as it had gone in.

With no one declared the victor, the men settled in to eating. Along with the intestines, often referred to as "boudins," they cut slices of liver and dipped them into skin bags of gall collected from the buffalo.

"Just appetizers," Mr. Quincannon said. "I'll join them for the main course of hump ribs."

I rode back, deciding I had no appetite for dinner and would just have tea with Aunt Avis and Uncle Walter. As I entered camp, I could hear Edward shouting at Barton.

"For God's sake, give it a go," he was saying. "What's the matter with you?"

"You promised you wouldn't force me," Barton said.

"What am I to tell your mother? Will she understand that you never once attempted to shoot a buffalo? And that I stood idly by and did nothing?"

"If I shoot at one, will you then leave me alone?" Barton asked.

"Certainly. Just come out with me and try it."

Barton went into his tent to change clothes. In the meantime, I asked Edward why he nagged his nephew so.

"We've been over this before, Ella," he said. "Allow Barton to become a man, will you?"

Barton had dressed himself in field clothes—corduroys and a broad-brimmed hat, and a hunting waistcoat similar to Edward's, but black in color. He stepped over to a cart filled with rifles.

"Hurry, Barton," Edward said. "It's getting late."

Barton reached into the wagon and grabbed a rifle by the barrel. As he pulled it toward him, it discharged. The blast burned his lower arm badly and the ball shattered the bone just above the elbow. He screamed and fell unconscious to the ground.

Bom and I rushed over and turned him onto his back. His arm lay at an awkward angle, with bone splinters poking through the flesh.

"This is bad," Bom said, wrapping a piece of cloth tightly around the arm above the wound.

"Bom, have Noel see to him," Edward said evenly. "I want you with me. We have buffalo to chase."

"I will get the doctor first," Bom said.

Edward leaned over the saddle and shouted, "I told you not to worry, Bom! Now mount up."

A number of men had come running and everyone stared.

"I don't want to miss a record bull," Edward said.

He and Bom rode away as Dr. Marking hurried over with his bag. Barton had regained consciousness and lay moaning.

"I'll have to remove the arm," the doctor said. "We'll need to move him next to a fire."

Gabriella's Journal

23 APRIL 1846, 2ND ENTRY

Barton fell unconscious again, thank God, and didn't come back until the surgery had been completed. I agreed to help, as I've always been inclined towards nursing people in one way or another. I don't know where it comes from, but I recall the night I assisted with Millie McConnell and her husband, Martin. I often wonder how his arrow wound healed, knowing full well that it looked incredibly bad the night they came into our camp.

Dr. Marking worked a miracle on Barton. The upper arm had been badly shattered, the entire bone above the elbow having split nearly to the ball of the shoulder. After giving Barton a strong dose of morphine, he worked well into the night removing splinters and searing blood vessels to shut off the blood flow before removing the arm with a heated knife.

At the conclusion of his work, he asked that a horseshoeing pliers and a large wagon bolt be delivered to him. As there was no way to suture the wound properly, he gripped the pliers and seared the stub of the arm with the bolt, glowing white-hot from having been in the fire.

Mr. Quincannon had arrived shortly after hearing the gun discharge, but stayed out of the way, as he could do nothing to help. After the operation we sat with Barton, and Mr. Quincannon told him stories of the frontier and how it takes a brave man to make it through a serious mishap. Barton was comforted by our presence but asked two or three times where his arm had gone. I explained what had happened and he nodded before dozing off.

I laid my head on Mr. Quincannon's shoulder and wept. It seemed so unfair. We discussed the oddities of life and he ran his fingers through my hair and wiped tears from my cheeks. I felt comforted in his arms and raised my face to look into his eyes, when we heard a piteous bleat from nearby, a bawling that he said could have been made by only one thing.

A tiny buffalo calf appeared in the light of the fire, searching for its mother, who had been killed in the hunt. Mr. Quincannon lifted the little bundle, no bigger than a medium-size dog, to his breast and held it. I stroked its soft hair and it looked at me with large brown eyes.

"What in the world are we going to do?" I asked.

"It's a good thing we have the milk cow," he said.

26 APRIL 1846

We called her Daisy and she's doing very well on cow's milk. June doesn't seem to mind suckling her and Mr. Quincannon tells me that soon we will teach her to drink from a pail. He has already fashioned a little rawhide halter and she's fast learning to lead. I walk beside the carriage with her. I miss riding Whistler but Mr. Quincannon tells me that Daisy will soon be strong enough to keep up with us easily.

She seems to have got over the loss of her mother. I appear to have taken her place. She jumps about and is generally a pest, following me everywhere and butting me so that I'll lead her to the milk cow. I don't know why she doesn't consider June her new mother. It would seem only reasonable. But I'm learning quickly that "reasonable" is an elusive term out on this prairie.

Taking care of Daisy helps keep my mind off Barton's condition, which I fear is deteriorating. Whenever I visit him, he talks about the past and never the future. He laments not having told his brother that he loved him and wonders what life would have been like with different parents, ones who had accepted him.

"You have your life ahead of you to answer those questions," I told him.

He never speaks to that, but lies there as if alone. I'm trying to bring him out of his depression any way I can. I've brought Daisy to his bedside a number of times and she sucks on his fingers. This brings a smile, but a short-lived one. He's forever wondering of what use a one-armed man is.

The Rivet brothers have brought him any number of delicious offerings. He thanks them but eats very little. Pierre told him that he should consider becoming a chef, a career I believe would be very suitable. That cheered him up considerably, and for the first time since the accident he came to believe life was worth living.

This evening Walter came to visit Barton and tell him that he would be happy to hire him as a chef, once he is trained by the Rivets. This allows Barton something to look forward to once he's fully recovered. I said to both of them that I would personally see to it that Edward honored this decision.

"In fact," I said, "I'll go get Edward right now so that this matter is clear."

Barton asked that I not go for fear of aggravating him. I said the time had passed when I cared whether or not I aggravated anyone.

At Edward's tent, I was surprised to see that Bom was not standing outside in his usual position. I looked inside and discovered that the lamp resting on a table at the foot of the bed was very low. I stepped inside and Edward suddenly rose from under the sheets. Aunt Avis stuck her head up beside him.

I stepped back in surprise. Edward glared at me and said, "What are you doing here?"

"The better question is," I said, "what on earth are you two doing?" I looked from Edward to Avis, awaiting an answer.

Avis turned away while Edward continued to demand why I was in his tent. His favorite rifle lay propped up against the table. His two pistols lay near the lantern. I lifted one and cocked it.

"What are you doing?" Edward yelled. "Put that down!"

I turned the lantern up and stepped towards him.

"How long has this been going on?"

"We'll talk about this another time," he said.

I turned to Avis. "You tell me, then."

She began to cry.

"Is that why you bought me all those new clothes?" I asked. "Did it appease your guilt at all? Apparently not."

She begged me to forgive her, insisting that it had happened just this one time.

"It will never happen again," she said. "I swear to you."

Edward pointed a finger at me, his face drawn in rage. "This is quite enough," he said. "I demand that you leave immediately."

I walked over and leveled the pistol on his forehead. "Your demands mean absolutely nothing to me. If I were you, I would say no more."

Edward shrank back. "Please," he begged, "put the pistol down."

Avis leaned towards me, holding the sheet over her breasts. "Don't do this, Ella. Please."

"Tell me about after the duel," I said to her. "You were supposedly shopping when I got back to the hotel. Edward insisted that he had important business to attend to and put me on a carriage with Barton. Did you two meet on the boat?"

"What does it matter?" Edward asked.

I turned the pistol back on him. "You're right. It doesn't matter at all anymore."

Edward rose from the bed, covering himself with a sheet, and reached out his hand.

"Give me the pistol. Right now."

"You had better be careful, Edward," I warned.

"You wouldn't shoot me."

"You're very wrong," I said. "From here on, things are going to be very different."

Suddenly, Uncle Walter stepped in behind me. He stared at the scene for a moment, then said, "I suppose

I've suspected this all along. I just didn't want it to be true."

He picked up Edward's rifle and, pushing me aside, cocked the hammer. Edward put his hand up, as if to block the shot, but when Walter fired, it was Avis who took the blast square in the face from nearly point-blank range. I couldn't see for the smoke but could hear her gasping and thrashing in bed.

"Oh, God!" Edward yelled. "Walter, stop!"

Walter was looking for powder and ball to reload the rifle. I grabbed his arm and said, "Please, stop now."

He paused and looked at me strangely, then grabbed the pistol from my hand. He hurried out of the tent and Edward called for him to stop, quickly sweeping the second pistol off the table.

I stood in front of Edward, but he pushed me aside, yelling, "He's going to pay for this!"

As he spoke, a blast sounded from outside and I hurried out to see Walter's body lying near the doorway, the back of his head blown away. He had placed the pistol's muzzle in his mouth and pulled the trigger.

I stepped back inside the tent and found Edward back in bed with Avis.

Though I was sobbing, I said, "Are you quite satisfied now?"

He paid me no attention, but held Avis in his arms, rocking her as if she were asleep.

26 APRIL 1846

E dward Garr is a man in turmoil. He's lost the woman he truly loved and he'll never have the woman he wanted to own. Miss Hall informed me about his desires to get her land and if that wasn't enough, his involvement with Avis has made her sincerely hate him. I believe that he worries now that she will show up in his tent some night with a pistol. I find it interesting that she has borrowed one of mine and now takes target practice. She knows how to load and fire, and she seems to be getting pretty accurate.

Bom tells me that Garr awakens at night screaming. He paces and sweats and calls for tea and special meals, so much so that the Rivets have bags under their eyes from lack of sleep. But their eyes don't look nearly as bad as Edward Garr's.

Bom takes the blame for everything, as he was off talking with Jessie when it all happened. I told him that Garr and Avis were likely having their affair long before St. Louis, but he still contends things would have been different had he been doing his job.

Both Barton and Robert Colville are improving remarkably. Barton seems resolved to healing himself as quickly as possible so that he can learn the culinary arts. He wants nothing to do with Garr and doesn't want to dwell on the incident. He told me that as soon as he heard the shots, he knew something bad had happened. He had seen Avis leaving his uncle's tent late one afternoon and had been too frightened to tell anyone.

"Maybe it would have ended the same, no matter what," he said.

We buried Walter and Avis on a hill overlooking the river, but not side by side. Miss Hall wouldn't hear of it. Standing near her uncle's grave, she sobbed while J. T. Landers read Scripture.

Garr stood with the group for a while, but before the reading had ended walked off by himself and stared into space. He waited until we had all left the gravesites to return. He must have stood on that hill for an hour. He wouldn't even let Bom be with him.

We buried them both a good six feet in the sand, then Lamar and I dug up cactus plants and planted them on and around the graves. Miss Hall came up while we worked and wondered if that was a common thing to do. "It keeps the wolves from digging," I told her. J. T. Landers said later that as we traveled he had noticed a few sites where cactus had been growing unusually close together and stated that he now realized we had passed a number of gravesites along the way.

While we finished Avis's grave, I considered the irony. She had worried all the time about wolves getting her, and in the end, they still might. If they're able to dislodge the cactus, they can dig a long way down.

After we left, Garr went back and stood guard for some time. He wanted to be perfectly certain the wolves remained at a distance. I can't imagine that he wouldn't know they would be back and trying their best once he left. I've seen them lay down on their sides and scrape out under the cactus until it toppled over, then begin digging from above. But that happens most often when they can smell the corpse and know their efforts will reap rewards.

He stood guard and they stayed away as long as he

remained on the hill with his rifle, his beloved Whestley Richards pill-lock, the same weapon that Walter had used to shoot Avis. The wolves were privy to his aim, as he had shot one or two of them before. He didn't come into camp until well after dark and I know that Bom doubled whatever it was he uses in his tea to help him sleep.

There hasn't been much discussion during travel. The carriage was taken apart and stored in two carts, along with Walter and Avis's three trunks full of belongings. No one had any idea what to do with them, but burying them on the plains didn't seem proper.

Garr is trying to pretend that Miss Hall doesn't exist. I've noticed that he says nothing to her and that they never eat together. Though Garr's appetite seems intact, hers is suffering. Nothing I've said has made any difference, and though she thanks me for my concern, she has made it clear in no uncertain terms that she needs a lot of time to herself.

Bom tells me the situation is very troubling, even for him. I thought upon our first meeting that nothing could bother him, but he's likely not experienced these circumstances before. Certainly he's been around affairs, but none that ended as quickly and tragically.

He says that all Garr talks about is Oregon. He wants to reach Fort Vancouver as quickly as possible. It seems obvious, as he spends most of his time in camp drilling his men. Bom says that Colville brought them down from Quebec in Canada to St. Louis. Most of them are discharged British soldiers who are not happy about the Oregon situation. I always knew they were a bunch of Hudson's Bay renegades, but soldiers they'll never be.

I haven't approached him regarding his remarks about finding a new guide, but I would suppose that's still on his mind. I don't believe he wants to spend any more time with me than he has to. It might be the best for all concerned.

I'm eventually going to ask Miss Hall about her plans. I don't know if she's still interested in painting Indians or not. I don't see her sketching much, just riding by herself or sitting alone during camp hours, taking care of Daisy. The calf even sleeps in her tent and the two have grown very attached. The few times I've offered to help her with the feeding, she's been silent.

Bom says she isn't talking to anyone, so I won't approach her again until he says he believes the time to be right. I can see that she's still confused about whether she should be mourning her aunt or enraged with her. I know her uncle's death, especially by his own hand, will haunt her to the grave.

I believe she should do what I did in handling my father's leaving: Accept that it's over and done with—there's nothing more to it than that. Bom has told me that such things are never over and done with, but I say that they are. I believe that she can be like me and put it all behind her and never look back.

We'll reach Bent's Fort in another day. We've passed a number of caravans headed back to St. Louis and there will be even more to come. I've learned that war with Mexico is as good as begun and troops on both sides are preparing for battle.

Since Bent's Fort is on the north side of the river, there'll be no fighting there. But American dragoons will certainly use it as a base of operations. I hope we can get in and out without involvement.

I decided to keep us moving longer than usual today so that we might reach the fort well within daylight hours tomorrow. Though everyone is tired, no one complained about the extra travel. There is a sense of lost purpose here. The incident with the Dodges has taken the spirit out of us all.

Lamar returned early from his scouting trip and announced that we were being followed by Arapaho. He said that while praying last evening, a vision showed him a warrior with a black bow and arrows. He didn't tell me at the time, as Miss Hall had gone up on the hill with us, as she has been doing lately.

Before leaving this morning, we discussed his vision. I asked him if the warrior he saw had black stripes on his face and forehead, and wore raven feathers in his hair.

"I saw only the bow and arrows," Lamar said, "but they were being held in the grasp of a very large black bird."

While with the Arapahoes, I knew a warrior named Kills It, whose medicine was the raven. His name translated into a phrase that meant "Whenever he feels like killing, he goes after it," which was shortened by traders. He and I never got along.

My troubles with Kills It began early in my life with the Arapaho and I haven't told Lamar everything there is to know. It's too complicated and he doesn't care anyway. He and I are friends and whatever else mixes in from the past is irrelevant.

I thought about Lamar's dream as a large party of Arapaho warriors appeared on the south side of the river. Kills It rode in the lead, his lance covered with paint and feathers. They were all stripped to breechcloths and moccasins, typical dress for hunting or war. Some had trade rifles but most carried bows and a full quiver of arrows. Lamar and I both agreed that they were hunting and would war on enemies if given the chance.

Though the Arapaho are generally friendly, Kills It always had his own followers who believed as he did: All whites needed killing—men, women, and children; a fes-

tering wound left over from childhood. His parents and
a brother had died at the hands of a trapping party, who
had thought they were Blackfeet. Ten years old at the
time, Kills It had made the sign for Arapaho just in time
to save his own life. He refused help from the trappers
and walked back to the village on his own.

I've always wondered why Kills It and his family were
out wandering around by themselves. He would never
tell me, but my guess was they had been part of a traveling band of Gros Ventres, an affiliated tribe who live
to the north along the Missouri, long-lost relatives allied
with the Blackfeet. Kills It and his family had been victims of circumstances and now he will always want to do
more than even the score.

But he wasn't the main leader in the village and didn't
want to be banished from the band if he made a decision
that cost everyone else. When I lived among them, there
were strict rules about taking matters into one's own
hands, especially if others might be affected adversely. I
knew in this case that Kills It was very angry that we had
spoiled their hunt, but wouldn't start trouble unless he
believed he could kill us all without casualties to them.

We stopped and I communicated across the river in
sign language, inviting them over to eat fresh buffalo
with us. Garr proceeded to denounce my intentions until
I pointed out that we could either feed them or fight
them.

He left in a huff. Kills It signed back to me that he
didn't care to eat with dogs. He and some of his followers would come across and speak with me, but there
would be no pipe ceremony and no sharing of food.

Lamar and I met them as they rode out of the river.
I gave my rifle and pistol to Lamar and Kills It handed
his lance and shield to a warrior with him. I told Lamar
to ride a distance away and wait for me. I didn't want

additional intertribal tension added to the problems at hand.

There was no cordial greeting. Kills It looked very similar to the day I left the Arapaho village, tall and well proportioned, his hair long and groomed with clay and bear grease, and topped with two raven feathers. His eyes were as penetrating as ever and his mouth tight, the ever present lines of black trailing across his face and forehead.

He had always been known as brave in battle and wore his marks with pride. I noticed two long knife wounds outlined in red paint, one along the outer thigh of his right leg and another on his left forearm. They were both relatively new and along with the old ones—also outlined in paint—his entire body looked like a crosshatch of old wounds.

"I believed when you left us that I was rid of you for good," he said. "I even said thanks to the Grandfathers. I guess I shouldn't have thought that way."

My command of the Arapaho language hadn't diminished during my time away. "We do not have to be friends," I said, "but we don't have to be enemies."

"Yes, we do. You come into our lands and disturb our hunts and drink our water. Your animals eat the grass and they also drink the water. No one invited you back."

I pointed into the far western distance. "We are passing through, to cross the mountains into other lands."

"You have come far enough," he said. "You should turn around and return to the land of the whites. It is that or go under. I will see to that, for I have warriors who feel the same and have strong hearts for fighting."

"I have not lost the fighting heart," I said. "And my men have heard from me about you. They are ready to see your blood, and the blood of anyone else who would cause trouble for no good reason. So if you wish to fight us, paint yourselves for war. I will do the same. Is that how it is?"

Kills It stared hard at me. "You would die in a land that means nothing to you?"

"This land holds good memories for me," I said. "But not of you."

"You talk very bold for one who leads men who are more like women. They are Britishers and cannot fight us and win."

"Are you going to talk, or fight?" I said.

Kills It pointed to the warrior with him. "I would fight you but promised Antelope I would bring his son home safely."

I was surprised to hear that my good friend among the Arapaho had a son so large. He had been but a small boy when I left.

"His name is Water That Stands," Kills It said. "You can see that he doesn't like you any more than I do."

"He doesn't even know me."

"He doesn't have to know you. I've told him about you."

Water That Stands sat his horse and watched us. I detected no animosity toward me. Kills It was just hoping he could influence me against the young man and Antelope, in hopes I would agree to turn the caravan around and go back to St. Louis.

"Believe me, the village won't be happy to know that you've returned to these lands," Kills It said.

"I would like to hear that from Antelope himself," I said. "Where is he?"

"He has become the head chief of our band and is discussing the future of our people if the whites keep coming," he said. "You might say that he would still call you friend, but many things have changed since you left."

Garr suddenly rode up on his black stallion, leading

Miss Hall's pinto behind. He had no business interrupting our talk and I told him so.

"Tell him we'll give them this horse if they'll leave," he said.

"That's not your horse to give," I said.

"It doesn't matter. Ella won't need it any longer, since she's going back to St. Louis."

"What are you talking about?"

"Ask her yourself."

"Even if what you say is true," I said, "we aren't bargaining horses, or anything else. Ride back to camp."

"You keep talking about giving them gifts," Garr said. "Have you changed your mind?"

"Why don't you give them your stallion?" I suggested.

"Don't be preposterous."

Kills It spoke no English and neither did Water That Stands, but both knew the conversation wasn't amicable.

"You and the Britisher are not friends," Kills It said. "Did he bring the pony for me?"

"It's not his pony," I said.

"The pinto looks to be a good horse, very good for hunting buffalo," he said. "I will take the pinto and also the Britisher's black stallion, and all your mules and horses, as payment for crossing these lands."

"What is he saying?" Garr asked.

"Order your men into formation," I said. "He wants to fight."

Garr hurried back and shouted commands. In less than a minute his men had formed a skirmish line and were loading their rifles.

"He has a very short temper," I told Kills It. "Decide now if you want to fight or not."

While I waited for Kills It's answer, Miss Hall took her pinto back from Garr and rode over to me. She handed me two small rolls of linen.

"Give them to the warriors," she said. "Maybe they are suitable presents."

I unrolled them both and discovered that one was a watercolor of Kills It sitting his pony, with the river behind, and the other of Water That Stands. Kills It's eyes widened. He showed the paintings to the young warrior, who quickly covered his mouth with his hand.

"I have heard that special people can do this," Kills It said. "Is she your wife?"

"No, but she has a gift."

Kills It rolled the paintings up and stared at Miss Hall.

"Is she a spirit?" he asked.

"No, but the spirits act through her fingers," I said. "Once she has seen you, she can create pictures of you old or young as well."

Kills It said nothing more, but turned his horse and rode back across the river, with Water That Stands right behind. They rode upriver a short distance, crossed, and became lost in the hills and evening shadows.

Gabriella's Journal

27 APRIL 1846

Through this difficult time I've come to realize that my work is my life. The incidents with Edward Garr and the tragedy of Uncle Walter and Aunt Avis muddied the waters, but everything is now very clear: I will proceed with my art and recede from Edward Garr.

I told him the other evening, in a place along the river

where we were alone, that I couldn't imagine anyone being as deceitful as he. I told him that I had once loved and cared about him, but his eyes were blank. I wonder at times if he has any feeling whatsoever.

All this could mean I will be returning to St. Louis and back home. I told him as much, but I didn't mention that the Rivets and Barton are secretly planning to join a caravan going back. I don't want to do that necessarily, but Edward has spread the word and everyone seems to think I've made my decision.

I am discouraged at having traveled this distance without achieving my goal of sketching Indian chiefs and warriors. But the paintings Mr. Quincannon gave the two Arapaho seem to have kept us from battling them.

The rendering I just finished of Mr. Quincannon talking to them has turned out nicely. I believe I will redo the sketch on linen and finish it in oil. That picture of them talking with the late afternoon colors behind them was all too striking. Had I known what they were discussing, I might have been less intent on sketching and more inclined to take cover.

Thanks to Providence, we avoided a confrontation and I will live at least another day to look for suitable subjects for my work. Mr. Quincannon suggests that there will be opportunity to do many more sketches and paintings at Bent's Fort. "All manner of trader and Indian passes through there," he said. "You can pick and choose among a variety."

We had a nice discussion this evening on the riverbank. He asked me if I was planning a return to St. Louis and I hedged a bit. He seemed disappointed that I should even consider it.

"You wouldn't have me travel further with Edward, would you?" I said.

"I'm going to check at the fort for anyone who wants

to hire on with me," he said. "We can get a caravan bound for Oregon and join up with others along the way."

He said that no matter how many decided to go with him, he was going ahead with his plans. He said he wanted to put Missouri behind him forever and settle in a new and promising land. Oregon had always been the solution.

"I told you when we left St. Louis there would be sacrifices," he said. "Hopefully the most difficult of them are passed."

"The warriors we saw today," I said. "They could make trouble."

"It does have me concerned," he said. "But I intend to go ahead."

"Do you realize," I said, "that in many ways you are no different from Edward? You are just as driven."

"But for different reasons."

"No, for the same reasons. You both believe your cause to be right and neither of you will allow anything to stop you."

"My cause is right," he said, "and his is wrong."

He got up and left me sitting there beside the river, listening to the evening sounds and peering into the scarlet twilight.

BENT'S FORT

Gabriella's Journal

Bent's Fort is constructed of adobe and stands one hundred and eighty feet square by eighteen feet high, with bastions on the northwest and southeast corners. The gateway rises six and a half feet and is seven feet across, made of heavy plank timber and covered with sheet iron bolted on for reinforcement. There is a sentry station with a belfry over the gate, complete with a bell for ringing at mealtime and a large telescope for watching anyone who approaches.

We made our entrance yesterday and drew many curious stares. There are a lot of men coming and going, many of them with families, but none with tricorn hats and British Empire red. No one seemed to care much, though, as the Oregon problem is the last thing on their minds.

The Spanish influence here is tremendous and there's a good deal of cultural intermingling. Everyone happily adopts other foods and styles of life to bolster their own. I find it too bad that the governments can't share the same interests as the common folk.

Edward has said nothing to me since the deaths of Walter and Avis. I moved into the fort with Jessie and Bom and the Rivet brothers while he and his men camped along the river. They stayed but one day before leaving.

Edward took all the carts and supplies. With him were his taxidermist, Norman Stiles, and Dr. Marking, as well as J. T. Landers, who didn't seem eager to go. They were

led by three mountain men hired as guides. Bom says
Edward spoke of a buffalo herd that roamed to the north.
Among them, the buckskinners said, was a white bull.

Bom thought it strange that Edward didn't take him
along. He thinks it just as well, though, as he likes the
fort life and is starting to relish a little freedom. He is
relaxed and talks much more with me now, and also with
Mr. Quincannon. Ever since Walter and Avis died, Edward kept him at a distance, not allowing him in his tent
or to stand guard at any time.

I am also much more at ease. I've begun my artwork
again and find more subjects than I can handle. Mr. Quincannon took a number of us to tour the fort. The owners
were absent but we met a number of servants, including
Dick and Andrew Green, and Dick's wife, Charlotte, the
cook. Charlotte and her best friend, a French–Indian
woman named Rosalie, are both delightful and filled with
stories. Bom and Jessie and the Rivets became fast friends
with them and everyone now comes to me to volunteer
for portraits.

Daisy has generated the most interest, though, and
everyone has wanted to feed her and groom her and otherwise dote on the little buffalo. Mr. Quincannon had to
forcibly discourage a buckskinner from taking her for
steaks. Luckily, he's one of the three who left on the hunt
with Edward. Otherwise I know Mr. Quincannon would
have had a serious altercation with him at one time or
another.

This morning a small herd of buffalo passed nearby
and a few wandered close to the fort walls. Everyone gathered to watch them, no one suggesting a hunt. Daisy gal-
loped over to a lone cow and began suckling. It seemed
the cow had recently lost her own calf because she happily took our little orphan on as her own.

I had been brushing her soft coat at the time and was

desperate to have her return. I couldn't bear to watch her cross the river by the cow's side and become lost in the herd. Mr. Quincannon suggested that I resolve myself to the fact that Daisy has found a new mother. I cried on his shoulder for a good long time.

"It's for the best," he said. "Daisy needs to be with her own kind."

I have to agree with him, but will never forget that little buffalo calf. If, even for a short time, caring for her took my mind off Walter and Avis, I will think of her always when I relive the trail to Bent's Fort.

This afternoon I decided to portray the buffalo cow and Daisy at her side, with the fort behind. I chose a medium of watercolor on parchment paper. I intend to do a large work in oils once I get back home.

Mr. Quincannon came down to join me and shook his head in amazement.

"That is a picture befitting a king's wall," he said.

I thanked him and said that if he knew any kings with whom I might do business, I would be obliged.

"I've learned that a band of Arapaho Indians will be coming in to trade soon," he said. "Their leader is Antelope, an old friend of mine."

"At last I will have the chance at some portraits of warriors," I said. Then I began to worry. "Will Kills It be among them?"

He said he thought Kills It would still be out hunting. I told him that if I got the chance to paint a portrait of his friend and possibly others, I would consider my work finished.

"You're not going back to St. Louis, are you?" he asked.

"I believe it's time for me to return home," I said sadly.

"But there's so much to see between here and Oregon."

"I'm sorry, Mr. Quincannon," I replied, "but I think I've seen enough."

I believe it's time to concentrate on my efforts to reach Oregon. Lamar is not at ease here and has taken to spending time by himself. I know him well enough to leave him alone.

I guess I feel the same way about Miss Hall. I don't see any way of talking her into going on to Oregon. It would be foolish and a lie to tell her that the hardest part was over. She might be wise to go back, though I wish things would turn out so that she could come along.

It's amazing to learn what this fort has gone through since I left the mountains. It has become a major trade center and landmark for travelers along the southern route. Brothers Charles and William Bent, and Ceran St. Vrain, are the owners. They have a good rapport with the regional tribes, especially the Cheyenne, as William Bent married a chief's daughter.

I know them only slightly, and have never met the third partner, Ceran St. Vrain, who is presently with Charles looking into cattle ranching across the Mexican border. I learned that from William, who returned just this afternoon with his wife, after a short visit with her people.

He greeted me in a friendly manner and we shared a meal in the dining room. He spoke about the trade business and then turned the subject to the problems with Mexico.

"There will be fighting, of that I have no doubt," he said. "Likely all-out war, but I have heard nothing official."

"What about the Indians?" I asked.

"They are very restless, as you can well imagine," he said. "Everything is changing very fast out here and they don't like it."

I told him about my encounter with Kills It and he said certain trouble would come from him.

"He's a war leader now, and respected," Bent told me. "It's not like the old days when I could get everyone together for feasting and trading. They're all ready to burn wagons now and I can't stop them."

"We'll rest a few days and be on our way," I said. "I just wanted to see Antelope before I left."

"He should arrive in a couple of days," Bent said. "Meanwhile, enjoy yourself. We're having a fandango tonight."

Quincannon's Journal

28 APRIL 1846, 2ND ENTRY

A number of old trappers and traders have taken up residence and evidently pay their way by hunting for the fort. They relive the old days with Taos Lightning and card games. Some race horses but most are past those days and complain of stiff joints from setting traps in winter water.

There's an order among these men that didn't used to exist. When I first came into the mountains I saw a lot of drinking and gambling at the old rendezvous sites, resulting in a number of fights and a few deaths. That doesn't happen here. If you don't behave, you get chased away to fend for yourself alone.

An old trapper told me before I left the mountains that if the Good Lord hated your guts, you'd die out in the open. It wouldn't be by cold, but slower—hunger and thirst. The wolves would just sit back and watch you linger. "They don't come and tear into the two-leggeds like the settlement stories would have you believe," he said. "If they know you're a goner, they'll wait till you're down and pissed your pants for the last time."

I had always wondered if he died peacefully or passed on naked and shoeless from eating the last scraps of his buckskin clothing while watching the grinning wolves circle him until it all got too blurry just before the end.

But it seems he hasn't died. Not yet. I discovered him late this afternoon, after leaving Miss Hall. Samuel Brandt, buckskinner from the earliest days, arrived late last night on a white mule, just in time for a card game with some old friends. They told me he had ridden down from Fort Laramie, where the trail is clogged with wagons headed for Oregon. He had been gone a month and needed to finish some business at the graveyard.

He's aged considerably. Most noticeable is his weight, which has easily fallen forty pounds. He never had the extra flesh to spare, and was called Bones by everyone who knew him. His face has gotten hollow and his hair thinned to nothing. Most noticeable, his smile is missing.

"Owen Quincannon?" he said when he saw me. "By all that's damned! I heard you'd turned corn cracker."

"I'm back," I said. "Headed to Oregon."

"There's no milk and no honey there," he said. "Sit a spell, if you've a mind."

We sat cross-legged next to a grave under a cotton-wood near the river. He was whittling a small wooden buffalo from a cutting of wild plum.

"Had to come back and give this to her," he said. "She left me last spring. They wouldn't let me put her in the tree, though, where she'd have preferred."

"Is it Red Flower?" I asked.

"Consumption," he said. "She'd been doing poorly for a spell. 'Spect she feels better now."

I looked across the vast open toward the mountains, where Pike's Peak rose toward the clouds. Somewhere across the mountains lay the Ute villages and Red Flower's homeland. Some of the bands traveled to the fort to trade. I knew Bones wished he could have taken her back to her people.

"There's nary but me left now," he said.

"What about your sons?" I asked.

"One got drunk and drowned in the South Platte. The other got shot by a whiskey peddler. Wagh! It's all cursed, by the way I see it. All of it."

"So why don't you head back to the settlements?"

"Like you did? You take me for a fool?"

"It's no fool who wants a soft bed on freezing nights."

"I can't rest nohow among corn crackers."

"Don't live near the farms."

"What else is back there?"

"You could settle along the river somewhere. Old Franklin, or such a place."

"I told you before, I don't cater to corn crackers, and you can't go nowhere back there that they ain't around. There's a plenty of them rolling out this way in their broke-down wagons. They're to blame for this ruination."

"It was ruined before they heard of it," I said.

"Like so much squat!"

"Samuel, we trapped all the beaver out," I said.

Bones Brandt had always paid attention only to his own beliefs. Today was no exception.

"It'll all come back in time," he said. "The corn crackers won't last out here and beaver will rise again and we can go back to the streams."

"Beaver will never come back. Nobody wants a fur hat any longer."

The old man's eyes darkened. "Don't you say that!"

"It's true and you know it," I said.

"I told you when you left that I figured you'd give up buffalo and go to soft hog. I see I'm right."

"I'm headed to Oregon, but not to farm. I'll trade with the farmers and the Indians there."

"What, and be a Hudson's Bay man?"

"The British are leaving Oregon."

"Like so much hell. There's talk that some of them will fight. Ragtags from the British army and Hudson's Bay."

"They can't fight everybody."

"They can make trouble for some, and I hear you're headed into it."

He told me that he had ridden past a Britisher and a bunch of no-accounts in red the day before, headed up the trail toward Fort Laramie. I told him about Sir Edward Garr and his ambitions.

"Did you talk to them?" I asked.

"I told them if they knowed what's best for their health, they'll steer clear of Fort Laramie. There's a Frenchman named Latour putting a settlers' army together. Says he's going to Oregon and drive out Hudson's Bay."

"He was supposed to be traveling with me," I said. "He won't take orders."

Bones laughed. "He'll chew them Britishers a new hole, I'd say."

He placed the carving into the soil at the top of the mound. At that moment a chickadee flew from the cottonwood and landed on the carving. It sang a little song, then flitted back up into the branches and sat looking down at Bones.

"She was always partial to them little birds," he said.

"Come along to Oregon with me," I said.

"I can't leave Red Flower here alone."

"She's with her ancestors. You know that."

"I'm for certain not far behind her," he said. "But they won't want me tagging along, and I've got no family no more."

I pointed up to the chickadee. "She'll come back for you, Samuel, when the time's right."

"She's got no call to go to Oregon."

"She'll find you, Oregon or wherever."

The chickadee flew off into the sunshine. Bones pointed over to where Miss Hall was working on the painting of the fort.

"She going along?" he asked. "If she is, I might consider it. You won her over yet?"

I couldn't believe it. Since coming to the mountains, Bones Brandt had always believed an Indian woman to be the best a man could find. "Them white women got too much religion to loosen up in bed," he always said. "An Injun woman wants you more than you do her. She'll care for you day and night, if you'll do the same for her." He didn't think that way about Miss Hall.

"What do you know about her?" I asked.

"While you were in the fort she came over here and painted my picture, slick as you please." He rummaged in his pack and pulled out a small parchment.

The image was of Bones at a much younger age, standing with his horse, wearing buckskins and a large hat.

"I told her about my third spring in the mountains and I'll be damned if she didn't catch it how it was."

"It looks good," I said.

He pointed to the crotch. "She got that just right, too. Kinda puffed out, wouldn't you say?"

I handed the painting back to him. "Yes, Bones, you're puffed out. Take care of that painting. Don't crumple it up."

"I figure to place it between two slabs of wood," he said. "I'll keep it in good shape that way." He held it tightly. "You think Red Flower will mind that I have it?"

"Why should she?"

He smiled. "Then it's settled. Ah! Did I mention, I saw your pa this spring?" He saw the look on my face and added, "You'd do good to look him up, you know."

"I didn't see him all those years before," I said. "Why should I now?"

"It's only fitting. He's near my age, you know, and living with the Utes."

"How long?"

"A fair piece of time. He asked about you."

"I'm headed straight through to Oregon," I said.

" 'Spect you are," he said. "But someday you'll wish you'd stopped to see him."

Gabriella's Journal

28 APRIL 1846, 2ND ENTRY

They call it a fandango. The Spanish women wear their finest perfumes and dress in white blouses called *camisitas*, with short, full skirts called *enaguas*. They adorn themselves with earrings and necklaces of gold and silver, and powder their faces. They line themselves along the wall and many of them roll short cigarillos for smoking.

Jessie has got to know Charlotte Green very well and has learned a lot about fort and frontier life. She told me that she wouldn't mind staying at the fort, but that Bom thinks she's too young.

She talked to me about it as the fandango got started. She encouraged me to join her and the other women as the festivities began, but I declined, as Mr. Quincannon was absent.

I watched with curiosity as the men formed a line across the center of the floor and began clapping to the music of two fiddles, a guitar, and a concertina. Three women accompanied them with little Mexican drums called *tombes*, and the crowd grew wild and festive.

I wore my blue dress for the first time in a very long while. A slim young lady with long black hair performed a Mexican hat dance to the loud whoops of everyone watching. Soon Charlotte Green and three other servant women were doing dances of their own.

I tired of watching and left the fort. I walked along the trail that led to the river, drawing the peaceful spring evening to my breast. The moon was full and the wind was soft over the plains. Some might say I was foolish for being alone, but I knew it wouldn't be long until Mr. Quincannon found me.

I stood and watched the Arkansas flow through the vast open, the hills filled with shadows and the cries of night birds. He appeared a short way from me, a blanket folded over his arm.

"Are you getting chilled?" he said.

"Why weren't you at the fandango?"

"It's a little raucous for me. At least tonight."

Though the air was warm, I allowed him to wrap the

blanket around me. He stood behind me and held me by the shoulders, his strong hands resting gently.

"Antelope and his band are arriving tomorrow," he said. "It's your chance to do some good paintings."

I was excited to get the opportunity but dreaded going back to St. Louis.

"You are an amazing woman, Miss Hall. Might I call you Ella?"

I felt his fingers brush my hair away from my neck, and his warm lips touch me just below my ear. I welcomed it. He had never seemed a stranger to me, not even at our first meeting on the island in the Missouri River. At that time it had seemed as if he was supposed to be there, having arrived to take me away from my captors and deliver me unto my new life, where I belonged, with him beside me.

"I believe it's good to dispense with formalities," I said.

He made me want to forget about going home, about everything but the moment. His touch was very exciting.

He continued to kiss me softly, his lips trailing to my cheek. I turned and lifted my lips to his and felt his arms encircle me, drawing me close. I pulled him to me tightly and allowed myself the pleasure of absorbing him fully.

He took me by the hand and led me downriver to a small grove of cottonwoods where the grass grew lush and soft. He spread the blanket and we sat down.

"I've waited a long time to be alone with you," he said. "I never thought it would happen."

He slipped my dress down off my shoulders and kissed the tops of my breasts, gently unbuttoning the back until dress and undergarments slid free. I pulled his buckskin shirt off and admired his chest and broad shoulders, caressing his strong muscles with both hands.

"It's been a long time since I've been with a woman," he said.

He removed my dress completely and allowed me to run my hands along his hips and buttocks, sliding his trousers down. He was large and yearning for me and we lay beside each other, touching and poring over each other's bodies. He explored my breasts and stomach and ran his fingers gently along my thighs. When he slid on top, I pulled him into me and sought his mouth with a sudden fierceness.

We moved perfectly together, our motion increasing. I wrapped my legs around him and a lifetime of holding back exploded within me. I felt uplifted in a way I had never known before.

We rolled up in the blanket and held one another while the stars filled the sky and the wind spoke in the leaves overhead. In the far distance came the sounds of laughing and yelling as the fandango spread outside the fort.

"You'll be missing a lot by not going to Oregon," he said softly. "And we won't be traveling with Edward any longer."

"What do you mean?"

"Bones Brandt told me that he passed him and his men traveling north toward Fort Laramie. I think he's in a hurry to reach Oregon and left you behind."

"That would be the best luck I've had on this trip so far," I said. "But I'm still concerned about going all the way to Fort Vancouver."

"Travel north to Fort Laramie with me," he said. "If you want to go back, catch a wagon train there. It's safer than down here, with war about to start."

BENT'S FORT

Gabriella's Journal

I watched the Indians' arrival with interest. As they approached from upriver, the fort cannon sounded a loud welcome. Young men dressed only in breechcloths raced their ponies in circles around the fort, yelling and whooping. It both surprised and scared me, but Owen assured me they were not painted for war.

Their leader and his subchiefs were all dressed in finely tanned skins and beadwork, and wore feathered head-dresses. They rode in order of ranking at the head of a long column. In the middle were the women and children, and the elderly. All their possessions were packed on travois pulled by horses, and more warriors brought up the rear.

Owen commented that the young men seemed to be circling the fort more than normal and yelling cries usually reserved for actual warfare. So much so that a number of men inside the fort took position along the walls.

William Bent and some of his assistants rode out from the fort gates. Mr. Bent motioned to Owen, and after mounting his buckskin, he rode out with them to have a meeting. I saw a warrior lead a pony forward that was pulling a travois. It held something covered with skins and was decorated with feathers and ribbon cloth, and a war shield hung from one cross-member.

Bom joined me, along with Dick and Charlotte Green.

"They tell me that there's a dead man on that travois,"

Bom said. "They're getting ready for a burial."

I would learn what had happened from Owen before long. We all watched and wondered while the leaders gathered around the corpse and talked. Antelope gestured towards the mountains and one of the young men raised his lance, yelling loudly. He was silenced by Antelope. He quickly turned his horse and left.

"Not going to be festive this time," Charlotte said.

The leaders dismounted and seated themselves in a circle, where they talked and smoked. The women unpacked the travois and set up the lodges, numbering nearly a hundred in all. They formed a series of circles across a large open area near the fort. Bom pointed out that Antelope and his family would occupy the central lodge of the largest circle.

One of Mr. Bent's men rode back into the fort, and after considerable time returned to the meeting with a pack string of five mules laden with goods, along with three good horses.

"Those are gifts for Antelope and the subchiefs, and also the dead man's family," Dick Green explained. "Something bad's happened."

I watched them unpack the gifts, a large collection of knives and awls and what Owen called "fusies," a style of rifle, along with powder and ammunition. There was also a lot of brightly colored cloth and bags filled with blue and red and yellow beads, and vermilion for the women's faces.

Other bags contained flour and sugar and coffee, together with copper kettles and pans for cooking. Two large kegs of whiskey were offered but refused by the leader. Owen told me later that Antelope was one of the few chiefs who wouldn't allow his people to drink what he called "white man's poison."

"That's one of the reasons why Kills It is attempting to

break away with his own band," Owen told me then. "A lot of young men prefer to make up their own minds about drinking."

Bom and the Greens went back inside the fort and I decided to walk through the encampment. I took my sketchpad with me and busied myself with drawing. There was so much to see that I felt I could never take it all in. The lodges were conical and supported by long, slender poles, the coverings painted in various bird and animal designs. The women went about their work with great skill and efficiency and didn't seem to mind my watching.

I noticed one of them staring at me. Her hair was long and loose, and she wore a skin dress with a beaded belt. She went into her lodge and came back out with the watercolor of Kills It.

"I knew it had to be you," she said in broken English. "My name is Willow Bird and I'm Kills It's wife."

I was taken aback. She told me that she had learned English from two different trader husbands before becoming Kills It's wife. She told me more about her life and her people, believing I would be interested and want to draw her. I asked her to pose with her teen-aged son, Hawktail.

When I had finished the piece, Hawktail left to ride horses with his friends. His mother said, "He is mixed with white blood, and you know his father." She pointed to Owen. "He was once my husband."

When the meeting was over, Owen told me the news.

"Edward shot Water That Stands yesterday," he said. "It was from a long distance and no one understands why. But if it wasn't for my friendship with Antelope, Edward and all his men would be suffering some terrible tortures right now."

"Where is Kills It?"

"He and his followers are off preparing for war. Antelope says he can stop him. The gifts seem to have satisfied the family."

I showed him the sketch of Willow Bird and Hawktail. He studied it, his eyes wide.

"She's alive?" he said.

"Why didn't you tell me you were married?"

"I'm not married."

"Did you leave her to go back to St. Louis?"

"No, she got rid of me," he said. "In their culture the woman owns the lodge and all the belongings, except her husband's war articles. She booted me out. I left for about a month and came back to talk to her, but learned she and Hawktail had been stolen by a Ute war party. I heard later they had been killed along with some other captives. I'm glad they're both alive, but I don't think she treated me fairly."

He told me that Willow Bird had been given to him by Antelope, her brother, for a wife. As Antelope's father and mother had both died of sickness, it had been up to him to see that his sister was well cared for. Owen had offered five good horses and a trade rifle.

"At first the marriage was good," he said. "But I soon learned that Willow Bird had always wanted to be Kills It's wife. He hadn't gained war honors yet, but soon after Hawktail was born, he led a successful war party against the Utes. She left me to be with him."

He said that he had been dishonored and to save face would have had to fight Kills It. He believed that no matter the outcome, Hawktail would have been scarred for life.

"Maybe leaving was the honorable choice," I suggested.

"Had I not left, they wouldn't have been captured," he said. "I learned later that a Ute war party had struck the village while Kills It and most of the warriors were on a war party against the Pawnee. He should have stayed home."

"None of that matters now, does it?" I said. "Don't you want to get to know your son?"

"I would, if that's what he wishes."

"Go and see him," I urged.

"I don't know if I'm ready."

"You haven't got a choice," I said. "If you're traveling on to Oregon soon, you had better get to know him now."

Quincannon's Journal

29 APRIL 1846

I have a lot on my mind now, not the least of which is Willow Bird and Hawktail. It changes everything so much. I want to spend time with my son and learn how he's doing. And then there's the matter of getting to Oregon.

I sent Lamar ahead with the men yesterday, right after learning from Bones Brandt that Latour was at Fort Laramie. I hope they can find him. We'll be a much stronger force all traveling together.

I told Lamar to meet me along the trail at Fort Hall. I want to spend some time with the Arapaho. When I leave I'll be able to travel fast enough to catch up to them, especially if Ella decides to go back home.

I wonder what I can say to change her mind? She seems to understand me better than I do myself. For someone without children, she seems to know what it's like to love them.

Seeing Hawktail has brought up a lot of pain. He was only four years old when I left. I remember him sitting beside his mother's lodge, watching me as I saddled my pony, tears streaming down his little face. When I came to say good-bye, he rushed into the lodge. He didn't want me to see him crying.

I've never forgotten that day. There was nothing I could do and the frustration of it all drove me into rages for weeks after that. Willow Bird had made her decision and it was final. I could have stayed in the mountains, but I had tired of fighting Indians and scraping for a living. I wanted better than what was being offered. Beaver prices were dropping already and the fur companies were going all-out for what was left. There were plenty of Americans cutting one another's throats, to say nothing of the Hudson's Bay Company.

I thought that returning to St. Louis would bring about better times. Maybe I could get the farm back. But the men who had swindled my mother out of our land had sold it to someone else who had no idea who I was or what I was doing there asking questions. I decided to leave that part of my life behind for good.

I managed a small trading house upriver for a man named Watkins, who succeeded in staying in business by catering to a market the bigger traders cared nothing about. Emigrants moving from one place to another are always in need of food staples—flour and sugar and bacon—and will trade plows or wagon parts, even horses, for what they need. Watkins then traded those items back to other emigrants or local farmers and made a large profit.

He spent most of his time in the city, trusting me to run his business. I thought about Hawktail a lot during that time, as the Watkins children and their cousins would come and go around the trading house. I wondered what kind of man he might have become had he lived and if he would have carried a lot of me with him.

Now I know that there's a lot of me in him. It scares me to think of approaching him. I wonder what he thinks of me. He has certainly been well cared for and I know he's being trained in his people's ways by any number of uncles, each of whom—in their tradition—is considered another father.

I will find the right time and place to approach him. I hope his grudge against me isn't too great.

Never before have I discovered that I knew so little in such a short time.

I look back on the evening in St. Louis when Owen Quincannon told Indian stories at the hotel and later informed me that my beliefs about savages in the American West were wrong. At that time I didn't know he had married one of them and had lived among them.

Willow Bird sat for her portrait this afternoon and I've got to say that she's one of the most intelligent people I've ever met. No one can say that her dark eyes aren't filled with wisdom. She said her time is counted in winters and that at the time of her first marriage, she had counted thirteen.

She wanted to know all about where I grew up and how I came by such a good pony. I believe she's quite impressed not just by my artistic talent but by my ownership of Whistler. Even the men took notice, though they came nowhere near me and asked no questions.

I agreed to paint Willow Bird sitting on my pony in exchange for a soft doeskin dress, finely decorated in porcupine quills of red and black and green. It's the finest garment I've ever owned, and that includes my wonderful blue dress. I wore my blue slippers with the new dress and Willow Bird laughed.

"How far are you going to walk in those?" she asked.

"They're for dancing," I said.

Before it was over, I had traded her the slippers for three pairs of moccasins, one of them an Apache-style boot that ran clear to my knees. "They're for if you ride in the tall cactus," she said. "And now I can dance in the slippers."

We finally got around to discussing Owen and she told me that he was a good man whom she loved dearly, but that he would have died had he stayed with her.

"My husband before him was killed by enemies," she said. "I didn't want that for him."

"Did you tell him that?" I asked.

"I tried to, but he said I was only making excuses."

"Then you really didn't want to send him away?"

"I didn't have a choice," she said. "The Creator has a plan for us all and we must live by it."

She explained that Kills It was soon to rise to power because of his love for warfare. Older leaders held power because of their dreaming, and not warfare, but in the years to come all leaders would have to be fighters.

"The old people say a time of much bloodshed is coming," she said. "Our leaders will have to spill more blood than our enemies if we are to survive."

I asked her why she didn't resent me, as I was of white blood.

"Our people have never decided who was good or bad by skin color," she said. "It's what's in your heart. But now there are a lot of people of different color than our own coming into our lands, some good, but many bad. We can no longer trust as we once did."

She told me that as a girl she used to hear stories of bearded men with white skin who wore metal shells harder than a turtle's back.

"They came across the big waters in huge boats and journeyed up from the south on medicine dogs, what we know now as our buffalo ponies. The Indian peoples in those lands thought they were gods. But they weren't and came only for riches. They brought with them men in long robes who said they carried messages from their god, but stood by and watched while the metal-shelled men tortured the Indian peoples."

She spoke matter-of-factly, with no animosity. What she was telling me was simply the way it had occurred and had to be accepted as such.

"But we will never understand," she said, "why it is that your people wish for so many things to make themselves happy but never are."

She sat and admired the painting of Whistler and her. She called all her friends and relatives to come and see it and smiled while they stared at me. One old woman looked at my hands and felt them with her own. She put my fingers up to her forehead and smiled. Willow Bird said she was making up a song about me.

It was ironic that we were having so much fun, while not far away, women were crying. Water That Stands would be taken for burial the following day. His war shield and all his weapons would be buried with him. His best horse would be killed and left beside the grave so that he might ride it across to the spirit world.

Willow Bird told me all this and asked me not to paint any pictures of those in mourning. I hadn't thought of it, as I wanted subjects in festive dress or in everyday living. I had already seen those in mourning and was told that the blood on their hands was from cutting off fingers and that on their arms and legs was from knife gashes.

"They will not wash until the mourning period is over," Willow Bird said. "That way the Creator knows they are giving of themselves in sacrifice so that Water That Stands might have a good life on the Other Side."

Gabriella's Journal

We are camped on a small tributary of the Arkansas, just north of a fortified village called Pueblo. It is a trading house similar to Bent's Fort, on a smaller scale. Owen tells me the two factions are in competition.

It's been a difficult day and the camp is a solemn one. Water That Stands was buried along the trail near the river, at his mother's request. He had been born in the same exact spot twenty winters before.

Willow Bird told me that the family would grieve for a long time, perhaps a year. They were all very bloody from inflicting wounds of grieving—cuts in their arms and legs, and often along the forehead. Willow Bird herself is missing the last joint of the little finger on her left hand. She cut it off with a knife when her first husband fell to the Blackfeet.

I stood with Owen beside the grave. Next to him was Antelope. Water That Stands lay in the ground, dressed in his finest war shirt, wrapped in robes and blankets, his weapons lying with him, his dark and sullen face painted for his journey to the spirit world.

"It was not a good way for him to die," Antelope told Owen. "I only hope that he is granted a good life in the Other Side Camp."

Antelope cut his hair and let it fall into the grave. Braids that had once trailed down nearly to his knees were reduced to uneven locks that reached just below his neck, tainted with blood from self-inflicted wounds along his shoulders and back.

I had learned a lot from Owen about the Indian culture and in particular the Arapaho. I had learned even more from Willow Bird, who gave me the name Woman Whose Hands Are Sacred. She believes my ability to paint portraits to be a special gift from the Creator.

I believe her and know that we are already good friends. She says that she has much more to teach me and that I should allow myself to learn as much as I can about her people's culture, for some day I will need the knowledge to survive.

One of the first things I learned is how to grind a little white seed up into powder and drink it with water to avoid pregnancy.

"We often have hard times when having a child wouldn't be good," she said. "In fact, those times would kill both the mother and the child."

She called the plant "stoneseed" and said it was plentiful in the foothills and mountains during the summer. She showed me the plant and said the seeds would develop in another full moon. I wished J. T. Landers was with us.

While Antelope sang a prayer to his deceased son, I looked out across the country to the towering mountains that lay just ahead. Pike's Peak rose high into the blue vastness, with sheer walls of high mountains running along both sides of the landmark.

We had left Bent's Fort soon after the meeting where the presents were exchanged. Antelope had invited Owen to their village, to talk over old times and also the future. He had been free to bring anyone else along that he chose. I thought long and hard about going straight back to St. Louis but didn't want to leave him just yet. It was difficult, as Bom had decided to stay at the fort and work with Dick and Charlotte Green.

"I'll be treated much better here than in Oregon," he

said. "When you get to Fort Vancouver, you write me."

I left a number of sketches and paintings with Barton and the Rivet brothers. They promised to see to it that Mother received them when they got home. I hadn't heard anything from her while in St. Louis, which I thought odd. She had promised to write daily and didn't take such commitments lightly.

To our surprise, Bones Brandt asked to come along.

"I figure to stay a while at Fort Laramie and then move on," he said. "I'm too old to get caught up in a war."

He looked far too old and skinny to have any strength, yet he saddled his own pony with ease and packed a large skin bag full of valuables.

"Don't worry about him," Owen told me. "He'll outlive you and me both."

We left, riding our horses and each leading a pack mule, traveling with Antelope and his band. I had plenty of sketchpads and watercolors to do a number of pieces. But I think the people are worried about me doing their portraits.

Antelope told Owen that they think me sacred but are afraid of me. They had all seen the picture of Water That Stands, and now he's dead. They worry that should I paint any one of them, they might suffer the same fate.

It was even worse that Water That Stands had fallen to a white man's rifle. Owen had explained to Antelope that none of us would ever condone Edward's actions. I'm certain Antelope thinks that by even traveling with such a man, we are accepting of his behavior. But because of their friendship, Antelope asked Owen to stand beside him on a very hard day.

According to Willow Bird, Water That Stands was Antelope's favorite son. He had been tutoring the young warrior in the ways of a medicine man, believing that when the time was right, his own medicine would be transferred to this special person. Now a senseless act had taken that happiness away and had threatened to make his heart very bad.

"It's a difficult test for him," she told me. "If he's to stay a holy man, he can't wish vengeance."

Antelope finished his prayer and said, "The man who killed my son must be very strange in the head to have behaved in the manner he did. Who shoots someone for sport? What honor is there in that?"

Antelope had not witnessed his son's death, but he had heard every detail from the young horse tenders who had gone searching for lost ponies. The report they brought back was that Water That Stands had ridden ahead of them to investigate a party of white men shooting buffalo. When he raised his hand to signal he wanted to talk, their leader dismounted from a black stallion and shot him.

Willow Bird says the Arapaho way of life is changing. According to their elders, the times when warriors rode for horses and honor against other Indian nations is ending. The coming of the wagon people has changed everything.

Now Antelope is being looked upon with suspicion. In honoring his friendship with Owen, he's being accused of accepting the white man's ways. Willow Bird says that she's convinced no one will step forward to demand he step down as leader, or to ask for his white medicine shield, a sign of great honor..

After the burial, we resumed the march upriver. Our destination is a special place called Manitou Springs. Indian people camp there without worry of attack by enemies. There is a general agreement, Owen says, that precludes any warfare from taking place there.

I'm anxious to reach the mountains. It's hard to keep my eyes off them. Heavy white clouds are now dropping

snow on their high summits. Owen says he will take me
over a divide called Ute Pass and then into some beautiful
mountain country before turning north and heading for
the trail towards Fort Laramie.

When we reach there, I will have to decide whether to
go on to Oregon with Owen or turn east with a caravan
and return to St. Louis. I must admit that I miss Mother
and home, but I love this traveling and the thought of
seeing new lands and painting portraits of interesting people. It will be a very difficult decision.

MANITOU SPRINGS

Gabriella's Journal

10 MAY 1846

The Boiling Springs, the place of the Manitou, is the most enjoyable of any place on
my journey so far. Beautiful foothills and mountains sur-
round a stream named for the bubbling waters that flow
clear and warm to the touch.

The people bathe naked and have no qualms about it.
I save my time for the later hours of the evening and
Owen often tracks me to our favorite pool, a large basin
enclosed within a group of trees.

One evening while in the water I heard soft, melodic
music. As the music drew closer, I saw Owen emerge
from the trees playing a large wooden flute.

"Do you know the story of the woodpecker?" he asked
me. "As the story goes, it's the woodpecker who is re-

sponsible for the love flute. A young man traveling along the river on an evening like this wondered how he could win the heart of a young woman he wished to marry. As he thought about it, he heard beautiful music coming from the trees. He searched for the source and discovered that a woodpecker had pecked holes in a hollow tree and the wind was playing songs. He cut a hollow branch from the tree and after making holes in the wood, taught himself how to play. He went back to the village and won the young woman's heart. That's the story of the wood-pecker."

"That's a good story," I agreed, "but what's your point?"

He removed his clothes and stepped down into the water. I'll admit, I always enjoy it when he comes to me naked. He took me in his arms and we kissed while the warm water bubbled all around us.

"I'm going to play that flute day and night, until you say yes to following me," he said.

I had no inclination towards arguing with him at the time. I was enjoying his strong arms and his response to me as I stroked him under the water. When neither of us could stand it any longer, we made love, while the birds sang evening songs around us.

Afterwards, we nestled in the warm water and Owen brought up having a life together.

"You've got nothing to return to England for," he said. "You've told me yourself that your mother seems to have abandoned you, that she didn't write you like she promised."

"I have to admit I still don't understand that," I said.

"Then what's keeping you from agreeing to go with me to Oregon?" he asked.

"I can't sell artwork to settlers," I said. "Perhaps when I've gained a following in England, I can return and we'll talk more about it then, since you refuse to go over there with me."

"How would I fit into your society?"

"Just fine, with a coat and tie instead of buckskins."

"Maybe you would fit better over here," he said. "You've told me before that you've often wondered where you truly belong."

All he said is true. I've never felt that I truly fit in. While growing up I used to sit on the beach, looking out across the Irish Sea, wondering where I came from, who I was, and where I was going. But more than wondering where I came from, I was aware a part of me existed somewhere else, far away from Lancashire.

"Yes, I've always been searching for something that was missing," I said. "Strangely, though, I knew I would find that part of me on this journey."

"You've found it?" Owen asked.

"Yes, I have," I said. "The missing part of me that makes me whole is you."

"I've felt the same way, ever since I first met you," he replied. "Why would you ever want us to be apart?"

"It's not that I would want that," I said. "But there are things I need to do before we can be together always. One of those things is to become established as an artist."

He stepped out of the water and left without saying anything. He doesn't understand that I need fulfillment as much as he does. Perhaps ladies of my class aren't supposed to desire things for themselves, but that's something I won't adhere to.

I know that Willow Bird has her own ambitions, but is unable to fulfill them. Even more than I, she is caught in a society that expects more from her than she can possibly produce.

She is the main reason I am so interested in these people. Owen was right, they are not the complete savages everyone thinks they are, nor are they noble and above reproach. They are no different from any other race of people: they have wants and needs and a desire to know what it takes to find happiness.

Though the villagers here are strongly opposed to the white movement into their country, they are very hospitable. Our stay has been more than pleasant and I fear I've used too many of my paints and sketchpads. I have painted the surrounding foothills and mountains many times. Willow Bird and Hawktail have both sat for their portraits, and Antelope as well. But none of the others will even come close to me.

Still, I have enough work and memories from here to last a lifetime. Perhaps I will travel back home from Fort Laramie and work to sell my paintings, then return by boat to Fort Vancouver and meet Owen there. I have no shortage of subjects to interest the English aristocracy.

Nothing in picture form can convey all that I have learned. Willow Bird has shown me so many things and has even included me in some of their sacred ceremonies. I have been in a sweat lodge once, and that's enough to last me forever. If that ceremony was meant to burn the old life out of me, it surely succeeded.

As I understand it, going into the darkness of a small round lodge covered over with buffalo skins is like going back into the womb. The darkness is penetrating, but not nearly so much as the heat. I sustained it through the sacred four rounds, but I don't know how. Perhaps I do. It truly was God above who came in answer to my prayers, along with the Arapaho ancestors who took pity on me.

Willow Bird sweats with her friends and relatives on a regular basis. She says that during the days before the Sun Dance ceremony, it's a daily occurrence. I can't imagine anyone being able to stand that ordeal day after day. Once was enough for me.

I will admit that, that one time, though, has changed my outlook forever. I have truly been reborn in a way. I don't see things the way I used to and am convinced that a Supreme Being exists and cares for all living things.

"If you take your time in the sweat lodge seriously," Willow Bird told me, "the Creator will always look down on you with favor."

To her way of thinking, we have only our bodies to offer the Creator in thanks for the divine life He has given us.

"When you give yourself to the Divine and do so without reservation," she said, "that is a measure of true faith. You will never again be afraid of anything in life, for you know how powerful the Creator is. Good things then come to you."

She told me all this while we waited for the rocks to heat up outside the sweat lodge. The small, round structure was made of willows that had been cut and planted into the ground in a large circle, then doubled over and the opposite end planted as well.

"Only one who has the right to build such a lodge can do so," Willow Bird explained. "No one else is allowed."

We watched the rocks as they heated to a glowing white. They were placed in a pit inside the lodge. When the time was right, we all stripped naked and entered the lodge, sitting in a circle around the pit of rocks. I'll never forget how those rocks glowed and how much heat they gave off.

An old woman entered and sat next to the door. She said some prayers and tossed cedar onto the rocks. The incense filled the lodge with a strong perfume that Willow Bird told me would drive away bad spirits and invite good ones in.

The old woman had a large kettle of water and a ladle. When she closed the flap, she said more prayers and poured water over the rocks. The steam was suffocatingly hot. Willow Bird had made me a switch from chokecherry branches and I used it along with the others to swat my back and sides.

The old woman continued to pray and poured even more water on the rocks. The heat was so intense that I felt I would burn alive. It took my breath away. Willow Bird had told me to lean forward and put my nose close to the floor. I did this and slapped my back and sides with the chokecherry switch.

"By so doing," Willow Bird had explained earlier, "you will become one with power of the heat and the spirits will be able to help you."

The ceremony began in late afternoon and concluded near nightfall. After each of the four rounds, we left the lodge to recover and gather strength. I have never been so tired and at the same time so exhilarated in my life. My senses were open to sights and sounds I hadn't experienced before and every bird's song was a mastery of music. The clouds in the sky seemed close enough to touch, and the green of the leaves and grass was so brilliant they seemed to glow.

I tried doing some new watercolors and discovered that I could bring out a better image by mixing colors more to the complexities I remembered from the sweat lodge. Willow Bird smiled broadly, knowing that I had benefited from my experience. Even old Bones Brandt, who spends considerable time alone, exclaimed at the richness of a new portrait I completed of him.

"Looks like I might just step off that parchment," he said.

There was a sadness to his eyes that I couldn't keep

out of the portrait. Try as I might, I could get no bright-
ness to come through.

"You create the image as it truly is," Willow Bird said.
"That is part of your gift."

She then asked me why I never painted a portrait of
myself. I told her I had an aversion to that. I've thought
about it and I don't know why, but I've never wanted to
see myself straight on from an image I painted.

"You look into the mirror without a problem," she said.
"Why not paint yourself?"

Willow Bird has a way of seeing into me that is un-
nerving. She seems to know me better than I do myself
and I often wonder if she doesn't have a gift of her own:
a gift of seeing into another's soul.

Quincannon's Journal

12 MAY 1846

I've spent considerable time with Antelope and have
discovered how much has changed between us since
our friendship began. He tells me that my time in
the settlements has made me the same as any other white
man and I argue that it hasn't.

Kills It hasn't returned with his warriors and there are
villagers who wonder if Ella and I aren't to blame.
Maybe Antelope needs an excuse to send me away.

He's preparing for a hunting trip. Before he leaves will
be a good time to tell him we're leaving. I'll miss the
friendship we once shared but I guess what they say is
correct: Time changes everything.

I'll also be saddened to say good-bye to Hawktail. I likely won't ever see him again, but I can't tell him that. I guess I shouldn't feel that way, as anything can happen in life.

We have developed a very good relationship, and though he spends most of his time with the horse tenders, our time together has given me considerable satisfaction. When I first approached him, I wasn't certain what his reaction would be. Now I feel that we've always been close.

The second day after we camped, I asked him what he thought of Parker. In my opinion my buckskin was as good a horse as any other to be found, and he agreed.

"I expected you to have a good pony," he said.

"How would you know that?" I asked.

"I might have been small when you left, but I already knew you very well."

That day we rode across the hills together. An early afternoon thunderstorm had cooled the air and brought a sparkle to the lush landscape. Hawktail led me up a small draw where a little creek gurgled through the rocks and wildflowers. In this little hideaway the wind was silent and the birds chattered in the trees.

"I come here a lot to sit and think," he said. "I used to dream that you'd come back to live with us."

"I had the same dream," I said. "You weren't old enough to understand at the time, but I had to leave. There was no choice."

"I knew that," he admitted. "I also knew that my mother made unusual decisions for reasons I couldn't understand. I know now that she was trying to protect you."

"I don't know if I can believe that," I said.

"But it's true," Hawktail insisted. "As a child, I had dreams of you dying in many different ways."

"What you were seeing was my pain," I said. "It was so hard to leave you."

"Maybe some of it was that," he said, "but not the other visions. I saw warriors charging you and trying to cut off your head."

For a moment I was shocked. Hawktail had just explained my dream to me. I had initially believed the dream to be a warning to stay out of hostile Indian country, but the meaning had been much deeper.

Willow Bird had once told me that her first husband, another trapper, had been killed before her eyes by Blackfeet Indians. She had escaped only by submerging herself in a beaver pond. She had told me often that she worried for my safety, but I had always assured her that I wasn't going back into Blackfeet country, that it wasn't worth it. Still, she persisted that I was in danger.

When she asked me to leave her lodge, she never explained that she believed it to be for my safety. Kills It had always expressed an interest in her and resented both me and Antelope after the marriage. I had always believed that she loved him and not me.

"After you left, I became angry at Mother many times," Hawktail said, "especially after we were captured by the Utes. I told her we would still be with our own people if she hadn't wanted you to leave."

I asked him how they managed to escape, and he told me that the Ute warriors had left for war against the Pawnee and Kills It had then attacked the village at dawn and taken them back.

"Mother had no choice but to marry Kills It then," Hawktail said, "since he was the one who had rescued us."

"Do you have dreams about Kills It?" I asked.

"He scares me, so I don't think about him."

I suggested that we head back to camp so there would

be no concerns about us. I knew it wouldn't be long until I would be leaving for Oregon. That same feeling of dread came over me.

We untied our ponies and I said, "You know that it's not possible for me to stay now, either."

"I've known that from the time you came to the village," he said, sadly. "But I'll always love you as my father, and I'll keep you forever in my heart."

Gabriella's Journal

20 MAY 1846

Yesterday we were prepared to leave, but our plans changed abruptly when Kills It returned to the village with his warriors and announced that a war party of Utes was two days behind.

He said that the war party was large enough to wipe out the entire band. No one became anxious immediately, as we were camped at a place of sacred waters. The tribes that frequent this area have an unspoken rule prohibiting warfare anywhere near the site.

"Before they arrive," Kills It said, "I want to give a feast."

He said that the feast would be in honor of his victory over Edward and his soldiers. He had caught up with them and had forced them to turn back towards the east. Then he and his warriors had taken fresh meat. He wanted to give the feast so everyone would know he was a truly good war leader.

He told Owen to ask me if I was sad that the one I would have married was now leaving America.

"She would never have married him," Owen insisted.

Kills It laughed. "He's a coward and not worthy to take any woman. And since you were with him, you're the same."

"I doubt your victory," Owen said. "You just need to make your people think you're a warrior."

Kills It's eyes turned hard and his jaw muscles turned rigid as iron. He walked away and soon Antelope came to our camp.

"It's not good to stir everyone up," he told Owen.

"Not everyone," Owen said. "Just Kills It. He had it coming."

"My people are divided as it is," Antelope said. "You make it worse."

"I won't be insulted," Owen said.

"I can understand that he would insult you," Antelope said, "but you should disregard it."

"There was a time when you would have taken my side," Owen said.

"Times have changed," Antelope said. "You know that."

Owen looked out towards the mountains with hurt in his eyes. "Maybe we shouldn't have taken your invitation to come with you to the village."

"But you accepted it," he said, "and now you will have to stay until the Utes have left the area."

"No, I think we should go now," Owen said.

"You might escape the Utes," Antelope said, "but Kills It and his warriors will catch you quickly. He has everyone believing that you are the reason the Utes have come, and that if you leave now, it will be to help them fight us."

"And everyone believes this?"

"A great many do," Antelope said.

"It seems he has more power here than you," Owen said.

Antelope turned rigid but held his tongue. "I told Kills It that to believe you would fight with the Utes was crazy. He said yes, that it was crazy, but he doesn't want you here, and that's a way to turn all the people against you. He says he knows you will have to stay until the Utes are gone and that to keep peace with him, you must attend his feast.'"

We had no choice, and tonight Owen and I sat with Antelope and Kills It and a number of high-ranking warriors around a fire. For me to be seated with them was very unusual, as women rarely eat with the men, especially in times of important council.

The discussion dealt chiefly with the Ute problem. I couldn't understand a word that was said, but Owen told me later that the men disagreed about whether or not there would be fighting. Most of them believed the Utes would respect the Manitou in the Boiling Springs and go about their way, perhaps hunting buffalo. The other men said that they had no business in Arapaho lands for any reason, and that they knew it. Fighting would surely happen.

The discussion ended when the feasting started and Kills It began an oration about how he had found Edward and his soldiers and forced them to go back towards the east. I knew Owen didn't believe him, but I couldn't understand why not.

"Because he's talking about gaining glory," Owen told me. "If he believes Edward to be no more than an old woman, then what honor would he gain in fighting him?"

Owen never said what he thought to the others. He accepted his bowl of meat, as I did, and we were asked to take the first bites, for the sake of conserving peace between Owen and Kills It.

The meat had been stewed with roots and tasted sweet.

Owen asked what kind of meat it was and Kills It said he had shot a young bear with his bow.

"I've eaten bear before," Owen said. "This isn't bear."

Kills It shrugged and suggested that it might be mountain lion. Owen threw the bowl on the ground and stood up.

"You've fed us human meat, haven't you?"

I looked at Owen and realized he had determined something I didn't yet know about or even understand. It confused and frightened me, as well as set my stomach to churning.

"Did you feed us Edward Garr?" Owen demanded.

"Sit down," Antelope said. "There will be no fighting."

Owen took some deep breaths and sat back down. Kills It grinned broadly. I turned away when I saw a warrior carry the heads of J. T. Landers and Dr. Noel Marking to the fire and drop them. Two other warriors brought Norman Stiles forward. He had been gutted out like an animal and his body, mouth, and eyes stuffed with grass.

"We tried to make him look alive like he did the birds and animals he put stuffing into," Kills It said. "But we couldn't."

I covered my mouth and nose and struggled not to vomit. The images of the three men, especially Mr. Landers, rose vividly in my mind and I couldn't comprehend what had been done to them.

Owen turned to Antelope. "Why would you allow such a thing?"

"My people are angry about the death of Water That Stands," he said. "Now they feel avenged."

"But none of these men shot Water That Stands," Owen insisted. "Edward Garr did."

"That is true, but he gave Kills It the three men to save himself," Antelope told Owen. "It was a trade that everyone thought fair, if the Britisher agreed to turn back from our lands."

Owen saw me clenching my fists. I yelled out loud in rage, attracting everyone's attention.

"What is she doing?" Antelope asked Owen.

"Expressing her anger at Edward Garr, a man who betrays everyone he meets. If you believe he left your lands, you're all fools."

Kills It leaned forward and spat at Owen. "You are the fool! Maybe we should cut you open and fill you with grass, also. Then your woman can have you hanging on her wall."

There was laughter. Owen said, "You and I should decide between us who gets filled with grass. Or are you too cowardly to fight on your own?"

Antelope stopped the confrontation. "We are at the Manitou, a sacred place," he said. "Whatever needs to be settled will happen after the Utes are gone and we have moved camp."

BOILING SPRINGS RIVER

Gabriella's Journal

24 MAY 1846

The Utes arrived two days ago and set up their camp less than a mile downriver. Antelope and his subchiefs went to meet with their leaders but were told there would be no negotiations for peace. Since that time the village has been under siege.

Antelope announced to the people that all but the children would go on half-rations. The village was getting low on food supplies and the time for gathering roots and hunting game had begun. But everyone knew that if a hunting party left to get meat, the Utes would eradicate them.

Kills It blamed Antelope for the bad fortune. "If you hadn't invited these white people," he said, "this would not have happened."

Antelope told him that we had nothing to do with the Utes coming across from their lands to hunt buffalo, but most of the villagers agreed with Kills It. In winning the argument, Kills It had come a number of steps closer to becoming the main chief.

Against Antelope's wishes, Kills It called a second meeting with the Ute war leaders. He told Antelope he didn't want him to go along, as his thinking was tainted by his friendship with Owen, who could barely restrain himself from challenging Kills It to fight. But he realized that should he win the encounter, Kills It's followers would likely make short work of him.

When Kills It returned from the meeting, we learned that he had planned for us to die anyway.

"The Utes will leave us alone if we offer them someone to kill," he said. "I propose that the three whites be given over to them."

Everyone but Antelope agreed. I grabbed Owen's arm, but he said that we had no choice but to pack our belongings and follow Kills It to the Ute village. Bones Brandt seemed unusually calm.

"If I'm to die," Bones said, "then it's good that I go with my wife's people."

Before we left, I said to Kills It, "You may have sentenced us to die for your own sake, but remember that I once painted a picture of you. I have your spirit."

His face paled. When he got his composure back, he said, "You cannot make me die. I will burn the image in a fire."

"Your spirit will burn with it," I said.

We were taken by a selected group of Ute warriors. Owen said they were the camp patrol and would see to it that we were watched closely until it was decided how we would die. Bones had learned a good deal of their language but could get none of the villagers to show any compassion. There would never be a time, one of them told him, when the Ute people would not seek vengeance against the Arapaho for past grievances, and it didn't matter that he had once been married to a Ute woman.

We were marched through the village and insulted in every way. Children threw stones and struck us with sticks, while the women spat on us and tore at our clothes. We were taken to the river and tied to cotton-woods, where the women began piling campfire wood at our feet.

I went through many emotions and found myself turning numb, awaiting sure death. A group of warriors gambled with small, notched sticks, and after a winner was declared, he walked over to me and started to tear my dress off.

At the same time Bones kicked at a small boy who was sticking him in the leg with a knife. The warrior turned from me and walked over to him. He took the knife from the boy and plunged it deep into Bones's thigh. The old buckskinner didn't even flinch, but spat in the Ute's face.

The warrior called for two ponies, and Bones's eyes turned wild, but he said nothing. A number of warriors took him, struggling, from the tree and tied two long ropes, one to each of his ankles. The other end of each rope was tied to the saddle of a separate pony.

While this was happening, the same small boy walked

up to Owen and fitted an arrow to his small bow. The camp women urged him to take careful aim.

The first shot stuck in Owen's buckskin shirt. The boy's mother stepped forward and ripped his shirt open. The next arrow penetrated the flesh and muscle of his upper chest and hung awkwardly while the women all laughed. I screamed at the women and called them cowards, but they ignored me.

Bones lay on the ground, resolved to his fate. His leg bled profusely and I believe he was losing consciousness. The two warriors made certain the ropes were tied securely to their saddles and prepared to kick the ponies into a run in opposite directions. The intended result was that Bones's legs would split and tear off.

Before they could execute their intentions, a small group of riders appeared and the warriors froze. An older white man with long hair, dressed in beaded and quilled buckskins, stepped down from his horse and asked one of the village men what they were doing.

Owen stared at the white man, turning pale. After a moment he yelled, "Father, is that you?"

The man walked over and stared at Owen for a long time.

"Where's your mother?" he asked finally.

"She's been dead for some time," Owen said.

"Why did you come out into this country?"

"Just passing through is all."

"To Mexico?"

"Oregon."

"You're off the main trail. No son of mine would make that kind of mistake."

"And no father of mine would live among a people who were once friendly and now barbarous to the extreme."

"You don't know what's happened to these people," he said.

"Killing everyone you can isn't going to solve any problems," Owen said. "You should know that by now."

"If you stay out here long enough," Owen's father said, "you'll learn that you really don't know anything. You just live one day to the next and see the changes and learn there's not a thing you can do about them."

After carefully removing the arrow from Owen's chest, he ordered that I be untied and that Bones be cut loose from the ponies. I almost fainted with relief.

It seemed odd to me at the time that the Utes would obey a white man, but Bones told me later that Owen's father, known as Strong Hand, had earned numerous war honors in fighting Ute enemies. He had even killed white trappers and traders who refused to do business fairly or who wouldn't leave Ute lands when warned.

"He's turned Injun in his own right," Bones said. "He don't want nobody moving out here and changing all this."

Owen did not hug his father, nor did his father attempt to hug him. Instead, they stared at one another. There was pain on both faces, but neither could make the move to do anything but shake hands.

We spent the night in the Ute camp as the guest of Strong Hand, who owned a lot of property and had the right to demand we be treated well. In the course of less than an hour we went from facing torture and death to dining on choice cuts of fresh buffalo and elk.

Owen said his chest wound was more troublesome than threatening. Bones's knife wound was treated by an older woman gifted in herbal medicine. She did as well as she could, but the cut was deep and painful.

The Utes were a shorter and stockier people than the Arapaho, but other than the physical, I could see no difference in their ways of life. Their lodges were painted in similar designs and their men wore the same kinds of medicine charms to help them in battle. But they had always been enemies.

Owen said little all evening. He told me that we would begin our journey to Fort Laramie as soon as possible. He didn't know what would happen next, but believed the Utes would still require a measure of satisfaction against the Arapaho, unless some trading and peace negotiations could take place.

I don't believe he spoke more than a few words to his father, barely a thank-you for saving our lives. I can't help but think that their years apart might have produced a chasm neither of them can bridge.

Quincannon's Journal

25 May 1846

I listened to war drums throughout the night, and with the dawn, took my place with the other warriors while an old medicine man said prayers and danced under a grizzly bear robe. My father told me that I would be looked to as a leader against the Arapaho forces, and that I shouldn't fail to show strength and courage.

Stripped to moccasins and a breechcloth, I stood still while my father painted me in war designs of lightning and elks' feet. My face was all black and red and three eagle feathers hung from the trigger guard of my Hawken, and three more from the handle of a battleax.

My pony was painted in similar designs, and when the

medicine man came past each of us shaking a gourd rattle, we mounted to face the Arapaho.

Not long ago I was with Antelope, discussing our friendship and old times. Now I was facing his young men. He hadn't stepped forward to stop Kills It from handing us over, so I don't feel I will ever owe my old friend anything ever again.

I can't really blame him. His future as main leader is at stake. My feeling is that he's already lost his position and he just doesn't know it yet.

Antelope wasn't going to fight, of that I was certain. He's of an older age and stays in the camp to help sing war songs with the medicine man. The Utes were already doing the same thing and my father was among the singers. His son, Black Horse, five years my junior, received the same paint as I did from our father. He watched me for a long time, no doubt wondering how I would fight.

Ella was also watching and worried not just for me but for Hawktail. I told her a number of times that he was too young for battle.

"He must prove himself stealing horses first," I said. "He hasn't even done that yet."

Though I felt sure of my belief, I did worry that he might be pressed into going his first time. I didn't really believe it would happen, but I couldn't be sure of anything.

We lined up facing one another and the chanting began. Some of the warriors carried handheld drums and others beat on their shields with their bows. Kills It rode back and forth on his pony, whooping loudly, showing his bravery to his followers.

Finally a warrior from among the Utes rode out to meet another from the Arapaho. They charged each other straight on, their ponies running full speed.

The Arapaho carried a lance and raised his shield as

the Ute shot an arrow at him. The arrow deflected upward and the Arapaho warrior rammed his lance into the Ute's leg.

The lance head pierced the warrior's leg and penetrated his pony's ribs. Horse and rider went down. The Arapaho rode past the Ute warrior, who was trying to rise, and slammed a war club into the side of his head. Then he quickly dismounted and with a brief stroke of his knife, cut across the front of the dying Ute's forehead and ripped a chunk of hair and scalp free. He held the trophy up and screamed to the sky.

All the warriors from both sides rode forward to engage in battle. Men yelled and ponies screamed and the air quickly filled with dust. The chants of death songs began with the killing.

I saw a warrior with arrows in his back and side, struggling against a foe who was tearing at his scalp. I fired my Hawken at an Arapaho who rode up beside me and aimed an arrow at my chest. He fell backwards off his horse and lay still.

Through the dust and confusion I noticed that Kills It was circling the battlefield in an effort to reach me.

I rode toward him, fighting Arapahoes along the way. When I reached him, Kills It got down from his horse and challenged me hand-to-hand.

I dismounted and slapped Parker on the rump to send him off. Kills It tossed his shield aside and came at me with a large knife. I had nothing but the battleax, and instead of swinging it, I reached in quickly and touched him on the arm.

He knew that I had counted a great honor against him and yelled with rage. He charged me and thrust the knife toward my middle. I dodged sideways and touched him again.

I had intended to count coup four times, but Black

Horse stepped in front of me and sought to prove himself. Kills It was waiting for him. When my half brother reached in with a stick to touch him, he felt the big knife's blade slice deep into his abdomen.

Black Horse doubled over and fell to the ground, his blood staining the trampled grass.

Kills It turned to me and smiled. "Why don't you try it again?"

"I'm content to see you go through life with the shame of my coups against you," I said.

Kills It charged me, white-eyed as a rabid wolf. As he lunged, my ax caught him on the forearm, slicing the muscle to the bone. The knife fell to the ground and he picked it up with his other hand, his eyes still wild.

When he came again, his knife raised high, I buried the ax straight into his forehead, right between his eyes, and let him fall past me. He did not go to the ground and writhe in a death throe, but stayed on his hands and knees, trying to rise.

I had heard stories of warriors who refused to die, of men who had lain on the battlefield still breathing after legs and arms had been removed, once for a long while after the head was taken. I had thought the tales to be far-fetched. But I saw in Kills It the most startling demonstration of strength that anyone could imagine.

Warriors on both sides stopped their fighting to watch Kills It rise to his feet and face me, the ax protruding from his skull. He could stand but a short time before falling forward to the ground.

The Ute warriors cut off his fingers for trophies, and even before he was dead, one of them cut out his heart, to gain Kills It's unusual medicine. They left me the scalp, but I didn't want it. Instead, my father came forward and ripped it free, saying he would spit on it every time he thought about Black Horse, who now lay dead beside me.

25 May 1846

The camp rejoiced in victory but grieved for the losses at the same time. Owen told me that forty-three young men had died and another fifteen were injured. The Arapaho had lost that many and more.

Men and women, both, went into mourning, cutting their hair and themselves with knives and awls. The keening was terrible and lasted until late afternoon, when the Scalp Dance began.

I watched while the warriors, Owen among them, circled a pole in the center of the village that had been adorned with scalps taken in battle that day. They sat and waited while painted women approached the pole and sang victory songs, then made room for a warrior on horseback who rode around the pole and told war stories.

I wondered why Bones Brandt wasn't in attendance and went off to look for him. I found him down by the river, resting against a large cottonwood tree. He greeted me with a smile and asked me to sit down. While the drums beat and the dancing continued, we looked across to the mountains where thin clouds trailed into thin wisps above the peaks.

He said there was a time when he would sit with his wife and they would talk about the land—how it could be so beautiful yet so harsh, and so soft and gentle, like a mother who fed her child with tender care, and how she shuddered when warriors killed one another on battlefields and soaked the soil with blood. Then the wives and mothers would mix their tears with the blood and earth, and the sky would send lightning and rain, and the cycle would start all over again.

"I figure it will be that way till there's no tomorrow," he said, looking into the distance.

He rubbed his leg and moaned. It had swollen considerably, and even though he had changed the heavy herb compresses many times, they couldn't stop the bleeding.

"Red Flower's grandfather used to say that the mountains and sky are the only things that last," he said. "I figure I saw this country at its best. Can't complain."

He said he had long since tired of telling people what things used to be like, but believed that I somehow knew.

"Otherwise you wouldn't paint them pictures the way you do," he said. "You can see what was in a man's eyes when he was younger and you can get it through them paints you use. I ain't never seen nothing like it."

"Do you have anything that belonged to your wife?" I asked.

He took a large blue bead from a pouch that hung around his neck. It felt warm in my hand. I held it for a while and gave it back to him.

"I'll be right back," I promised.

When I arrived back from our tent, twilight was spreading across the mountain sky in scarlet ribbons. He took the painting and stared at it for a moment, in shock.

"That's exactly how she looked," he said softly. "That's just how we both looked the day we was married."

He handed me the bead and asked that I keep it.

"She would have given it to you herself, had she been here," he said. "The way I figure it, she already knows you somehow."

I left him beside the river, clutching the painting. He told me not to mind about him, that he would make it back to camp in due time.

"You get back to Owen," he said. "He's a good man."

In fact Owen had come looking for me and I met him at the edge of camp. He said he thought it best if we went back and helped Bones get to his bedroll. When we reached him, his head had slumped forward and his hands had released the painting.

As the sky darkened, Owen dug a deep hole in the sand and we laid his friend to rest under the tree where he died. From the branches came the twitter of little birds, and as we finished we looked up to see a pair of chickadees flit off into the waning light.

THE BAYOU SALADE

Gabriella's Journal

29 MAY 1846

Yesterday we packed the mules and saddled the horses without fanfare. Owen had stretched Kills It's scalp across a small hoop to dry. I hate looking at it but he reminds me that we must keep it because should we meet any more Utes, or any of the tribes to the west, we will be welcomed as an ally.

Owen's father didn't even see us leave. He's in mourning and has cut his hair and carved lines into his arms and legs with a knife. Some of the young warriors who watched Owen battle Kills It stood at a distance and watched us leave. Otherwise there was no good-bye as we renewed our journey towards Fort Laramie.

At the edge of camp, Owen took a last long look up the trail toward the Manitou, where smoke rose from the

Arapaho campfires. He had thought about saying one last good-bye to Hawktail, but then realized he couldn't do that. He had fought with the Ute against them, so we are now both considered mortal enemies.

Even Antelope would now turn his back on us. Especially Owen. It's as if the old friendship between them never existed. Though Kills It had caused the problem in the first place, Owen could have chosen not to fight. But then the Ute people would have had cause for mistrust.

I wish things could have been different, but it seems there's no way to predict what will happen at any given time out here. The weather changes rapidly and the fortunes of travelers even quicker.

There are many good memories to treasure, along with the bad. I will always remember my friendship with Willow Bird and the many things she taught me. I saw her standing with the other Arapaho women just before the battle, urging the young warriors to be brave. I know she saw me as well and I wonder if her heart was just as heavy.

Though I might never see her or her people again, I have my sketchpads and watercolors to remember them. I have much to transpose that will stand as a testament to the things I saw and did while in the camps of the Arapaho and the Ute. I'm certain Owen has his past memories to deal with now as well.

I feel sorry for him. As a child he had never known his father properly, and now as an adult, it will never happen. The two men seem to have everything in common but no emotional bond. They have separated themselves from each other totally and there seems to be no foundation for a reconciliation.

Now he has to face the additional reality that he will likely never see his son again. I know that pains him deeply and sense that he doesn't know how to talk about it. All he can say is that Hawktail has grown into a fine young man and that he will someday make his people very proud.

That evening we camped near a beautiful little stream called Plum Creek, at the headwaters of the South Platte River. Owen shot a small deer and we roasted the loin and back legs. He laid out the remainder of the meat on branches to dry.

We both fell sound asleep and didn't awaken until late this morning. Owen was frying more meat when I decided to go for a walk.

The day was open and warm, the bees and butterflies filling a little meadow where the trail ran. I wondered what lay over the hill ahead and walked to the top. There, next to a wagon track, I discovered one of Edward Garr's rifles, with his initials engraved on the stock.

The stock below the engraving was cracked and the hammer bent. I called Owen and he came running. He suggested that it had likely fallen under one of the carts. Edward was never one to have his guns repaired. He merely discarded them.

We looked down the hill from where the rifle lay and to my surprise I noticed remnants of tattered clothing strewn everywhere, along with the remains of three large trunks, each one smashed to pieces. I recognized one of the ripped dresses.

"This was Avis's favorite dinner gown," I said. "I can't believe it. And look, some of Uncle Walter's things."

"Sir Edward must have grown tired of hauling their belongings," Owen said.

Owen stood back while I walked through the scattered memories. Tears came as I relived that night in Edward's tent. I turned to rejoin Owen and stumbled over a shoe. Regaining my balance, I noticed a white envelope lying in the grass. I picked it up and recognized my mother's

handwriting—a letter from home, addressed to me at the
Planters' Hotel in St. Louis.

The envelope had been opened. Curious, I took two
separate letters out and read the first one:

3 MARCH 1846

My Dearest Gabriella,

*I do hope this reaches you before your departure for
the mountains. I have searched my soul since your
leaving and have come to the conclusion that I have
been wrong in keeping important information from
you all of your life.*

*I do hope you'll agree that I've tried to be the best
mother I know how. I hope you also realize how very
much I love you. I've always loved you as if you were
my very own child. But, Gabriella, you are not.*

*You were given to us by a lady whom your father and
I made agreement with to conceive for me, as I knew I
could never have children. Your father also thought it
prudent that you not know, as he has always felt un-
settled over completing his end of the agreement.*

*Your true mother is a friend of mine from schooldays
and resembles me in looks and attitudes. I had lost
contact with her for many years.*

*Her name is Lucy James and she wrote me from Fort
Vancouver, your very destination, where she is working as a nurse among the Indians. She had promised
never to bring up the matter of our agreement but
wrote that she wanted desperately to learn what she
could about you, as she had been thinking a lot about
her past of late.*

Unfortunately, I kept the letter all this time without advising you. It is enclosed and you can see for yourself that what I've told you is true. I am so sorry that I waited so long.

This past winter I wrote Miss James back, telling her of your plans to travel with Edward to the Oregon territory and suggested that when you arrive, she ask you her questions in person.

Perhaps I'm presuming too much by believing you would even want to meet her. I hope you do. I do hope as well that you'll forgive me for keeping this from you, and that nothing will change between us.

Please write me at your earliest convenience.

Take good care.

All my love,

Mother

I sank to my knees, gasping. Owen hurried over to me. "Did someone die?" he asked.
"Yes," I whispered. "My whole identity."
"What are you talking about?"
I handed him the letter, and while he read, I looked over the second piece of correspondence. It had been four years since my real mother had written.

FORT VANCOUVER
BRITISH COLUMBIA
10 FEBRUARY 1842

Dear Ann,

It has taken me considerable time to muster the courage to approach you. I know that I promised you I

*would just go away and allow you and yours your
lives. But believe me, I cannot leave it lie.*

*You see, I am haunted by a little face. These past
years especially I often see her in my dreams and
wonder what her life has been like. What did you
name her? What does she like to do? Does she love the
sea?*

*I am certain she has brought you much joy, and I am
certainly glad for that. However, you must understand
how driven I am to learn as much as possible about
her. As I am presently working as a nurse among the
native peoples here, I cannot help but wonder how my
child has fared in life.*

*Would you do me the honor of corresponding with me
about her?*

*Please forgive me for the intrusion, and I hope and
pray that you see fit to tell me about the child, now
certainly a lovely young woman.*

Thanking you for your trouble, I am sincerely,

                                      Lucy James

Putting the letter aside, I rose to my feet and began to
wander around. I must have looked very dazed because
Owen came after me and asked me if I was all right. He
took me in his arms and told me that he would help me
find her, if that's what I wanted. I was too shocked at first
to shed any tears, but later they came streaming down
my face.

My anger at Avis and Edward for hiding the letter was
soon overcome by a form of relief that is hard for me to
understand. It's as if a lot of questions I have always asked
myself over the years have been answered.

But only partway. I still need to know why my real mother would agree to do such a thing. On some level I suppose I should be grateful that she did make the arrangement. I suspect it was for money, or for some kind of compensation that would simplify her life.

Owen and I walked and talked and he reminded me that whether or not I ever find her, I am my own person, and in his estimation, a special one. Perhaps his view is prejudiced. But I must say that there are times when he makes me feel entirely whole and fulfilled.

After I regained a sense of composure, we sat near the little stream and listened to the birds. Owen picked a handful of small purple daisies and handed them to me.

"For the most wonderful and talented lady I know," he said.

I hugged him and wept again. So much had happened so quickly. I felt at once eager to take off and hurry towards Oregon, and at the same time hesitant. Owen is right in advising me not to hold a great deal of hope of finding her. He says that there are a lot of Indian tribes along the northwest coast, and as the letter is four years old, any number of circumstances might have changed.

He confided to me that as a child he often wondered about his father, sometimes thinking that a true father would never go off and leave him. After much soul-searching he came to the conclusion that true family is not always formed of blood.

"I couldn't understand why there was no man to call a father in my life," he said. "When I got to the mountains, Bones Brandt gave me what I had been missing. It didn't take long until I began to feel whole."

"I always loved Mother and I know she cared a great deal for me," I explained. "She must have wanted a child very badly to have made the arrangement she did."

"Why didn't they just adopt a child?" Owen asked.

"I don't think they wanted anyone to know they couldn't have children," I said. "In the society where I was raised, people look for the smallest reasons to pass judgment."

Owen asked me if I had ever wondered through the years about my identity. I knew what he meant. It's a sixth sense about belonging somewhere other than where you are.

"Yes," I said. "I can remember as a child and a young adult, sitting alone on the beach, gazing out across the Irish Sea. Somehow I felt drawn across, and though I never made it, I wonder now if my true mother is Irish."

Owen chuckled. "If you turn out to be as Irish as me, look out, world."

Gabriella's Journal

20 JUNE 1846

I have nothing else on my mind now but reaching Fort Vancouver. Owen has taken a well-used trail across the mountains towards a post called Fort Hall, a major stop on the Oregon Trail. He believes we will arrive easily by late July, which will give us ample time to reach our destination before winter.

Owen is so wise about the wilderness and survival that I wonder if he has an equal. He is so aware of what could happen ahead of time that he precludes problems by making sound decisions far in advance. We are traveling slowly and stopping at selected locations to allow the horses and mules to graze and fatten up. We'll be crossing some challenging country before we get into the Oregon forests and the animals will need to be as strong as possible.

We are in a beautiful mountain park known as the Bayou Salade—or Salt Fork, as it is sometimes called. The area supports a great number of deer and elk, and at times buffalo will climb up here for the lush grass.

As I watch Whistler enjoy himself in the tall grass, I think of the journey along the Santa Fe Trail and how it took substantial weight from him. The closer to Bent's Fort we got, the worse the grazing conditions. When I recall that, I'm reminded of J. T. Landers. I refuse to dwell on his demise but will remember him as I knew him—an eager little man with a passion for botany.

It saddens me to realize that he will never see these beautiful mountains, with all the many wildflowers that grace the meadows and hillsides. He would have been immersed in his collecting all hours of the day, and it would have been difficult to have made him move on with us.

"I could spend the rest of my life out here and never collect every new specimen there is to catalogue," he once told me. "This beautiful land is an endless study."

There will be many other naturalists who travel this region, no doubt, but none with more verve. And I would dare say none with a greater expertise.

In my mind he was gifted not only in taxonomy but also given to a deep sense of duty to nature. He knew all the plants and the reason why they exist where they do. He realized their connection to the whole and deeply lamented the fact that many of the species would not survive the western migration.

I will never in my life meet an individual more troubled by change, especially when it pertains to the degradation of the natural environment.

I also miss Barton Strand and the Rivet brothers, as well as Bom and Jessie. I hope they're all doing well and looking forward to each day. Perhaps I'll see them again someday.

As we travel, I am putting to use the knowledge gained from Willow Bird and her friends among the Arapaho. I have a forked stick that she gave me and have been digging breadroots from the moist soil. Mr. Landers found some of them in the hilly regions before we reached Fort Hall and I know he would have been enthusiastic to study the other plants I'm collecting for our stews and for future use.

There is a dainty flower called a spring beauty that grows profusely in the mountains. Small leaves emerge from the ground in a rosette, along with dainty flower stalks that produce delicate rose and white flowers. They grow from corms, some of which are bigger than my thumb. When cleaned and baked in the warm coals of a fire, they are far tastier than any potato to be found anywhere.

There are numerous other plants whose roots provide a wealth of sustenance. Willow Bird gave me two large deerskin bags and I've filled one of them already. There are any number of plants related to the common carrot that inhabit the meadows and lowlands. Yampa is as sweet and succulent as any root one could find and would hold its own in a Thanksgiving feast.

25 JULY 1846

This game of survival is very difficult for me to get used to. Having come from a background of plenty, I had never imagined struggling to make it through each week and having to fight off wolves and coyotes to keep our horses so that we might make our way to a fort or settlement where food and rest are easier to manage.

Things have changed so much since leaving the Bayou Salade, and our fortunes took a turn for the worse. We celebrated the Fourth of July by crossing the Colorado River and meeting the largest bear, I believe, ever known to mankind.

The water was high and we had to swim alongside the horses, holding their manes, so they wouldn't go under with our weight. We had nearly made the crossing when Owen's pony took a sudden turn in the water and headed downstream. Owen held on and waited until the horse found another place to leave the river.

The mule he had been leading snapped its rope and broke free. Upon climbing onto the shore, it was attacked by a grizzly who burst from a thicket. The huge bear swiped at the poor mule with a massive forepaw, knocking its head into pulp. The mule screamed and kicked and fell back in the river, but the bear jumped in and pulled it out as though it was a sack of feathers.

In the process, my root bags were lost, as well as our camping equipment and all of our food. I watched it all float down the river as the grizzly tore into the dying mule and began feeding. My clothes, along with my precious collection of sketches and watercolors, had been packed on my mule. Luckily, Whistler had chosen to turn and follow Owen's pony, and we had no trouble once out of the water.

"That mule should have smelled the bear, too," Owen said, sick with disgust at losing so many valuables.

I feel ill-tempered a great deal now that I'm sleeping on the ground with just a thin blanket. And I can't get over losing all my hard-earned roots. I had prided myself on having collected them and will find no more where we're headed. The country is much drier and those plants don't exist here.

Owen keeps saying that we're nearly to Fort Hall. I don't believe him anymore. I think he's been attempting to pacify me for the last two weeks. Maybe he thinks that if he really tells me how far it is and what kind of country we're going to cross, I'll lie down and die. Perhaps he's right.

He says this is nothing compared to the wasteland on the other side of Fort Hall, so I might as well enjoy myself while I can. I can't see his humor and he knows better than to cross me in the mornings after I've been awake all night wondering what's going to happen next.

It's not only the discomfort of going without sufficient covering, but also the constant worry that we will be left without the remainder of our necessities that makes rest impossible. Owen always sleeps, as he terms it, "with one eye open," so that trouble is avoided. Even so, he manages to rest somehow and assures me that should there be real trouble, he will be ready for it.

We haven't met any Indians and Owen believes we won't before we reach Fort Hall. They are to the south, hunting buffalo, he says. At one time they would have been here, but most of the herds have migrated away from the Oregon Trail, which is not far to the north. Our troubles are caused by predators.

The coyotes present more trouble than the wolves. They sneak into camp at every opportunity for any morsel of food they might find. Owen always carries one or two bags of salt and we have to be careful not to leave them on the ground or they will disappear.

The other morning, while cooking elk meat and beans together in a stew, I noticed a coyote watching me closely. I knew better than to turn my back for too long. Owen laughed and told me that I should do what he does. He'll wait for the rascal to pick up the bag and then yell, "Hey!" then watch the scared animal drop it and scamper off.

I told Owen that one of these times his yell wouldn't do any good. That happened yesterday morning. I maintain it was the same coyote simply out for vengeance, but one of them skulked into camp and picked up the bag. Owen yelled and the coyote simply ignored him. He was lucky the bag was too heavy for long transport. When he gave chase, the coyote finally dropped the bag. But Owen was in the far distance, running in zigzag lines, his arms waving in the air.

Quincannon's Journal

2 AUGUST 1846

I've seen transformations in my life, but none as astounding as Gabriella Hall's change from the afternoon teas of the British elite to the evening thunderstorms of the Rocky Mountains. She's lost none of the grace and charm that is her trademark, but now exhibits it in a doeskin dress and knee-high moccasins.

I'm willing to believe that she now shares more in common with her biological mother than she does with the parents of her previous life. From the tone of her true mother's letter, she appears to be a woman whose calling is to help those in need. It's not hard to see where Ella comes by her desire to nurse sick or injured people.

Our troubles have taken her mind off Fort Vancouver for the time being. It was unfortunate to have lost a mule and the bulk of our possibles, but we'll get by. She'll be stronger as a result, and when we reach the real tests of the trail, she should make it through with flying colors.

We're not far from the fort and still haven't met up with Lamar and Latour. I don't know if they ran into Garr somewhere along the trail or not, and have no way of knowing. Bear River and the main trail is another long day's ride. Then once we cross over to Soda Springs it will be just a hop and a step to Fort Hall.

Ella has been different since the Colorado River crossing. Maybe she sees life as a flash in the pan. Last night I got her to open up a little about what's on her mind. She's spending a great deal of time staring into the distance, maybe wondering who she is now and who she will become once we get to Oregon. I can understand her concerns. I had no idea that we would be running into my father until it happened. He saved our lives and I still don't know how I feel about him.

"I used to believe that life could be predicted," she said as we talked. "Now I don't believe the word 'prediction' has any true meaning, other than perhaps a desire or a false hope in something."

"Are you expecting something?" I asked.

"It's not that I expect anything," she said. "I just don't know what to expect."

"You'll discover that to be true every day out here."

"I think it's doing something to me," she said. "Perhaps I'm becoming more accepting of Providence."

"You'll find these mountains to be a pretty good church," I said.

"What if it all makes me somebody different?" she asked.

"You won't change any," I told her. "You might become more fulfilled after meeting your mother, but you'll still be the same great lady I know."

"Stop buttering me up," she said. "I want to feel sorry for myself."

"We haven't got time for that," I said. "We've still got a long way to go."

FORT HALL

Gabriella's Journal

23 AUGUST 1846

We reached Fort Hall two days past, quite late in the morning. The post reminds me of Bent's Fort on a smaller scale, with people milling around everywhere and travelers coming and going.

The surrounding grasslands are lush and many herds of horses and cattle roam the area. The proprietors trade fattened and strengthened oxen for the worn-out beasts the settlers bring in. They make quite a profit, I'm told.

A large number of emigrants were camped along the river. The scene was similar to any of the gathering points:

Men working on wagons and shoeing horses while the women washed clothes and tended children.

We had no sooner arrived than two horsemen came galloping towards us. One of them was Mr. Latour. He greeted Owen rather curtly and commented that he was ready to go to war.

"Are you declaring your own?" Owen said.

"What, are you a traitor?"

"I'm just asking. Where's Lamar?"

Mr. Latour pointed to the fort. "He's in talking to the Hudson's Bay people. He's like you. He doesn't want to start something. But I say it's already started."

"Did you find Edward Garr?" Owen asked.

"He's only a couple of weeks out on the trail," Mr. Latour replied. "He picked up more men here and maybe more at Fort Boise. He wants war and I do, too."

"Two weeks is a big start," Owen said.

"I plan to travel day and night with the men. Do you think you're up to it?"

Owen thought a moment. "Do you know where Garr plans to set up his resistance?"

"The Columbia, of course. Where else?"

"Where on the Columbia? Surely he won't go clear to Fort Vancouver."

Latour laughed. "I intend to arrest him long before he gets to the Columbia, in the name of the American government. We'll hold him until Oregon can put him on trial."

"You haven't got that authority," Owen said.

"Garr doesn't know that. So, do you plan to join me or not?"

"We'll talk more later," Owen said.

"I can't wait long." Mr. Latour studied me and smiled. "So, you're dressed for the mountains now. I wouldn't have thought it of you."

"Life is full of surprises," I replied.

Latour left and Owen rode to the fort. He told me to find a camping spot I liked and picket the horses and mules. I might have told him to do it himself, but I rather enjoy my newly learned frontier chores. The horses like being led to water and combed after long rides and I've come to believe they will go to no ends to please when treated well.

I rode through the main encampment, studying the emigrant women at work. They all looked tired and emaciated, and I decided they had not fared well in their journey so far.

I discovered a little pocket of grass among a colony of cottonwoods and brush along the river and had no sooner cared for the stock than a woman with a baby walked up to me. I was flabbergasted to greet Annie Malone.

"Boy, do you look different," she said. "Are you still painting pictures?"

We hugged and I said that I would never stop painting until the day I died.

"In that dress, some people might want to make that happen soon," she said.

She explained how Indians had harassed them all the way, stealing stock and trying on occasion to set fire to the grasslands around them in an attempt to stop their progress.

"I can see their anger to a degree," she said. "I remember how it was to be pushed off our lands in Ireland."

She told me that she had given birth to her child, Mary Elizabeth, the same day that Martin McConnell had died from his arrow wound, just a week after leaving Round Grove.

"He never recovered, even after that good doctor operated on him," she said. "We got to the same spot where he was wounded and right there he up and died. Said good-bye to us all and closed his eyes. He let out a long breath and was gone. The Good Lord wanted him to end his earthly days there, I know that for a fact. I had the baby that night and held her the next morning when we buried him."

Sean was with a group of men, discussing the route they would take to Oregon. Annie told me there had been a lot of meetings since arriving at the fort. Brothers Jesse and Lindsay Applegate, and a frontiersman named Levi Scott, had been trying to persuade emigrants to follow them along a new trail. They had left two weeks earlier with a caravan of wagons.

"They're calling it the Southern Route, or the Applegate Trail," Annie said. "It's supposed to be a shorter way into Oregon."

I asked her about the possibilities of war with the British and she said no one seemed to know for certain, but Fort Hall was a Hudson's Bay outpost and the men in charge were seeking to have everyone turn back.

"No one's listening to them," Annie said. "We're all headed to Oregon, war or not."

She invited me to their camp and I accepted, grabbing my bag of sketchpads and paints, which I never leave far from sight. I followed her to her mother's wagon, where Millie McConnell was rubbing her eyes with a kerchief. She brightened up and hugged me, then explained that she was getting ready to see another emigrant woman off, a friend named Martha Rush.

"She and her daughter decided to go the main route," Millie said. "They'll be leaving soon and it will be hard to tell her good-bye."

After meeting at Fort Laramie, she and Martha Rush, herself a widow, had become fast friends, sharing the hardships of their lives and helping one another while traveling.

"She's come to be like a sister," Millie said.

I asked Millie if she and her friend would mind sitting for a portrait. She blushed and said, "Can you take a little of the gray out of my hair?"

"Anything you want," I said. "I'll even add some curl."

Annie insisted her mother change clothes in the wagon before going over to the Rush camp.

"This painting will hang on our wall when we get settled," she said.

"No," Millie said, "it will hang on *my* wall."

Martha Rush, along with two daughters and a daughter-in-law, were hanging newly washed clothes on a makeshift line to dry. They greeted me cordially, and after changing clothes, Millie and Martha stood in front of the wagon, holding hands, dressed in their Sunday best.

I painted a small canvas for each of them and they thanked me graciously. Martha presented me with a knitted sweater and one of her daughters handed me a new mirror, freshly unwrapped from a box.

Later I painted another scene and entitled it "Pioneer Women Saying Good-bye." It depicted Millie and Martha Rush, hugging one another, their faces stained with tears. They stood next to a wagon where two young children, with their small and lively dogs, looked on from the seat above.

The children introduced themselves as Pearl and Katie McCord, daughters of a widowed barber named Silas McCord. They are ten and eight, respectively, with blue eyes and blond hair and big smiles. They told me that their mother had perished from cholera far back along the trail, even before reaching Fort Laramie. I found it interesting that they hadn't died as well.

"All of the people in the wagon train died but us and Papa," Pearl said. "He buried twenty-one people and we thought we would die, too. But we didn't even get sick."

"You are very brave girls," I said.

"We traveled by ourselves until we caught up with another wagon train," Katie said. "We miss Mama, but it would have been real hard if we didn't have Rufus and Jake."

I bent over and petted them both, fine little terriers with wagging tails. Rufus was a West Highland white terrier, common to the Scottish Highlands and bred for digging into holes after varmints. His ears were perky and sharp and his eyes bright. He looked like a miniature white wolf with a broader nose, a stocky body, and strong, stubby legs.

Jake, his partner, was a cairn terrier mix, also common to the Scottish Highlands. His coat was brindled and his ears drooped at the ends.

Katie told me that Jake's mother was a pure-blood cairn and that the father was "just visiting."

I asked the girls why the dogs' dark, bright eyes followed my every move.

"They wonder what's in your bag," Pearl said. "They're hoping for treats of some kind."

Katie admitted that they maintained a stock of dried beef tidbits for the dogs, and rewarded them after each day's hard traveling.

"Sean Malone shot a buffalo once," Katie said. "They really liked that."

I've noticed a number of dogs roaming the camps, most of them much larger than the terriers. Pearl said other dogs don't make a bother, as Rufus and Jake work as a team and had even chased off a badger on the Sweetwater River.

I know that I certainly haven't seen the last of the McCord sisters and their terriers. They said that their father wanted to take the Southern Route and I promised them I would paint them both with their pets, and their father as well. They wanted me to see how he used his barbering skills to keep the little dogs groomed.

Millie and Martha Rush said one last good-bye and the wagons going the regular route pulled out. Millie waved her kerchief and blew her nose, then announced that she was good as new and ready to travel on as soon as possible. She had known they would take the Southern Route, as Sean had mentioned the night before that the settlers in Oregon needed men quickly to fight the British.

She began cooking and insisted that when Owen came back from the fort, we join them for their evening meal. These pioneers drink much more coffee than they do tea. I was offered a cup, and after it was poured, I had only to look at it before requesting that extra hot water be added.

I sketched a number of scenes around camp with Annie watching me. I've concluded that she would like to learn to paint. She has some sketches she completed on the trail but is too shy to show them to me.

She let me hold her baby and for the first time, I felt as if motherhood might be a calling. Before long little Mary became hungry and Annie took her to her breast.

Owen arrived back from the fort with Lamar, who is happy to be back in our company. I believe Lamar is a good influence on Owen. Without his Delaware friend, Owen has been lax in saying his morning and evening prayers.

I believe Lamar had trouble traveling with Mr. Latour. He comments that the Frenchman fails to use good sense and endangers everyone at times.

Owen did say that Mr. Latour is right: Edward wants to make trouble for the emigrants along the Columbia. The fort proprietors made no bones about that. In fact, they seemed in support of him.

"We've got to move quickly to catch Latour," Owen said.

"What do you mean 'we'? I want to take the Applegate Trail," I said. "It's shorter."

Owen frowned. "We have to stop Garr, you know."

"What about my mother?"

"We'll have plenty of time to find her."

"You don't understand," I said. "I need to reach her as soon as possible."

"Going the Columbia route will likely be faster."

"Not if you're fighting Edward's soldiers."

"That won't take long."

"You can't know that," I said. "Leave it to Mr. Latour."

"I need to be there."

"I won't be going with you," I said. "I'll travel with Millie McConnell and the Malones."

"You won't be better off with a bunch of wagon people," he warned. "They can't move nearly as fast as we can on horseback."

"It will be far safer," I insisted. "I won't be going to fight a war."

"You don't know anything about crossing deserts. You'll die."

"No, I won't," I said. "I'll live to see my mother. I've promised that much to myself."

We're out of Fort Hall three days, following the Snake River and traveling as rapidly as possible. Mr. Latour and his men left the very evening we arrived at Fort Hall, without even telling Owen or Lamar. Owen still feels an allegiance and wants to catch up with Mr. Latour and the men. I argue with him daily about the route we will take. The Applegate cutoff will appear soon and he'd better have made up his mind to go with me.

I believe he will. Lamar says that he thinks there will be no war. From what he learned at Fort Laramie, the British don't believe Oregon to be worth fighting for. You can't prove that by any of these settlers. And Edward is going to fight just for the sake of calling himself a commander.

Another factor that will keep Owen with me is the emigrants. These people listen to him and know that his stories of deprivation on these trails are real. They've prepared themselves by stocking up on provisions at the fort. They've also elected him captain of the wagon train, and with that title he has the authority to make major decisions for the good of all.

But I believe the most effective argument towards keeping him with me is how I keep him snug at night. Though the days have become excessively warm, the elevation and the nearby mountain keep the nighttime temperature moderate. Still, he says that I make the bedroll "very toasty," in his words.

I haven't discussed Owen's indecision with anyone. As far as the men are concerned, he's with them until the end of the trail. They have said that they would like to catch up to the Applegate-Scott caravan, but Owen feels we are too far behind them to accomplish that. He won't give anyone false hopes about anything. At times I believe he's too frank with them.

Young Sean Malone looks up to Owen like an older brother. It was Sean who was instrumental in getting the other men to make Owen the captain.

"You should give Sean more of your time," I suggested to Owen. "He could be of help to you."

"I haven't got time to train everybody," he said.

"You haven't got time to do it all yourself, either," I told him.

"Have you ever crossed a desert?" he asked me. "Have you ever crossed mountains when the wind would freeze bare skin instantly? Since you haven't, you shouldn't be telling me how to operate this wagon train."

He went on to say that he had buried a lot of people who wouldn't take the right precautions before traveling into the desert, or before crossing hostile Indian country. We spent an extra day at the fort trading for dried salmon that a band of Cayuse Indians brought in. Though the settlers were as anxious to get going as we were, everyone agreed that the extra food would benefit us greatly.

After crossing that arid land east of Fort Hall, it's good to be traveling next to water again. When Owen told me in the pouring rain of the Narrows that I would see cloudless skies and pray for moisture, I thought it a tasteless joke. Now he tells me that we will be leaving this river to take a journey across a desert that makes the lava beds look like a park.

I feel I have entered a different section of the West. From Bent's Fort on to the Rocky Mountains and across, nearly to Fort Hall, felt like the backbone of the region, as the Indians describe it. The lofty peaks are a world unto themselves, unimaginable in scope and breadth. This part of the trail towards Oregon will have its own personality, I believe, and it will be a challenge.

Quincannon's Journal

27 AUGUST 1846

I sat with Lamar at the fire tonight and ate fresh antelope with him. He told me that when he was growing up, the frontier was an invisible line that stretched gradually each year, past the Appalachians to the Ohio. Then, at a faster pace, it had moved on to the Missouri. Suddenly the roads to Oregon and California and Texas were lined with wagons and the world as we know it now is forever changed.

"There is talk about war in all these places," he said. "You are my friend and I will fight beside you if you want, but what would I be fighting for? The new ways of living are not for me, and whether you know it or not, they don't suit you, either."

He's right in some ways. I prefer to live where freedom lives, but I know that is an elusive term wherever governments establish and grow in power. Oregon and California and Texas all want their independence, but they won't be getting everything they're fighting for. What everyone is moving to get away from is going right with them as they travel across the mountains and deserts. Some of these people will be the new leaders, the ones with the power and the right to make decisions for others. And they will make decisions that will not please everybody. But now the Pacific Ocean will stop those who want to start over again from going someplace else.

I can't be alone as much as Lamar. He and others like him—Indian and white—can stay off by themselves for weeks without bumping into another soul. I need the interaction with others to get going. I like the solitude of the mountains, but I don't mind a settlement at the bottom of the hill.

Maybe the coming of so many will ruin it all. Lamar is convinced of it. I can see his point, as his people have been totally displaced. He insists that the Plains and mountain tribes will suffer the same fate. I tell him there's too much land for that to happen and he says that I underestimate the capacity of my people to migrate into new territories.

Lamar and I have been friends since first coming to the mountains together. The friendship will never end but the association likely will. Lamar isn't interested in moving into a country where the population is going to be higher than where he left.

"I didn't know so many wagons were coming across," he said. "The only place where the white people won't fill it up is in the middle, where the high mountains are. That will surely happen in time, also, but not while I'm alive."

"Who will you live with?" I asked.

"There is a band of Nez Percé coming to the fort. I will go with them into the Yellowstone to hunt buffalo and to visit the Absaroka, the Crow people. They are friendly with the whites, so there will be no fighting, and one of their leaders invited me to live with them. He wants to adopt me as his brother, as I saved his child from drowning in the river at Fort Laramie."

We talked about the best places to live in the future

and found it hard to believe that I would last long where people stayed in one place.

"We've traveled around the mountains so much," he said. "How could you look at the same scenery for months at a time?"

"If it's the right scenery, I'll manage," I said.

"The lady who paints is good scenery," he said with a smile.

He asked me if I wanted him to go as far as the Oregon boundary, in case we met Edward Garr and his soldiers.

"I'll let Latour do the fighting," I said. "He's come a long way to do it and he won't be denied."

Lamar and I won't say the word "good-bye," as that has a finality to it that neither of us wants to face. It is highly likely that we'll meet again somewhere in the mountains. I know until that day comes, I'll certainly miss him.

THE HUMBOLDT

Gabriella's Journal

31 AUGUST 1846, 1ST ENTRY

The country has changed to greasewood and sagebrush. I don't know that J. T. Landers would have had the fun with this country that he did with the plains and mountains to the east, but I'm told by one of the ladies that the desert blooms profusely in the spring of the year and is an inspiring sight to anyone. This late in summer one would never know that any beauty ever existed here.

I will never get over how Edward gave Mr. Landers and his other friends over to Kills It. Every time I see a flower in bloom, I think of Mr. Landers and wonder if he now rests peacefully in eternity. Annie and Millie have both comforted me over the issue. We were talking one evening about ghastly sights along the trail and I couldn't hold back.

When I told Millie that Dr. Marking had suffered the same fate, she broke into sobs. Martin had told her that the good doctor had given him another two weeks of life, time enough to finish the business of telling everyone he knew and cared for how much he loved them.

I would be interested to know if Edward has trouble with his men now, since they have all witnessed his betrayal of others in the group. Had they all known, they would likely have abandoned him at Bent's Fort.

I often think of Bom and Jessie, and of Barton Strand and the Rivet brothers. I hope they're all content with their new lives and aren't worried about betrayal and death at every turn.

I don't believe anyone on this journey has that concern. As the caravan's captain, Owen calls a meeting every night to discuss concerns that anyone might have about the journey and how we might all contribute as a whole to make the trip easier. He has just left for tonight's meeting and said that he might be later than usual, as he had some issues to bring up himself.

I know one of them to be the Indians that are always around us. We were warned before we left that we would have trouble with them. Our party of thirty wagons is big enough to keep them from attacking all-out, but they still persist in harassing us. They cannot be seen, as they hide among the rocks and brush, waiting for an advantage.

Owen instructs the guards to keep the livestock near the wagons at all times. He in fact stands guard himself a great deal of the time. Last night, a stray ox wandered back into camp with nearly a dozen arrows protruding from its sides. There had not been enough damage done from the arrows themselves to cause death, but it would eventually die, as the heads had been dipped in poison.

Owen put the animal out of its misery and all the settlers had a difficult time keeping their dogs away from the carcass. The night passed without incident and as of this evening, we have had no further trouble. Owen says he believes the Indians are trying to lull us to sleep. They are a branch of the Shoshone tribe referred to as Diggers, who live in the desert and gather what they can to eat.

As far as I'm concerned, they are no problem compared to a few members of our party—namely, the "most reverend" Bertrand Rowe, a minister who feels called to reach the new Promised Land, and his wife, Guynema.

I met Mrs. Rowe two days ago, a frail-looking woman who always keeps to herself. I saw her sitting next to a wagon, cleaning a flintlock rifle, and asked her if she minded if I sketched her.

"Why would you want to do that?" she asked suspiciously.

"I find you an interesting subject," I said.

"Find somebody else," she warned, and pointed the barrel at me.

"Would you shoot me?" I asked.

"No, but the gun might go off."

"She acts that way toward everybody," Annie explained later. "She keeps to herself and pouts."

Annie said that the Rowes joined their wagon train back at Round Grove. While Reverend Rowe preached to a small congregation, Mrs. Rowe told a group of women that she lamented having to pull up stakes and travel to "who knows where." She complained that she couldn't adjust to the new foods along the trail, but had done very well, thank you, in the hickory forests of southern Missouri, feasting on catfish, collards, and cornbread.

As soon as the reverend learned his wife had expressed her discontent, he took her aside and, according to Millie, must have put the fear of fire and brimstone in her.

"She never once complained after that," Millie said. "It makes you wonder."

The night Dr. Marking took the arrow from Martin McConnell's shoulder, Mrs. Rowe commented to Millie that she should get ready to bury her husband, as he had the look of death in his eyes, and that she was never wrong about such things. She had even commented to Martin along the trail that he should just give it up and go to the Lord, and stop causing everyone so much grief.

Needless to say, that didn't endear Millie to the woman, or Annie, either. The two paid Guynema Rowe a visit and told her never to come close to Martin again. Millie emphasized her point by saying, "And if you ever point that rifle at me again, I'll wrap it around your scrawny neck."

To hear Annie tell the story, I felt sorry for Millie, as she is usually such a gentle soul.

"After chewing Guynema out," Annie said, "Millie went to her wagon and said two rosaries."

I've noticed that Mrs. Rowe's husband often puts extreme demands on her. He sits in camp, whittling small animals or smoking his pipe, while she gathers wood, builds the fire, and prepares the meal. This evening I saw her ask him for help and he quickly picked up a Bible and said that he must be about the Lord's work.

The men show him respect because of his dress and position, but I note that none of them have befriended him, not even the ones who feel compelled to listen to his sermons. Owen says that the reverend is doing his best to divide the group. His small cast of followers are considered "God-fearing citizens," while those who don't agree with him are "heathens of Satan, damned to Hell."

My belief is that Reverend Rowe wants to lead the party. He must be a failed man who has turned to the cloth in an effort to make people respect him. But he can't hide behind that guise forever.

Mrs. Rowe's only friend seems to be a large red hen she calls Henrietta. She keeps the bird on a tether and walks her quite often, penning her up at night inside their wagon. The McCord girls wanted to pet Henrietta one afternoon, but Mrs. Rowe would have none of it.

"She's a persnickety bird," she said. "If she smells your dogs on your hands, who knows how she might react."

The girls offered to wash their hands with lye soap, but Mrs. Rowe still wouldn't give in. Pearl commented to me later that she was thinking about allowing Rufus a fine chicken dinner, but Katie said, "Just because Mrs. Rowe's so mean, you don't take it out on Henrietta. She's a good hen."

Katie went on to say that she had considered the matter and thought that Mrs. Rowe might be suffering from a condition she called "shyness sickness," which to her meant "a problem much worse than just being shy."

I thought Katie to be quite perceptive. Mrs. Rowe had likely come from an isolated family and as a result, is sadly lacking in the social graces. In addition, her husband won't allow her to develop any friendships and she finds it necessary to push people away. I've decided that if anyone can break through Guynema Rowe's barrier, it will be Katie McCord.

31 AUGUST 1846

I've had little time of late to do much of anything but manage this caravan and grab winks of sleep and a few bites to eat. Most of the settlers are good, hardworking people with a common goal and the fortitude to achieve it. But there are a few who want nothing more than to cause a stir, and they have been duly warned.

At the meeting this evening, I informed the troublemakers that should any serious problems occur and complaints be lodged, the accused will be brought before a jury of their fellow travelers. After discussion, a vote will be taken and will follow democratic process. Should the vote determine that the accused is making it too difficult for the rest, that member will be given a warning. Should that same member be voted against twice in a row, he will be expelled from the caravan.

The Reverend Rowe immediately spoke in protest. When he started calling me a blasphemer, I stopped him and said that he was out of order. When he hit me with the Bible, I lodged a complaint against him for interfering with my duties as captain of the train. Twelve men immediately volunteered to form a jury.

Reverend Rowe got the message. All of his group were there but not a single one voiced an opinion. The jury voted unanimously against him and he was warned that he had but one more chance. I never saw a man bite his lip so hard or stare with such hatred.

The second item of business was the Digger Indian problem. The majority of the men are in favor of shooting them on sight. If I could determine that the same few were the culprits, I might agree. But we seem to be engaging different bands, and killing some who are just watching us will not solve the problem. I can't agree with eradicating them all because it "looks" like they might cause trouble.

Our best solution is to keep a tight watch, as we have been, and travel clear of their lands as soon as possible. I plan to suggest night travel when we reach the Black Rock Desert. This will save energy for everyone, as well as the livestock. I still don't have a good feeling about our passage across that wasteland. There's not much forage here for the livestock and I'm certain there will be even less farther ahead.

Gabriella's Journal

4 SEPTEMBER 1846

True to my prediction, Katie McCord has managed to break through the sullen personality of Guynema Rowe. Katie and Pearl had spent an evening in camp harvesting grass seeds from colonies of prairie sandreed that grew in abundance in the swales and along the ridges. I remembered the species from plants growing along the sandy Santa Fe wagon road.

The grass was far too coarse and dried out for the livestock, but Mrs. Rowe's hen appreciated the attention Katie gave her. She ate from the small girl's hand as if there would be no other meal for the remainder of the journey. Meanwhile, Pearl stayed back at the McCord wagon,

struggling to keep Rufus and Jake from helping Katie with
the hen.

Mrs. Rowe came out of the brush carrying a jackrabbit.
She seemed to expect to find Katie tending to her hen.
The reverend had left to read Bible passages from a nearby
hill. Millie told me that he had decided since no one
among us was worth saving, he would plead to the Diggers, expecting them to come forth and be saved.

Katie jumped out of the wagon, expecting to hear Mrs.
Rowe's wrath. I watched with curiosity as Mrs. Rowe offered a leg of the rabbit to Katie, so she might make the
terriers happy.

So for the past few evenings the McCord girls have
been collecting grass and shrub seed for Henrietta while
Mrs. Rowe takes her long-barreled rifle into the sagebrush
after jackrabbits. It's a fair exchange, and except for the
reverend, everyone is content with the arrangement.

I find it interesting that Mrs. Rowe is suddenly paying
much less attention to the reverend. He's not eager to
question her on it, for fear of causing a problem in camp.
Should he be called to the nightly meeting for any reason
and the vote go against him, he would find himself hunting his own jackrabbits.

The traveling has been difficult and everyone is suffering. It's been some time since I had a decent meal and a
good long drink of water. There are springs at various
intervals but they are often nearly dry and we must ration
what we find.

As the travel becomes more difficult, Mrs. Rowe has
taken to walking farther and farther out into the desert.
It's not just in the evenings now, but also during the day.
She often returns to the wagons with directions for Owen
on how to reach a spring that's flowing or a large pool of
water in one of the streams.

Never once in all this time has the reverend mounted

his horse and ridden out to see where she was, and never, as far as anyone knows, has he asked her if she would care to ride in the wagon with him. He has always tied his horse to the back and planted himself on the seat, paying no attention at all to Mrs. Rowe."

"Why do you suppose he married her?" I asked Millie.

"A reverend traveling without a wife is suspect," she said, "as surely as is a priest traveling with a niece."

Last evening in camp, Mrs. Rowe arrived from a long walk with three rabbits and gave two of them to the McCord girls. After skinning the one she had kept, she asked the reverend if he might drive the wagon over to a stand of dead cottonwoods a distance away, so that she might get some wood. He refused. So she refused to go for the wood or to cook the rabbit. Instead, she climbed into the wagon and began wailing at the top of her lungs.

Knowing everyone's eyes were upon him, Reverend Rowe could do nothing but sit beside his wagon and pretend to read the Bible. Seeing he had no effect, he stood up and began preaching in a loud voice, quoting Scripture. Still Mrs. Rowe continued to howl. Finally, she tired herself out and fell asleep.

Equally tired, the reverend made himself a bed under the wagon and poured kerosene on the ground all around himself in hopes of avoiding snakes and scorpions.

The following morning, the reverend still refused to take the wagon over to the trees for wood. This time Mrs. Rowe made no sounds of any kind, but sat on the ground and refused to move. Owen did what he could to persuade her to come along. Even the McCord girls and their terriers had no effect. She refused to talk to anyone but sat by the wagon with her rifle and wouldn't budge.

The caravan left with the reverend driving his wagon. We all watched Mrs. Rowe and saw her take off across the hills to the north. Millie said that she would show up later as she always did, while Annie maintained she had gone into the hills to die. I knew Mrs. Rowe better than that and worried that she might be contemplating some-one else's death.

Owen had a meeting and it was decided that the Rowes had to solve their own problems. The McCord girls begged their father to go after her, but he said they had enough problems of their own. He seemed as convinced as I was that Guynema Rowe needed no one's help. Be-sides, she had left her pet hen in the wagon, and had anyone thought about it, they would have known she would never desert that precious chicken.

That evening she arrived in camp, having traveled par-allel to our course all day. Many offered her food and drink, but she refused them all. Instead, she strode up to the reverend and asked him where he had put his Bible. Alarmed, he searched everywhere in the wagon. She told him what a fool he was and said she had taken it and had left it back at the base of the biggest cottonwood in the grove of trees at the last camp.

"You should have taken me to those trees," she said.

If we had not been standing there, I am certain he would have struck her. Instead, he saddled his horse and rode off in the sunset to get his Bible. Mrs. Rowe waited for him to get out of sight, then, after leading their team of oxen and putting them into their traces herself, she drove the wagon out from the caravan.

I went with Owen and a number of others to try to talk her into turning around.

"Leave me be," she said. "I'm not going anywhere."

True to her word, she drove the wagon a distance off the trail and unhitched the oxen. From where I stood with Owen, I couldn't tell for certain what she was doing inside the wagon. She had taken Henrietta out and had tied the hen by the foot to a sagebrush plant. I realized shortly that after going back inside, she had doused everything with kerosene.

The wagon went up in flames and everyone gasped. The only thing Mrs. Rowe saved besides her hen was her rifle. She left with it in the crook of her arm, holding Henrietta with her free hand against her bosom, and was soon lost in the darkness.

Reverend Rowe arrived at a gallop soon after and asked what had happened to his wagon. Owen told him that after executing her last act of defiance, his wife had left for parts unknown with the flintlock cradled in her arm.

Reverend Rowe wisely chose to remain in camp.

This morning the reverend is gone and no one knows which way he went or whether we'll ever see him again. But Mrs. Rowe did arrive back in camp, waving to us from a distance and laughing, carrying three jackrabbits by the hind legs.

Quincannon's Journal

4 SEPTEMBER 1846

I miss Lamar not just as a friend but also as a partner in travel. These settlers are a rugged bunch but they haven't yet learned the fine points of traveling the wilderness. There should be less card playing and more traveling.

I can understand that the children are pressed and become exhausted after a hard day's march, but they're much more resilient than their parents think and can handle the rough spots as well or better than anyone.

Sean Malone has been able to fill in almost as well as Lamar, except that he cannot scout. He would make a good one had he any previous experience out here. As it is, I have to go ahead and leave him to manage any trouble that comes up until I return.

He can see trouble coming and knows how to check it. A couple of settlers were arguing over stock, which occurs often, and he told them if they couldn't handle their trouble peacefully, without fighting, he would bring it up at the nightly meeting. No one wants to come before a jury, and so the men settled it.

Surprisingly, one of the men admitted to wanting the other's horse and to trying to trim the hair around the horse's brand. This could have been construed as thievery, but it's hard to hang a man from a sagebrush plant. Instead, the abused party insisted on administering a punishment of ten lashes. The guilty party readily agreed and exposed his back over a wagon wheel. The sound of the lash against bare skin terrified the women, and the man bled a good deal, but he'll live and he won't be sent off on his own. I also doubt he will covet anyone else's horses for a good long while.

The tension within the group would be much worse if it weren't for the McCord girls. They are a kick. Pearl and Katie argue as much as any two kids, but they seem to respect one another and other people as well. The trip is certainly boring for the most part; riding in a wagon, or walking ten to twelve miles a day, is no one's idea of a good time. They rely on their terriers to keep things jumping, and the two dogs never let them down.

I think Rufus has taken a liking to me. Pearl keeps his white coat as clean as she can, but it's a chore. He greets me by standing up on his hind legs and putting his forepaws out in a digging motion, his way of saying, "Hello! I would sure appreciate it if you petted me a lot."

Jake is equally exuberant and carries a favorite small stick around to show me, prancing around while his little tail whips back and forth furiously. You would think that both dogs were part retriever, as they love to fetch a stick and then get into a tug-of-war with it. Their growls and snarls aren't as bad as they sound and the winner gets to bring the stick to me for another round.

Silas McCord has started calling me "Uncle Owen." He's a good barber and a fair hand with a rifle. He helped me drop a dozen antelope the other day, he and Sean Malone and a small man named Riordan. We hid in the sage and got them to come to a white flag. Silas dropped two himself, one at a dead run.

He cuts my hair when I request it. "You keep the girls and the dogs happy," he told me. "That's worth a free barbering now and again." He trimmed Ella's as well. At first she was reluctant, but after she saw how mine turned out, she relented. He didn't take much off, but it pleased her and gave her a fresh feeling.

She's been using the roots from soapweed to cleanse her hair. Some people call the plant Spanish bayonet, and there's no shortage out here. But there are no spring beauties or bitterroots. And breadroots and yampa that she collected in the mountains have already dried up out here. A shame she lost everything.

She learned a lot of things from Willow Bird and talks of her often, a little too often as far as I'm concerned. I realize that she's the mother of my son, and that she's done a great job raising him, but I can't forget how I was forced to leave, and I find it frustrating that Ella can't understand that.

She told me that Willow Bird kicked me out because she feared for my life. She says that Willow Bird believes that all her husbands will die young. Maybe she's right; they all have so far. I argue that she might have told me her feelings at the time. Instead, I believed she cared more for Kills It. Now I'll never really know the truth.

The journey to Oregon is foremost on my mind. Finding Ella's mother there could be difficult. The country is huge, and there are a great many Indians in any number of places who need tending. Every form of disease has struck them and nurses from Fort Vancouver regularly travel hundreds of miles to care for the sick.

There are a lot of things to think about in getting Ella to her mother. The desert is the first problem, and it's now right in front of us.

THE BLACK ROCK DESERT

Gabriella's Journal

10 SEPTEMBER 1846

It is a strange place, this desert, with open holes of salt and mirages that make the open vastness appear to be one large ocean. The sage has given way to more greasewood and other forms of rank brush. It is a struggle to ward off despondency as we work desperately to conquer this most difficult of passages. There is little to break the monotony of sand and heat, and as we are crossing during a particularly bad time of year, we can only expect the worst.

I have kept Annie Malone's baby for two days while she suffers terribly from drinking alkali water. I cannot nurse the child and am glad that she takes water mixed with mild herbs and roots. There's no one else to care for little Mary, as Millie drank of the same pothole, along with some of the other emigrants. We've been stopped four days to allow for their recovery.

Owen was scouting ahead and said that he never dreamed anyone would partake of that foul bog. He's been thirsty many times before and can stand it far better than most of us.

Guynema Rowe carried bags of fresh water from a spring she had discovered nearly five miles away. She said she traveled faster afoot than on horseback, as the stock were all suffering from lack of food and water. Each day we remain in one place means more concern over reaching the mountains.

Mrs. Rowe is to be commended for her tenacity. Owen helped her carry the water, as did Sean Malone and a number of emigrant men, those who hadn't succumbed to the temptation to drink the bad water. None of the horses or oxen would touch it, though their tongues were hanging out.

We've noticed that the caravans ahead of us aren't moving as rapidly as we are. Likely our four-day stop will allow them to gather distance again. Owen had considered riding ahead to meet with them but realized it wouldn't do us any good. They are likely having as difficult a time as we are and won't have any food or water to spare.

A young settler traveling alone in a mule-driven cart passed us early this morning. The cart, similar to the ones we used along the Santa Fe Trail, was filled with goods of all kinds. He offered a number of dresses to any woman who would take them, plus a blanket and a baby's wrappings. He had gone off the trail to find a suitable spot to bury his family and had conceded there was no place without sand and alkali.

Owen offered to let him travel with us, but he wanted

to reach his own group. He asked Guynema Rowe if she wished to travel with him, as he knew her to have been with some of the people in his group back at Fort Laramie. She thanked him but declined. He clucked his mules into a lope and departed, wishing us good luck.

Mrs. Rowe and the reverend must share an interesting past. Though she is to be given credit for helping to find water, she has of late become sullen and distant. She allows the girls and their terriers to visit her, but no one else. Pearl told Millie that Mrs. Rowe has decided that the only pure creatures under heaven are children and animals. Everyone else, including herself, is so badly tainted by sin as to have no chance for redemption.

"She told Katie and me that the day of reckoning was at hand and that few would survive the Second Coming," Pearl explained. "She was crying."

Yesterday, before we got started again, I attempted to talk with Mrs. Rowe. She lifted the rifle at my approach, but left it pointed towards the ground.

"Stay back, lest you become as tainted as me," she warned.

"You are a good woman," I assured her. "Everyone thinks so."

"No, I'm good for nothing, or the Good Lord wouldn't have put me on this desert to suffer as a banished woman. He wouldn't have allowed the devil to talk me into burning our wagon and chasing my man away."

"The reverend left of his own accord," I said.

"He would be here now if I hadn't caused him so much grief. Likely he's dead and his bones bleached white somewhere along the trail."

"I'll bet he's back at Fort Hall," I suggested. "He had a good horse and plenty of food and water."

"There's nothing you can say that will make it right," she insisted. "I'm damned to eternal fire."

I went back to my camp to take a watercolor from one of my packs. When I returned, she was holding Henrietta in her lap, crying softly. She looked up at me and wiped her eyes.

"Doubt if blubbering will help," she admitted.

I handed her the watercolor. "I know you told me not to paint your portrait, but I thought I would take a chance at trying to catch you as a younger woman."

She stared at the painting in disbelief.

"How could you have known how I looked, or that I had a favorite brown dress just like this?"

"I can't explain it," I said simply. "I just knew."

"Satan did this!" she cried. "There's no other way."

She held the piece away from her by her thumb and forefinger, taking quick steps towards the coals of a fire. With her free hand she rustled the coals with a stick and dropped the painting into the small flame.

The watercolor burned readily, and before I could stop her, Mrs. Rowe held her hands into the fire. She stepped back and examined her blistered fingers with satisfaction.

"I reckon that will purge them," she said.

I urged her to wrap the burns but she said she needed to allow time for full cleansing.

"And don't talk to me again," she warned. "Child of the devil!"

Millie and Annie believe I should adhere to her wishes and stay away from her.

"If she chooses to come to you, so be it," Millie said. "She's no doubt a good woman, but touched in the head."

I have decided not to worry about it one way or the other. Should Mrs. Rowe decide she wants to be friends again, that will be fine. Otherwise I'll consider her to be just another casualty of the desert.

10 SEPTEMBER 1846

I find myself in the same situation I've endured so many times in the past. Though I've always respected the desert, I seem to underestimate its effect on me. It seems a man can endure thirst and tell many tales about it, but he just doesn't realize how much discomfort the experience creates until he puts himself through it once again.

I had wrongly assumed that we would be traveling at a much faster rate. I should have known better. Families cannot possibly get going in the morning in anywhere near the time of adults alone, and there are a number of elderly who are having a very difficult time. They have lived hard lives and their joints aren't working well. Even though the younger men help them, they just cannot seem to keep pace.

A group of emigrants offered to separate from us and travel behind at their own speed, but I won't allow that. Too many things can happen. The younger men don't mind doing the extra work and the older settlers are getting used to accepting the help.

A large number of these younger men are Kentuckians who've decided they want to start over in a less settled land. Many of them have inherited their grandfathers' long-barreled rifles, the same rifles that were used against the British at New Orleans. These young frontiersmen can shoot the head off a buzzard over a half mile away. I've heard such stories and thought them all to be exaggeration. But now I've seen it myself, and it's still hard to believe.

Needless to say, any antelope we encounter fall quickly. Unfortunately, these have been few and far between. The caravans ahead of us have no doubt scared them far back off the trail.

Because of the food and water situation, I have emphasized to everyone how important it is to get across the desert as quickly as possible. It not only saves the oxen but keeps everyone stronger as well. We are about to the point where night travel will be the most expedient. But no one can adjust to that immediately, so I'll work into it by gradually altering our times of rest.

The emigrants ahead of us must be having a harder time of it than we are. We've come across a number of dead oxen, barely picked clean by predators. The skies are filled with vultures, and they often press the issue by landing next to our horses and cattle while they are lying down.

There's no use in wasting ammunition on them, so I allow Pearl and Katie McCord to unleash their terriers. It's quite the sight to see Rufus and Jake scramble after the birds, often lunging into the air at them as they raise their large wings and flap away. Though many of the birds are huge, I don't believe they want to take the chance of letting one of those furry monsters clamp onto them.

Those two dogs have also decreased the rat population considerably. It's not unusual to see one or both of them digging sand out of a hole faster than their prey. I've seen Silas reach in and pull a dog out by the tail. He won't let Pearl or Katie do it; they are left to watch and worry, afraid their pets will become lost in the ground forever. Those two dogs aren't afraid to go after anything.

I will say that Silas has them well trained. They will sit and stay on command, and remain in position until he releases them. They aren't as well mannered for the girls, though, who work constantly to keep them out of trouble. They provide a lot of amusement for the camp in a situation that would ordinarily leave everyone severely discouraged.

I haven't yet told anyone about the body of a man I discovered while scouting three days ago. He had apparently become separated from the caravan ahead of us a number of days ago. He was nothing but a skeleton covered with ants.

If I tell anyone, it will be Ella. She's been strong through this long journey and, if the truth were known, she gives me a lot of strength to boot. We have long discussions in the evening and there's not much we haven't covered. I've discussed death with her before and it helps. I've known men on fur brigades who saw a lot of terrible things and wouldn't talk about it. They just held it all in. I learned later that they exploded from within and either killed themselves or someone else.

I've decided to leave Sean Malone in charge of the wagons most of the time now. I'll be out ahead scouting every day, looking for water and game and dead people, trying to keep our own group from having to witness more than they need to.

18 September 1846

Owen has devised a schedule he says will benefit both us and the livestock. We travel throughout the night and sleep for three or four hours just before sunrise, while the air is cool and still. We are all exhausted and have no trouble falling asleep. When the growing heat of early day arrives, we wake to travel until midafternoon, when the heat has built to its zenith. We get what rest we can until late evening, when the sun is falling, then resume our march.

Traveling at night has proved to be much more comfortable than I expected. The cool wind helps me forget my thirst, but I don't believe it does much for the children. As acting grandmother to Pearl and Katie, Millie has taught them every trick she knows to help their suffering, including sucking on pebbles and telling them stories throughout each night as we travel.

The moon shines brightly through these strange and testing nights. The rocks and brush stand out in the distance like black ghosts. Nearer the wagons, trotting coyotes often appear, and after watching the struggling oxen, disappear into the surrounding shadows and lift their noses to the starlit sky to yap and howl.

Owen says they seem to know which of the livestock is nearest death, and when the carcass is left behind, gain their meals with no exertion. The men strip the best cuts of meat, lean and sparse as they are, and the women cook them without complaint. The coyotes devour what's left, with some competition from vultures and crows, and leave the bones clean to bleach in the sun.

We have no trouble seeing where we must go, as the bones of oxen from the caravans ahead of us litter both sides of the trail. Even during the latest of midnight hours, the moonlight gleams off the skulls and rib cages that lie contorted on the desert floor.

The packed ground is in places as smooth and hard as porcelain. Had we sufficient food and water, tramping through this stark wilderness would be an interesting experience. Instead, we wonder if there will be even one oxen left before we reach good grass and water.

Many of the emigrants have taken to feeding their oxen the straw stuffing from their mattresses. They dole it out a little at a time and find that it gives the animals some strength.

The horses seem to fare much better. They are not pulling wagons and have not been ridden during our march. I lead Whistler behind me and the little pony keeps a stronger stride. I feel certain he has seen times equally stressful, perhaps with an Indian war party crossing another desert, or at the end of a bitter winter when the grass was gone and the temperatures low.

Owen continuously tells me stories of mountain men and survival during freezing winter storms or crossing wastelands under a blazing summer sun.

"The trails into California and the Gila country are all tough and without grass or water," he has said. "I've sucked the pulp from many a cactus to stay alive."

Though I suppose I could stomach eating a lizard or a rattlesnake if my life depended on it, I'm not certain I would resort to eating my moccasins and doeskin dress. But then I've never gone without food for nearly a week.

I have no fear of dying while with Owen. He knows too many tricks of survival. The other morning, near a dried-up streambed, he noticed a bulge in the sand. After digging a short way down he pulled out a large skin bag filled with pemmican.

"You can find these at almost every stream crossing, if you know what to look for," he said. "During times of plenty, the Indians bury these so that when the pickings become sparse, they'll have a food supply to fall back on."

Most of the emigrants had tasted pemmican somewhere along the trail. Many declined, as they said the sweet taste would only heighten their thirst. Owen told them the dried berries would provide good nutrition, but didn't press the issue.

Of course Rufus and Jake would have eaten the entire bag if given the chance. Pearl and Katie gave them small bites and Rufus was warned repeatedly to be gentle when taking the offering. He has a tendency to snatch quickly and gulp, often not concerned about the tips of someone's fingers.

Though none of us has eaten enough for some time, or received sufficient water, we're faring far better than anyone who might choose to negotiate this trail only during daylight hours. The darkness has its drawbacks, however.

Owen has told all parents to be certain that any children walking alongside the wagons are wearing shoes. If they have no shoes or theirs are worn through, they are to stay in the wagons, as scorpions are everywhere. These odd creatures look to me much like large spiders with crab claws and long tails that curl up over their backs. Some are small and white and others very large and coal-black, with all kinds of variation in size and color in between. They scurry about after the sun falls and can produce a terrible sting. Owen says the smallest are the deadliest, and you must shake out your shoes and boots after leaving them on the ground for any length of time.

Of even more concern than the scorpions are the rattlesnakes. They are active at night as well, but are more inclined to stay away from the trail. They sense the vibration of our approach and slither the other way. I have already seen a number of them, one very large with a broad head and a diamond pattern on its back. It was swallowing a large rat. Sean Malone shot the reptile and measured the length of its body to be seven feet three inches long.

This morning just after sunrise, as we were getting ready to camp, the McCords' little white terrier rushed off after a jackrabbit. Pearl ran calling after her pet, her father close behind.

We heard a scream and a pistol shot. In but a few moments, Silas McCord was carrying his daughter back to camp. Blood oozed from two puncture wounds just above her ankle.

"That rattler was huge," Silas said. "Larger than the one Sean shot."

Silas was beside himself with worry. Katie broke into tears and Guynema Rowe, who hadn't said two words to anybody for the better part of the week, appeared with Henrietta under her arm.

"Lay your daughter down on the ground," she said to Silas.

She ordered him again and when Pearl was still, Guynema quickly cut the chicken's stomach open and placed the protruding intestines against the snakebite.

"Everyone leave me be," she said to the silent crowd. "I've done this before."

Owen said he had seen a Shoshone Indian perform the same feat with a grouse to save his own life. His son had caught one in a snare and as he had reached down to catch the bird, he was struck by a rattlesnake. The live grouse's entrails enveloped the wound on the warrior's wrist and effectively absorbed the poison.

Pearl lay still while Mrs. Rowe held her dying hen to the wound. In but a few minutes poor Henrietta had expired. Her entrails were green with poison, and though the girl became nauseated, she never approached death. After a short time she was up and around, scolding her dog for running off.

Mrs. Rowe buried Henrietta alongside the trail. I stood with her and told her what a great thing she had done by saving Pearl McCord's life. She said she was pleased to have been of help, though she didn't know where she would find another hen like Henrietta.

"There was no decision to make, though," she told me. "That girl's life was in certain danger."

Other women came to thank her for what she had done, and Silas McCord offered her anything he had that she might want.

"I just want you to watch those two girls closer," she said. "Not everyone's lucky enough to have kids."

"My girls have learned to cook and sew some," Silas offered. "They can be of help to you. And if you'll trust me, I'd be happy to cut your hair for free anytime you'd like."

Mrs. Rowe smiled. "I guess I could use that."

As he cut her hair, Silas offered to allow Mrs. Rowe to sleep in the wagon with the girls. He had been sleeping out on the ground anyway and said that the extra space was being wasted. She said she would consider it.

After her haircut, Guynema Rowe walked into the desert and returned with a sprig of blackbrush. She cut the outer layers off the stem and gave the McCord girls the inner cambium. They chewed it and declared it sweet and tasty.

I had tasted cottonwood gum and found this to be similar, if not a little coarser. It would do for a desert situation where every bit of nourishment helped.

I was pleased to see that Mrs. Rowe wasn't turning me away and no longer referred to me as the devil's child.

"I know how you did it," she said. "You took something I own, like a hairbrush, and held it in your hand, didn't you?"

I admitted I had taken her hairbrush and apologized for not getting her permission first.

"My grandmother could do that," she said. "She could know all about you from a button or a thimble. But she didn't know how a person looked when they were young."

"I can't explain it," I said. "It's always been there."

"I'm sorry I burned the painting," she murmured. "Will you do another?"

I agreed that when we reached the mountain, I would do many more. As it is now, I'm so thirsty most of the time that I would rather drink the watercolors than paint them across a parchment.

THE SISKIYOU

Quincannon's Journal

25 SEPTEMBER 1846

The Oregon mountains have called for nearly a week, and through the distant haze, they have become a reality. Water on the breeze this morning brought every oxen's head up and they strained in their traces, bellowing to be freed.

I wouldn't allow them to be released, though it was a

pity to watch them yearn for refreshment. Had they taken off at the first smell of freshness, they would have collapsed well short of their goal.

There is enough water here to keep us going until we can reach the lake region and stop for good grazing. I have been waiting for this for over a month and so has everyone else. No one could deprive us of it.

But a surprise awaited us as we drew within sight of the stream. A line of marching men appeared, with a man on a black stallion leading them. Ella mounted her pinto and rode up to where I sat watching.

"It's Edward, isn't it?" she said.

"Without a doubt," I told her.

"How did he get here?" she asked.

"I suppose we'll know soon enough," I said. "You should stay out of the line of fire."

"I won't let you face them alone."

"I won't be alone," I assured her. "Tell the Kentuckians to ready their long rifles."

Garr ordered his men into a long line. As they stood at attention, I counted but seventy-two. I knew there had once been closer to a hundred of his soldiers and I wondered where the others were.

I searched around to see if more were flanking us, but the desert was bare.

I rode within earshot of Edward Garr and asked him what he thought he was doing.

"You'll turn around and go back!" he yelled. "In the name of the British Crown!"

"We're set to unhitch oxen," I warned. "Get out of the way or get run over."

"You are receiving your last warning, Mr. Quincannon," Garr replied. "I'll have no more discussion."

"I'm thirsty," I said. "I'm coming ahead."

"Prepare to fire!" Garr yelled. He dismounted and leveled his rifle on me.

I kicked Parker into motion just before the shot came. The ball whizzed past me and I could see Garr reloading.

Back at the wagons, Sean Malone and the Kentuckians had taken position. Seeing the soldiers readying their weapons, they quickly opened fire.

Garr's soldiers began to fall, kicking and screaming like babies. After another round from our long rifles, they ran toward the timber like so many rabbits.

But Garr wouldn't be stopped and again leveled his rifle at me. Before he could pull the trigger, a ball slammed into the stock, shattering it and causing a misfire. In the distance I could see the men cheering for Guynema Rowe.

I charged Garr on my pony and he quickly mounted his stallion to retreat with the survivors, leaving his dead and wounded soldiers behind. I saw no purpose in wearing my buckskin down chasing after him.

Robert Colville stood up and staggered forward a few steps before falling to his knees. I dismounted and helped him to lie down. A ball had passed through him, some three inches under his right breast. The wound was bleeding profusely.

"It's mortal," he gasped. "I was foolish to follow him."

"I thought you were up on the Columbia," I said.

"Sir Edward learned of the Applegate cutoff at Fort Boise. We surprised Latour and his men, killing all but one. They fought well and killed twenty-nine of us. When we asked one of Latour's wounded about you, he said you had taken a different route."

Colville asked me to help him sit up. I did and he peered across at the line of Kentuckians marching toward us. I told him that their grandfathers had stopped the Redcoats at New Orleans.

"We thought we could easily stop you here," he said. "We marched night and day to reach here. A settler in a lone cart who was begging for his life said he had passed your group, so we killed him and waited for you. There weren't supposed to be any Kentuckians with long rifles."

Sean and the Kentuckians reached us and circled around. I explained who Robert Colville was and how he and Garr and the others had come to be at this place, trying to stop our progress. No sooner had I finished talking than Colville expired.

We buried forty-eight dead right where they lay. There were six others mortally wounded who would die before nightfall. One soldier, shot in the hand, began running across the desert. No one fired at him and he became lost in the distance.

"What are we going to do about Edward Garr?" Sean asked.

"If he wants to try it again with what few he has left, let him come ahead," I said. "For now, let's get to that water."

Gabriella's Journal

28 SEPTEMBER 1846

Water never tasted so good. We've been here three days, recuperating and rejoicing for having crossed the desert. Owen and the men have killed a number of deer and we've been feasting. Our fortunes have definitely changed for the better.

Tonight we celebrated with a dance, much like the one I remember from Round Grove. Sean and Annie were playing, together with a number of men with fiddles, guitars, and banjos. The tunes ranged from lively to slow.

I got my blue dress out of the saddlebag and washed it. The wrinkles were so deep I thought it ruined, but Millie showed me a trick. She raised the dress on a stick above a large kettle of steaming water and brought it back to looking like new.

I danced with Owen a few times, hoping to get him going, but he was too preoccupied with the journey.

"We're taking too long here," he said. "We should be back on the trail."

"For heaven's sake," I said, "give these poor people some time to celebrate."

"We can celebrate in Oregon City," he said.

"Why can't you relax a little?" I asked. "This isn't like the old days, when you had to get your furs to market or lose to the competition."

"It's still a matter of losing to the competition," he said. "It's late in the season. By the time we get to the mountain passes, we'll be fighting bad weather. That's strong competition."

"The Applegates have made a road for us," I said. "It's not as if we'll be blazing our own. You said that yourself."

"New roads always have their problems," he replied. "We're pulling out at first light."

He stopped the dancing and made the announcement. There was a lot of disappointed murmuring and some of the celebrants retired for the evening. Others decided they would make the most of their last night of relaxation, and the dancing resumed.

I followed Owen out to check the stock and make certain the guards were watching everything carefully. The Indian threat here wasn't as severe, but should we lose any oxen or horses at this point, we would never succeed in crossing over the mountains.

"It doesn't make sense to come this far and squander the rest of the trip," he said.

"There's no one who wants to reach Fort Vancouver more than I do," I said, "but I don't understand why you're pushing these people so. They have every right to rejoice."

"Have you forgotten that I've been on journeys like this before?" he asked. "A lot can happen. If you don't believe me, just wait and see."

"I believe you," I said. "But I think you're unsettling everyone. Besides, you said yourself that the oxen need to fatten up."

"Some of them are past fattening up," he said. He pointed to one with its head down, standing knee-deep in grass but not grazing. "That one is so far gone that eating the grass has killed him."

He explained that starving animals often use up so much of their body's reserves that once they reach food, digesting it takes so much energy, it kills them.

"The ones that will make it are never going to be the same," he said. "Whether or not these people realize it, nothing's going to be the same."

"Try to look on the bright side," I said. "We've gotten this far and we're past the sagebrush and greasewood. What can be worse?"

"I don't think you understand," he said.

"No, I don't think you do," I told him. "I've wanted you to take this dress off me ever since Round Grove. Now's your chance to do it."

He didn't hesitate. It had been a long trip across the desert and we had had only a few opportunities to be alone. It hadn't been much fun worrying about spiders and snakes. Tonight would be different, nestled together in the soft grass under a moonlit sky, both of us so eager that we could barely contain ourselves.

Gabriella's Journal

20 OCTOBER 1846

Owen couldn't have been more right. We've been traveling through some of the most beautiful country I've seen yet and we can't make but four to six miles per day. The trails are steep and the oxen so weary that they stop in their traces and heave for breath and energy. There's little grass along the trail. It's all been eaten by previous caravans.

We skirted Goose Lake and the south end of Tule Lake, and then the lower Klamath. We're into the Siskiyou and have already seen a number of abandoned wagons, many missing the wheels and tongues, saved for use, no doubt, as extra parts. We've passed continuous lines of belongings that the owners decided must be left behind if their journey was to be successful. Among the most common objects are dressers and beds and stoves, and a lot of farming equipment.

There was even a piano beside the trail, resting slanted against a tree. Pearl McCord pounded on the keys and it made an awful sound, nearly as bad as Rufus howling to the off-key music. How they managed to get it across the desert I'll never know. Owen commented that items of

that sort were the reason so many oxen fell by the way-
side.

The deeper we get into the mountains, the more difficult the trail is to negotiate. I've never seen so much
rock and timber, almost obliterating the sky in places.
And the rain has started, a steady drizzle that soaks me
through to the skin.

The trail has become very steep and the rain makes the
footing treacherous. The tired oxen would struggle under
dry conditions but must now endure slippery rocks and
loose soil, draining precious energy.

One hill proved particularly difficult. The wagons had
to be pulled up one at a time, using as many as twenty-
three teams of oxen. Still the poor animals could barely
make the summit and had to be rested for the rest of the
day while other teams were hitched to more wagons. It
took three days to complete that climb.

Yesterday we were forced to stop for downed timber
across a creek. Owen believes that the rain has contrib-
uted to unstable ground conditions and the soil is shift-
ing. He showed me where piles of trees and rock had slid
down from the hill above the streambed, blocking our
passage.

I passed the time with Millie and Annie and Guynema
Rowe. We drank tea mixed with coffee to break the bore-
dom of taking one or the other straight. Millie had stories
of old Ireland and Guynema told of the Missouri country
and the life she misses so badly. She stated that she should
have burned the wagon at Fort Hall. Had she the chance,
she would have turned back around for her old home at
that point.

I find Mrs. Rowe to be most hospitable when the conditions are the worst. She was hard to tolerate when we
were recovering at the edge of the desert, complaining
about all the laughter and gaiety. But both under the hot

sun of that wretched desert and now on this narrow trail in the heavy mist, she seems to be doing just fine.

My theory is that she believes life should be all suffering and no pleasure. No doubt she had been forced to marry the reverend, and now that she's free of him, her concern is over not getting enough turmoil in.

She prides herself on her ability with her rifle. Even the Kentuckians respect her eye. She comes and goes as she pleases, searching the surrounding hills for anything and everything. The steepness of the terrain doesn't seem to bother her. I've never seen anyone who could walk equally as fast up a hill as across a level plain, and over such long distances.

While the men worked to clear the trail, Mrs. Rowe left our group and arrived back a couple of hours later with three large marmots, which everyone calls woodchucks.

"I guess these will do where there's no deer or elk," she said. "They'll sizzle in the pan."

No one will pass up food of any kind. Once again the rations are thin and everyone goes to bed hungry—except the McCords. Their terriers are forever in the rocks, yipping and digging for rodents. They catch chiefly ground squirrels, with an occasional marmot, and stop their hunting only to sleep at night.

Our slow travel was brought to a standstill this morning. We were traveling a treacherous grade around the side of a steep mountain when Owen discovered the trail ahead blocked by rock and timber. There was a lot of complaining. Many of the wagons were barely able to maintain balance on the steep and narrow trail, putting severe strain on the oxen. Everyone worked to place rocks and timber branches behind the wheels to steady them. Sean Malone had the most trouble, as his wagon was very close to the edge.

Annie took the baby from the back of the wagon to

feed her. Sean had left to cut tree branches and would soon return to place them behind the wheels.

The rain began falling harder and I suggested to the women that we find some dense pines for shelter. We had just got settled when someone yelled that the Malone wagon was rolling.

The oxen bellowed in their traces as they worked against the pull of the wagon. One of the wheels had slipped off the trail and the cargo weight began pulling everything over the side.

Sean Malone dropped his load of branches and ran, yelling, to the wagon. Two men were cutting the terrified oxen loose and the wagon was just going over the edge when Sean jumped inside.

Annie screamed. She handed Millie the baby and ran downhill towards the rampaging wagon. I followed, calling out for her to stay back.

The wagon rolled and bounced down the steep hillside. Everyone yelled for Sean to jump, but he stayed inside.

At the bottom, the wagon slammed backwards into an embankment. Sean let out a yell. Annie and I climbed into the front of the wagon and found him pinned under a load of household goods.

Upon impact, the dining-room table had tipped up on edge and come to rest with the legs sticking out the back, embedded in the bank. Sean was sitting upright with his back against the table's top. The cargo had gone flying into him, including the windowpane for their living room. My stomach felt empty clear down through my soul.

The glass had sliced into him at a perfect right angle to his body, cutting him in half at the waist. He sat trapped, his back against the table. The window, intact, protruded from his abdomen and lay resting atop his knees.

Blood seeped everywhere and there was no way to stop it. Once the window was removed, Sean would die almost instantly.

He looked at us, dazed but coherent.

"Where's little Mary?" he said.

"I took her out of the wagon, Sean. I already took her out," Annie said.

"I wish I'd have known."

Annie cleared the way to him. She seemed to want to embrace him, but was afraid to.

"I can't feel my legs," he said.

Owen pushed everyone aside and climbed into the wagon. He took one look and held his breath.

"Do you know what's happened, Sean?" he asked.

"Looks like I've got a window through me," he said.

His eyes began to glaze over with shock.

"Can I hold the baby?" he asked.

Little Mary settled into his arms and he told her how beautiful she was and what a wonderful woman she would become in this fair new land.

"You'll play fiddle and mandolin and banjo. Everything," he said.

Annie sobbed into my breast. Sean handed the child back to her and held out his arms.

"We can hug," he said. "It won't do no harm."

Owen and I left the wagon. We could hear them talking and crying together. Then Annie stuck her head out and asked that we join them.

Inside, Sean extended his hand to Owen.

"I want to thank you for all you've done for Annie and me," he said. "This is a helluva way to end things."

Millie joined us in the wagon. She held her rosary tightly, tears flowing down her cheeks.

"The Good Lord has seen fit to take you along with Martin," she said. "Pray for us when you get up there."

Sean looked at everyone and shook his head. "There's so many things I wanted to do." He took Annie's face in his shaking hands. "Had I known, I'd have spent more time with you."

Annie was holding up well. "You have nothing to be sorry for, Sean Malone."

"I ain't good at saying it, Annie, but I love you."

"I love you too, Sean. God be with you."

Sean Malone died peacefully with his head on Annie's shoulder, touching their baby. Owen and some of the men wrapped him in a tarp and laid him on a door. We buried him in the rain while the oxen breathed clouds of vapor and the wagons stood stark on the steep trail in the Oregon twilight.

ROGUE RIVER

Gabriella's Journal

7 NOVEMBER 1846

It is near dark and the rain has broken for a time. I have too much sense to believe it will stop even for a day. Each morning dawns gray and dismal. Clouds hover over the mountains and the thick and endless timber is layered with dripping water. Our breath forms heavy clouds and numb hands work to recover circulation. The only reason anyone sleeps is from exhaustion.

The farther we go, the more dreadful the trail becomes. Oxen are dying at an alarming rate. The pull is too much for them and there is little grass to be found among the rocks and timber.

As a result, many belongings are being dumped beside the trail. Books and reading chairs long cherished are thrown aside. All manner of kitchen furniture and equipment are tossed. They keep just the bare essentials.

Silas McCord wrestled a mahogany trunk to a clearing above the trail and dug a hole. Pearl and Katie stood by with their dogs, sobbing uncontrollably. Everything their mother had thought dear was in that trunk, including the family Bible on her mother's side.

Owen helped Mr. McCord wrap the trunk in canvas and secure it with ropes. They lowered the trunk into the hole and covered it over.

Silas hugged each of his girls. "We'll be back for it soon," he promised.

I stood with Annie Malone on the trail and remarked how hard it must be to leave something so dear in a hole on a wilderness mountainside. She only shrugged and rocked her baby.

She had left their family wagon and all its contents at the bottom of the hill where Sean died, and had never looked back. All she had taken were clothes and blankets for the baby. She had even left her precious fiddle behind. Owen had wrapped it carefully and packed it on one of our mules.

"When we get through this," he said, "she'll wish she had it."

She is still quiet and drawn into herself. She holds her baby tightly and periodically breaks into tears. Millie McConnell is perpetually saying the rosary. The beads are no longer black, but worn slick to the brown wood underneath.

It is a somber journey, yet alive with the firm belief that trail's end will bring comfort and the expected gratification of a bountiful land. Owen assures me that the rains will eventually end and that an early spring comes to this region. A number of settlers are talking about planting apple and cherry trees. The harvest in a climate such as this should be extraordinary.

That is all, literally, that keeps some of the emigrants alive. The elderly have become sick and many of them cannot function without help. The Kentuckians carry them to and from carts that Owen and the men have constructed from broken-down wagons. They encounter each day with the conviction it will be their last.

We passed a lady from a previous caravan who had got lost in the rain and was standing beside the trail. Her rain-soaked gray hair was matted against her leathery face, and her clothes were worn and tattered over her skeletal frame. Her vacant blue eyes were red from weeping. She said that she was searching for her lost husband.

Owen asked her name and we remembered having passed a splintered wooden grave marker early yesterday that read: ARTHUR COLLINS, A GOOD MAN, REST IN PEACE.

"Are you Mrs. Collins?" Owen asked.

"Yes, Lizzie Collins," she said. "Do you know where Arthur is?" She clutched Owen with her bird-thin fingers. "Please, do you know where he is?"

Owen said he would look and hoisted her into the wagon with Millie and Annie. She sat on the edge of the seat and looked in all directions, calling her husband's name. That evening, as we made camp, she laid down beside a tree and died.

Owen wrapped her in a tarp and tied her across a mule. He wished to find a more suitable way to transport her but time would not permit it. He found a piece of door beside the trail and chopped a marker from it and handed it to me. I'm not as good with a knife as I am with a brush but I managed to carve: LIZZIE COLLINS, DEVOTED WIFE, REST IN PEACE.

Owen rode back along the trail and returned shortly after midnight. I don't know how he found the original grave in the dark but he has an uncanny ability to feel things that he cannot see. I suppose it comes from life in the wilderness when survival depends on all the senses working perfectly together.

He takes it all in stride, never complaining. Sometimes he reminds me of Guynema Rowe—both being more at ease with themselves when everything is a life-and-death struggle.

After being at Bent's Fort and then Fort Hall, I would venture to say that Owen represents the majority of mountain men who still remain in the wilderness. They're like the wolves that roam the mountains and plains, always on the prowl for food, their instincts ever alert to danger.

Men like them cannot rest for any length of time. They must be on the go, following old trails and reliving hard-fought battles and nights without sleep, protecting their horses from Indian war parties. Soft-lit hotel rooms and quiet streets cannot provide for nerves that need to be on edge, and that's probably why Owen couldn't last in the settlements.

It is good that he's along on this journey. Though the men are bone-weary, they continue to have their nightly meetings. Important decisions have arisen from their conferences.

The settlers have all made arrangements to take along only what they deem absolutely necessary and are consolidating it in carts or wagons. Many have decided that the clothes on their backs are enough. Though they curse the road and the men who carved it out, they still believe there's a rainbow at the end of it.

11 NOVEMBER 1846

The rain has lessened but the trail remains horrendous. It's a daily task to remove fallen trees and rocks from our path. My feet are swollen from the cold and endless walking. Whistler is enduring and manages to discover wisps of grass and scattered shrubs throughout the forest. He's a fighter.

Owen rides ahead endlessly and returns for Kentuckians to help him clear the way. Everyone has resigned themselves to a day at a time, no more. Guynema Rowe, usually always on the go, has stopped her hunting. The woodchucks have gone into hibernation and the squirrels and chipmunks are so sparse that it isn't worth wasting her precious energy to range out after them. Even if she was lucky enough to bag one, she couldn't cook it. With so much timber in every direction, there's none dry enough to burn.

The McCord girls cry almost continuously. They care little about their own hunger but both are very concerned about Rufus and Jake. The little dogs have lost considerable weight and haven't the energy to dig in the rocks. Pearl carries Rufus in her arms much of the time. Her father protests and insists that she ride in the cart with Katie and Jake, but she's afraid the single yoke of oxen will tire and die.

Yesterday at noon Owen bled some of the mules, cutting them at selected veins along the leg. He filled two tin cups with blood and after pouring it in a pitcher, diluted it heavily with water. I was able to swallow a mouthful.

Mrs. Rowe made a blend of grass and moss and mixed

it with blood water. After digging under a log, she recovered handfuls of dry pinecones. They popped and burned and brought the grass soup to a boil.

She doled out small cupfuls, first to the McCord girls, and instructed the brew be sipped very slowly.

"Otherwise you'll wretch it up," she said.

Per her instruction, I drank a half-cup and discovered myself revived a great deal. I certainly wouldn't recommend it for every day but it does serve the purpose to ward off starvation.

Owen says that it's important to counteract hunger before intense weakness develops. Then it is difficult to think and delirium sets in. He maintains that it is almost impossible to starve on the plains or in the foothills, but that the thick woods are deadly.

The game remains at moderate to lower elevations most of the year, except for herds that cross high mountain passes in midsummer. In the most extreme situations there is always the inner bark of the cottonwood and the numerous plant roots along the rivers and stream courses to fall back on.

In the high mountains the soil is sparse and much of the vegetation is woody. There is little to feed any animal except the rodents who frequent the rocks. Anyone who travels at this altitude in other than the warm seasons is risking death.

I know these mountains to be lower than the Rockies in the interior, but to me they have been equally grueling. No one can tell me that the hottest of deserts is more of a challenge, not when there are plenty of ants to eat.

13 NOVEMBER 1846

We've had grass and blood soup for three days. Then two oxen died last night and were immediately butchered. One of the carts was chopped up for firewood. The meat added to our strength and for the first time in many days, the McCord girls relaxed. Rufus and Jake were back to normal, wagging their tails and looking for treats. They pestered Owen endlessly, knowing he would oblige them.

We began the journey this morning refreshed and in good spirits, but soon ran into serious difficulties. We spent the better part of the day taking the carts and wagons apart and carrying them and the goods over a huge rockslide that had blocked the trail. I walked over the slide with Annie and Millie and the McCord girls.

We had just reached the other side when we heard a rumbling behind us. Rocks began moving downhill. Owen was right below the moving hill with three Kentuckians, removing the hoops and canvas covering from the last wagon. I screamed as a mass of rock and mud tumbled down where they worked.

The rest of the men were reconstructing the wagons and carts. They dropped everything and rushed past me. Annie had a strange look on her face. My stomach fell down to my knees.

Rufus and Jake began barking, running over the rocks as fast as they could go, and I started after them.

By this time the slide had covered the wagon completely and there was no way to tell where it was within the rubble. Men scrambled along the hillside, removing rocks and pieces of shattered timber, looking for any sign of Owen or the three Kentuckians. Pearl and Katie McCord arrived and pointed to where Rufus and Jake were frantically barking and digging.

I rushed over and began turning rocks aside as quickly as I was able. Soon everyone was helping me, and the back of the wagon began to appear. I dug until my fingers bled and soon we heard Owen's voice calling out that he was alive.

First came a table leg and then Owen's arm and shoulder. Upon hearing the rocks tumbling down, he had quickly climbed under the table for cover, shielding himself from much of the debris that rolled over the wagon. He was badly bruised and shaken, and his right arm hurt him terribly, but we could find no broken bones and no deep cuts or scratches.

The three Kentuckians were not so lucky. The rocks had shoved all three of them against the bank on the opposite side of the trail, crushing them. Rufus and Jake had found where they were buried, and after the men discovered their bodies, they laid them out carefully and covered them back over.

The camp settled into shock. I helped Owen wash at the creek while Millie and Guynema Rowe worked together to brew a strong tea. While Owen sipped the strong brew, I cut a sling for his arm from one of my dresses.

"I feel strange," he said. "I almost died on my birthday."

"Today's your birthday? Why didn't you tell me?" I asked.

"I didn't see it as important."

"That's nonsense," I said, helping him arrange the sling. "Everything about you is important to me."

I laid my head against his shoulder and he held me with his good arm. I wanted to be strong but couldn't hold the tears back. I've never felt so panicked and sick with dread as when I saw that hill sliding down.

The strong tea helped Owen relax and soon he fell asleep. I joined Annie and Millie at their wagon, and Guynema Rowe came soon after me. Two of the men had left young widows. One was named Lucy, heavy with child, and the other Lily. I listened while Annie and Millie talked to them about carrying on.

"I can't," Lucy sobbed. "I can't bear to be without him."

"Oh yes you can," Millie assured her. "You'd best be thanking the Good Lord that you're still alive to have his child."

"But what will I do?"

"You've got two strong arms and two strong legs and a good head on your shoulders," Millie said. "Oregon City is looking for women like you."

"We'll all stay together and work at laundry or such," Annie said. "We can help with one another's children."

"I told Mace not to drag us out this way," Lily said, with clenched fists. "Now he's gone and gotten himself killed!"

"You can throw a fit of anger now, if you've a mind," Millie told her. "But come tomorrow you should ask the Good Lord to help you get along that trail and start over."

They talked half the night, sharing their pain among them. I left to join Owen atop a nearby mountain. We walked along a deer trail that took us to an opening in the trees, where we sat on a rock outcrop with a good view of the sky.

The clouds had parted and the stars shone brightly. The moon was but a small crescent hanging over the distant treetops.

"I never thought we'd see the sky again," I said. "What a sight!"

"You haven't seen anything yet." Owen pointed to the

north, where a glow of light had begun moving up along the skyline. "The real show is about to begin."

I watched in wonder as the light grew increasingly brighter, flowing across the sky towards us in long, ghost-like streaks of white. Soon the cloudlike movements became tinged with blue and red, with an occasional burst of green.

"The Northern Lights," Owen said. "Pure magic in the winter sky."

I marveled at the glorious show of beautiful color. At times the lights seemed to flow just overhead. I stood up and raised my hands into the air, hoping that I might feel the lights slip through my fingers on their way past.

"I used to sit in the cold, high up in the mountains along the Three Forks of the Missouri River," Owen said. "The lights would come down from the Arctic. I once saw a big white owl glide overhead through the color. There was a man named Clayborne with me that night and he started to cry. The next day he was killed by Blackfeet Indians."

"There will be no owls tonight," I said, and we held each other tightly.

I've decided that Providence is a scheme no one can predict or understand. Strong people don't always survive. Owen is among the strongest and he couldn't have known in any way that the mountain wanted to kill him. He's still with me now because Rufus and Jake decided they also wanted him around for a while longer, and what the Indians call the Great Mystery wanted it, too.

14 NOVEMBER 1846

I've never been so sore in my life. I guess I'm lucky even to be alive. It feels like the whole mountain fell on top of me, then churned and chewed me up. I should have more than just some bruises and scratches, but I twisted my right elbow pretty bad and I can't use it.

I'll keep it in the sling for a while and see what I can do left-handed. I never thought for a moment that hill would slip again. But none of the land I've ever crossed has ever once told me ahead of time about its surprises, and I've been luckier than some.

I feel bad for the Kentuckians and their widows. It's hard to understand how I lived through that and they didn't. I was lucky enough to be in the wagon and they weren't. I'd like to think that's all there is to it, but there's got to be more. This is not the first time that I've survived something that should have taken me, and saw those with me go. It doesn't make any sense.

I can't say I've accomplished all that much in my life and there's any number of people who wish I wasn't around. So I don't understand why I'm still here today and a lot of my friends are not.

I can still hear those Kentuckians screaming as the rocks rolled over them. Just as the slide started, one of them said, "Watch out, Quin! There's a landslide!" and another one said, "Oh, God! We're dead!" I thought I would go this time and crawled under that table out of instinct. That wagon was partly crushed, but it should have been crunched to kindling.

At first I didn't know if I was dead or alive, in all of the mud and the darkness. I knew I was safe when I realized that you don't feel pain when you're dead.

I had hoped that the Kentuckians had made it, also, but deep in my gut I knew otherwise. I had enough room to breathe and the rocks were loose enough so that air got to me without a problem. But no one would have found me if those two little terriers hadn't been around.

It makes me think of that hot day on the Cache la Poudre River when three of us were trapping and the sky suddenly filled with strange clouds. Briggs and Kestrom and I were out in the open when the thunder started. They wanted to finish checking our line and insisted I go back down to camp and cut elk steaks and bring them back for roasting. I didn't want to go, so we drew straws. I lost.

I mounted my pony to leave just as thunder boomed overhead. The horse bolted and I hung on with all I had, but I got bucked off. Heavy hail started, pea-sized but getting bigger fast. I ran for a nearby cave, thinking how lucky I was to have been bucked off next to good shelter.

I began to think about Briggs and Kestrom. I yelled for them to run to the cave, but they kept getting struck by hail that kept coming bigger and faster. They were yelling and I saw Kestrom's terrified face as he fell and reached out toward me.

Then it all turned white and the noise was deafening. It came so thick and so fast and so large that the world outside seemed only a wall of falling ice. I hoped I was dreaming but the storm kept up and I finally sat down with my back against the cave wall and held my hands over my ears and screamed.

When the storm ended, I watched a huge grizzly amble from the recesses of the cave past me and out into the ice-white afternoon. I waited for the bear to be gone and waded out into hailstones knee-deep and as big as my fist. Briggs and Kestrom were bashed beyond recognition, their buckskins a mass of blood and pulp. I found my pony in the same shape and saw one of the others in the distance. The grizzly was dragging it through the slop.

It took a full day before the hail melted enough for burial, and I spent that night fending wolves away from their bodies, praying the grizzly had gotten full of horsemeat. While I dug graves, I thought of the times other friends had been standing right beside me and had taken Blackfoot arrows or balls from Hudson's Bay rifles. It made me feel very alone.

I'll be sore from this rock-beating for a good long time. The hard travel won't make healing any easier and I hope my arm comes back to normal. It's swollen pretty bad, and though there's no broken bones, the joint feels like there's a fire inside.

I'll get through it and whatever else comes along. Physical aches and pains are something I can tolerate. The pain of survival is far worse.

Gabriella's Journal

16 NOVEMBER 1846

We arrived yesterday in the Rogue River Valley. This morning, for the first time in longer than I can remember, the sun is shining. Everyone is joyous but too weak to demonstrate. Owen and the Kentuckians greeted four settlers who arrived from the

Willamette Valley with food supplies and a herd of cattle. They told us that the Applegates, who had built the road, had come earlier with relief for the first wagons to leave Fort Hall.

We were treated to beef and biscuits and fresh vegetables. I found that my stomach had shrunk to the point that I could manage only half a plate of food. It felt so good to eat a hot meal. I slept the better part of the afternoon.

That evening, everyone rejoiced and ate beside roaring fires. A slight rain started, but it didn't last. Owen told me that another day in camp was all he would allow, as it is still a three-week journey to Oregon City.

That evening at the meeting Owen was voted down for the first time since leaving Fort Hall. No one wanted to depart in the morning, or the next morning, either, for that matter. They wanted to stay for however long it took to fatten up what was left of the oxen and mules and get themselves strong and rested for the last leg of the trip.

After the meeting, Owen was despondent.

"These people have come through so much," he said. "Why do they want to suffer more?"

"Can't you see, they're not fit yet to go another three weeks without stopping."

"We don't have to travel three weeks straight. Just through the Umpqua. Then we can stop again."

"Talk to them and take another vote tomorrow night," I said.

"Maybe we'll just go on ahead ourselves," he suggested. "I don't care to put myself through another wet hell."

"Give yourself some time to cool off," I said. "Don't explode at them."

He tested his sore elbow and grimaced. "Maybe I could use an extra day or two at that."

"Good idea," I said. "I have something for you. It's belated, but happy birthday."

I gave him a painting and he studied a portrait of Hawktail and himself, standing together. He held his rifle in the crook of his arm and Hawktail held his bow and arrows.

"That is truly nice of you," he said, smiling. "Thank you so much."

"I thought you might like something to remember him by," I said.

He hugged me with his good arm. "You are something, you are," he whispered.

The kind settlers who had brought us the beef and relief supplies decided to go back to their homes. I gave one of them a letter that I hoped would reach Uncle Walter's brother at Fort Vancouver. I had met Sir Reginald Dodge but once as a small child so I don't believe he'll remember me. Still, I think he should hear the news of his brother.

I also asked him to look into the matter of my real mother. I'm hoping he can tell me where she is once we reach the fort. It's a long shot, but I must give it a try.

When the men left, we all gathered together for a music session. A few people were dancing but most just sat and listened to slow fiddle tunes and haunting guitar ballads. Owen had told Annie earlier that he had brought her fiddle. She had smiled and hugged him, and said that she realized Sean would never want her to stop playing music.

She played a favorite waltz of Sean's, tears streaming down her face. Millie and the McCord girls sat nearby while Rufus and Jake insisted that Owen pet them.

I told him how glad I was that the two dogs had found him, and that I would do a portrait of him and the girls, together with the terriers, if he wanted.

"What I want," he said, "is for you to do a self-portrait for me."

"But I've never done a self-portrait."

"But you could. And do one of us together, too."

"You want me to do a lot of work," I said with a smile.

He smiled back at me. "Do the one of yourself first. That's what I want most of all."

OREGON CITY

Gabriella's Journal

5 DECEMBER 1846

I'm not used to the traditional Thanksgiving that is the American way, but I enjoyed myself in the Rogue River Valley. There was no turkey, but plenty of beef and biscuits and beans and various greens that Guynema Rowe had harvested from the river bottom. Since that day, however, a great deal has happened.

It began raining before we had finished our Thanksgiving meal and Owen suggested that we take to our beds early and get going before dawn. He had us all up and grumbling before we knew it, and on our way.

True to his prediction, the journey turned unbearable immediately. The rains came even harder than during our Siskiyou crossing, and while in the Umpqua, most of the oxen that had survived now perished in the rivers and thick mud of the lowlands. We were forced to abandon many of the last wagons and carts, along with the goods inside them.

We crossed the main stream over forty times in the length of just three miles. I never thought I would ever feel dry again. Owen had wrapped my paintings securely in canvas and had packed them in bags with ties. He kept them secured to the mules during our travel and tied them in trees when we stopped.

I can only begin to wonder how we maintained our sanity as we pushed through day after torturous day. There was no relief as we continued through that nightmare of swollen streams and pouring rain. The days passed in a watery blur and at times we made but two or three miles.

But everyone kept mouthing the words, "We'll reach the Willamette! We'll reach the Willamette!" to keep spirits up as much as possible. No one wanted to quit, not when we were so close to our destination.

Annie Malone and Millie McConnell had lost everything but their clothes and blankets for the baby. Little Mary is very strong and Millie says she'll survive when the rest of them collapse.

I feel sorry for Millie now. She lost her rosary in the rain and muck and uses her fingers to pray. She says it's a lot harder to keep track but that she isn't concerned.

"When you don't remember when you started praying and there's no end in sight," she said, "then you're always in the middle."

Owen and I lead our ponies and help the McCord girls carry their dogs. Those two pets are hardy and don't mind being lugged around like small sacks of flour.

Pearl has a phrase she uses in reference to the way Rufus shows his distaste for trying situations. His ears lie back against his head in a peculiar manner, which she calls "unhappy ears." I don't believe that little white dog has lifted his ears for a good number of days.

The rain finally lessened and settlers again came to our aid. We replenished our strength with fresh beef and potatoes and beans, and started the last leg of our journey anew. The going was much easier, as the valley was dotted with cabins and we were given shelter along the way.

Many in our group decided they had arrived at their new home, including Millie and Annie. There were a lot more settlers arriving along the Columbia to the north each day and the Umpqua Valley afforded land equal to the Willamette in fertility.

The Applegates, the road-building family, make their homes here. They have received a bad reputation and as far as I'm concerned, it's unwarranted. When some of the residents defamed them, I asked if they thought they could have done much better by taking the road to the Columbia.

There was no argument, as they knew I was right. They had taken the Southern Route to save time. I didn't have to mention that they had likely made the same mistakes as we had: resting too long in one spot, and believing there was all the time in the world to make it to Oregon.

After nearly a week's stay I wanted very much to continue ahead and look for my mother, but suggested to Owen that he might take the opportunity to go back and retrieve the buried trunk for Silas McCord and his family. He told me that he had thought about it but didn't want to bring it up, knowing how badly I wanted to get to Fort Vancouver.

I stayed with the girls and the dogs and helped Guynema cook while Owen and Silas retraced our steps back up into the mountains. They were gone a week and returned with the trunk tied securely to a mule.

"The going wasn't all that bad," Owen said. "We made good time and weren't bothered by Indians."

The girls were so happy to have their mother's things that they hugged the trunk and tied colored ribbons to the handles. They didn't even wait until all the mud was removed.

Owen met with the Applegates just before we departed for Fort Vancouver. He asked about the possibilities of opening a trading company in the valley.

"Would the settlers in the region be interested in trading furs for produce?" he asked.

Jesse Applegate, the eldest brother of the family, said the settlers had no desire to hunt for anything more than food and would have little time for that, as their main form of living would be farming the valleys.

"And the Indians aren't inclined to do business with anyone but Hudson's Bay," he said. "It doesn't matter who claims the land now, the old trade relations are still in effect."

He went on to say that we had been lucky not to encounter trouble with the Takelma and Tututumi tribes of the Rogue River country. The heavy rains had no doubt kept them in their villages.

The subject of Fort Vancouver came up and Mr. Applegate advised Owen that if we had business there, it would be wise to meet with the previous Chief Factor, Dr. John McLoughlin.

"He's always been a fair man and has taken land up at Oregon City," he said. "He can make arrangements for your business at the fort."

I was aware that the letter I had sent with the settler some weeks before was to have gone to Dr. McLoughlin. I was anxious to learn that my efforts might have helped me find my mother that much sooner.

Owen reminded me that even though war would not occur, informal conflict between the new Oregon government and the Hudson's Bay Company hadn't receded.

The present Chief Factor, James Douglas, might not be willing to help us in any way.

Still, I won't be dissuaded from my goal. I've resolved to find her. Since we've traveled this far, I will not be denied the chance, with or without the help of Hudson's Bay.

The day before our departure, Silas McCord organized a going-away party. Everyone gathered where one of the Kentuckians had already built a cabin. During the festivities, Mr. McCord broke the news that he and Guynema Rowe would exchange wedding vows. It turns out that Mrs. Rowe had never actually been a Mrs., but was the reverend's sister and had traveled with him at the insistence of their parents.

They had decided to call themselves married to keep people from gossiping about a brother and sister traveling together in the same wagon.

"Mother said it would keep me out of the eternal fire if I was to go with him to Oregon and have him find me a God-fearing man," she said.

"That was hardly fair," I said.

"I didn't consider him much of a brother," she said. "I had to remind him most every night that hell waited for men who bedded their kin."

"Why didn't you say something?" I asked.

"Say what? I wasn't brought up that way."

"I'm sorry you had to endure it," I said.

"It wasn't all that bad, once he understood about my rifle. After that, he wanted to get rid of me. So I got rid of him first."

Everyone joined in congratulating the couple, as well as showing their appreciation to Owen for the effort he had put forth in leading them to their new homes. Many wept at the memories of the hardships along the way.

Owen called for a moment of silence to commemorate

those who had passed on during the journey. One of the Kentuckians then led the group in "Nearer My God to Thee." Then, after a very large dinner, Pearl and Katie came forward with a cake.

"We think you're pretty special, Mr. Quincannon," Pearl said. "You didn't get to celebrate your birthday, except for getting out from under those rocks."

Owen sat down in front of the cake and thanked the two girls.

"We made it ourselves in a cabin and baked it in a real stove," Katie said.

The cake had fallen somewhat and the icing was smeared unevenly, but the taste held up. Owen blew out candles carved from pitch pine.

"We didn't know what age you were," Katie said, "so we got Pa to carve enough candles for a medium-old person."

Owen smiled and let her climb on his lap. "I surely appreciate it," he said.

"Where will you go?" she asked.

"I haven't decided yet," Owen told her.

"We know that you can't stay here," she said. "You've got to go climb more mountains. As long as there's mountains, you'll be going to them."

I believe that young girl about summed it up. I could see in Owen's eyes that remaining settled in a farming valley was something he just couldn't do. Perhaps it's a result of his childhood and the difficult times after his father left. He will no doubt never forget how it felt to see his mother's pain at losing their farm.

He hadn't been able to stay in or near St. Louis, and now with no opportunity for a trading venture here, he will likely look for another place to explore.

He told me in the Bayou Salade that there were few if any places left to be discovered.

"Most every place has been found and there will be settlement someday in everywhere that a house can sit," he said. "I'd like to see some areas grow, but it would be nice to leave others alone."

I watched the settlers laughing and eating together. When the meal was over and the dishes done, the musicians would break out their instruments. I asked Annie if she intended to play for dances in the valley once everyone got settled.

"Likely so," she said. "But I'll take it a day at a time."

I hugged her and Millie and the McCord girls and their dogs, and many others. We started out and I couldn't get them off my mind. We've traveled so far and been through so much it seems as if we've been joined forever. In fact, there's no one can say that we haven't become like family.

Gabriella's Journal

15 DECEMBER 1846

We came to the falls of the Willamette River and looked upon Oregon City, a bustling little town nestled against the hills just back from the water. There was both a sawmill and a gristmill and a number of buildings under construction. There were any number of bakeries and blacksmith shops, and a large boardinghouse with carriages in front.

Again I was reminded of Independence, except that the scene was one of triumph and celebration as opposed to anxiety. Wagons and children and dogs filled the streets, the mothers laughing rather than shouting, while men stood in groups and talked of their claims and how the crops would come in with all the rain.

It was easy to find Dr. McLoughlin's home, a large, two-story white structure of rectangular design. He met us in his study and asked how the trip had gone.

"We had a hard time," Owen said. "Some of them didn't make it."

"That won't slow things down at all," he said. "You Americans are a hardy lot."

I found Dr. McLoughlin to be one of the most interesting men I had ever met. Owen had told me some things about him but I wasn't prepared for his, literally, enormous presence.

In his early sixties, he was dressed neatly in a white shirt and black trousers, with black coat and tails, and he stood well over six feet tall. Layers of cotton-white hair spilled over his collar. His eyes were a piercing blue under heavy eyebrows that I imagine could appear very menacing if he were to become angry.

Yet his manner was light and friendly, and we shared an afternoon high tea with him while he spoke of Oregon and the Northwest, and how his affiliation here had been both good and bad for him.

"The land has been wonderful and the natives a source of interest and, at times, joy," he said. "I must confess, though, the growing political climate will likely do me great harm."

"I'm very sorry to hear that," Owen said. "I know how much you did for the settlers of this region. It's only fair that they reward you."

"I feel that the hardworking, common man knows me but is helpless to assist me in any way," he said. "I fear it stems more from the religious factions gaining power here. But enough about my troubles."

He produced the letter I had sent him with the settler and said that he had heard of Lucy James, and that the last he knew, she was living in a Chinook Indian village along the Columbia.

"It is my understanding that she is still a British subject," he said. "I would suggest that you visit with the Chief Factor at Fort Vancouver to learn of her exact whereabouts."

He said that he would send ahead a letter of introduction to James Douglas. Then his eyebrows furrowed and he grew sullen.

"There is another matter that needs immediate attention," he said. "Are you acquainted with a Sir Edward Garr?"

"We've had a long-standing rivalry," Owen said.

"So I understand." The doctor looked sideways at me. "The man is trouble, I won't hesitate to say it, and Hudson's Bay has done nothing to stop him."

Dr. McLoughlin explained that Edward hadn't come into town but that he had been sending threatening letters to various settlers, advising them to move out of Oregon. If they do not, he will visit them with his "officials" and physically remove them from the property.

"He is obviously ignoring the quest for settlement between Great Britain and the United States," the doctor said. "And to complicate matters, he conveniently stays on the north side of the Columbia and is therefore not approachable by the people he has challenged."

"I had hoped we might have stopped him a few months back," Owen said. "He has caused trouble along the trail from the beginning."

"Well, spare me all the history," Dr. McLoughlin said. "I am no longer affiliated with Hudson's Bay and cannot press an issue that directly relates to their interests, but I'm asking you to see what you can do to stop this man from causing further trouble. Some of the citizens here believe that I am somehow connected to him, preposterous as that may seem. Nevertheless, I am striving to assist you in locating Lucy James, so I would appreciate the return of favor in the matter of Edward Garr."

"We will travel to the fort as soon as possible," Owen said.

"Excellent," Dr. McLoughlin said. "I will send an envoy with the letter of introduction. I would be pleased to have you stay here tonight, and on the morn, you may take one of my personal canoes, given to me by the Chinook people. After you have attended to the Garr problem, you can take the canoe wherever you'd like."

Quincannon's Journal

15 DECEMBER 1846

D r. McLoughlin and his family have retired for the night and I sit here by the fire in his home, with Ella beside me, and we both write of what we've seen and done. His wife, Margaret, and his widowed daughter, Eloisa, who had been gone when we first arrived, prepared a fine meal this evening. David, a son, spoke graciously to us and excused himself.

I wonder if David doesn't like me, or maybe Americans in general. His father is being treated harshly by the political forces at work to control the new Oregon. Strange how it is that a group of people will go through dust and dirt and the winds of hell to escape governmental control and then quickly construct the same organization for themselves, as soon as they find a place to settle.

I don't believe that Dr. John, as most people call him, could have ever turned his back on anyone in need. He has given so much to the emigrants here that it's no wonder the Hudson's Bay Company saw him as more against them than with them.

It's all too difficult to put into proper perspective. Perhaps if the Company hadn't done him so wrong at different turns, he might have been harder on the settlers. I know that in the early years I was in the mountains, his men and we Americans fought tooth and nail for prime beaver grounds. No doubt he heard stories of our atrocities the same as we told tales about the things they did. Now all that has passed and this man who invited us into his home may soon be a man without a country.

I believe that the entire family sees Ella as both charming and unusual, and they were definitely taken by the beautiful portrait she painted of them this evening. In the blue dress and new slippers, she presents herself as any English lady is supposed to. But if they were to know how she can ride an Indian pony and shoot a rifle, they wouldn't think I was speaking of the same person.

I do hope she finds her mother. I don't know how long it will take and if we will even be successful, but I will do what I can to help her for as long as it takes to get the job done.

I often think about my father and wish I had the chance to meet him for the first time all over again. I want to think I would be more forthcoming, but I guess I don't believe he cared all that much that I arrived. Sparing our lives was the least he could do and it required virtually no effort.

Perhaps I'm being too harsh. I know that it's said that everyone should be beholden to their parents, but what if the parent doesn't care for the child? Is it necessary to try to make something work that's doomed from the beginning?

I'll never know the answers to the many questions I have. I hope for Ella's sake that her real mother rushes to her and holds her for a long time.

FORT VANCOUVER

Gabriella's Journal

18 DECEMBER 1846, 1ST ENTRY

We crossed the river in Dr. McLoughlin's canoe and put in to shore about six miles above the mouth of the Multnomah River, which is really the Willamette below the falls. The canoe is beautifully crafted white cedar and painted with the symbols of bears and seahawks and ravens.

The day was open and bright, with a slight breeze off the ocean. All forms of waterfowl darkened the skies, including white and gray geese, and ducks of every color and description. Numerous shore birds darted and flew along the water's edge, adding their sharp calls to the already deafening din.

We were met by Hudson's Bay representatives and taken by coach across a level plain and through a log town that housed the Hudson's Bay employees and their families. I again saw Independence, Missouri, except that the people were French-Canadian. The children ran yelling and playing and their mothers worried far less about their antics than did the women of the emigrant wagon trains.

We passed a number of apple and cherry orchards as well as vegetable gardens at rest for the winter. Lumber wagons sat everywhere and Owen told me that timber was fast becoming the most important product of the region.

At the edge of the plain, where it rises gently through grasslands to a level terrace, sat a large stockade containing a great many warehouses and shops, including lodging facilities for the officers and their wives, as well as guests arriving at the fort. The surrounding area provides for numerous farms and small cattle ranches, with possibility for a great amount of development. I can see why the Hudson's Bay Company is distraught at the turn of events.

The smell of fresh bread was strong as we were escorted to the center of the fort and into a large white house with a piazza covered with grapevines.

Chief Factor James Douglas greeted us coolly. He had agreed to see us only out of respect for Dr. McLoughlin, but declined to be of help in the matter of Edward's renegade notions until Owen made it clear to him that should there be further trouble, and possible casualties, he could be held accountable.

"Let me make this perfectly clear, Mr. Quincannon," he said. "I have never authorized or condoned the actions of anyone against the treaty signed by Great Britain and the United States. I might not approve of the agreement but will nevertheless abide by its contents."

"Has Sir Edward ever approached you regarding backing for his scheme to push the American emigrants out of Oregon?" Owen asked.

"That is Hudson's Bay Company business, and as such, is privileged information."

"We were told by Dr. McLoughlin that you would be

of help in the matter," Owen said. "It appears you could care less about maintaining peace with Oregon."

"I've heard no complaints, sir, by other than yourself," Mr. Douglas said.

"You no doubt will," Owen said. "By then it will be too late."

Owen said that we would be leaving, as no cooperation was forthcoming, and that the matter of Edward would be left to the Oregon authorities to handle as they wished.

"Oh, very well," Mr. Douglas said then. "Sir Edward Garr has been here on numerous occasions but I have given him no satisfaction. He happened to be in my office, once again trying to get me to change my mind, when Dr. McLoughlin's letter arrived by messenger. Since it pertained to him and his character, I shared its contents with him. He left immediately. You might ask me where he went, but I won't be able to tell you. I don't know."

"You don't have any idea?" Owen said.

"No. But in further reference to the letter, Sir Reginald Dodge was notified of your arrival. Would you accept his participation in this meeting?"

"We welcome his participation," Owen said.

My uncle was escorted into the room and took up a position in front of Mr. Douglas's desk. He looked at me with great displeasure. His opinion was that I had become a traitor to the British cause, and in some ways, he was right. But his main animosity stemmed from my association with Owen.

"What do you have to offer here?" Mr. Douglas asked him.

"I can clear up some issues on the matter of Sir Edward Garr, if you would please, sir."

"Very well. Proceed."

"Sir Edward deserves every consideration in this matter, sir, and had I the power to do so, I would throw this man, Mr. Quincannon, in chains."

"Pray tell, what for?" Mr. Douglas asked.

"He means nothing but trouble for the Crown, sir. Treaty or not, he is here to do mischief."

"My dear uncle," I said, "he's led settlers into the valley, nothing else. Unless you can be more specific."

Sir Reginald turned to me. "As you are, I would hope, a loyal British subject, and my niece as well," he said, "it causes me no slight concern to see you involved with Mr. Quincannon."

"If you have an issue with me," Owen said, "speak to me directly."

Uncle Reginald squared his shoulders. "Very well, I shall. And directly to the point. I cannot understand why you would consort with my late brother's wife and now my niece as well."

"What are you talking about?" Owen asked.

"Sir Edward made the matter clear to me," he said. "While traveling across the plains, my brother entered his tent and discovered you in bed with Avis. Whereupon you arose from under the covers, grabbed your pistol, and shot him dead. I have every intention of demanding justice in my deceased brother's behalf."

"Wait, Uncle, you should know the truth," I interrupted. "First of all, it was Edward, not Mr. Quincannon, who was in bed with Avis. Secondly, I entered the tent, not Uncle Walter. I was tempted to shoot Edward myself, but Walter came in and after killing Avis, left and shot himself. That is exactly how it happened."

Uncle Reginald's eyes grew large and he became even more enraged.

"Why would you say such a thing about my brother, your own flesh and blood?"

"My intention is not to defame him, but to bring Edward's part in this clearly to the forefront," I said. "I am sorry for whatever discomfort that may cause."

Mr. Douglas seemed unaffected. The matter was not of significant concern to him and he urged us either to conclude the meeting or to take our discussion outside his office.

"Have you no respect for the indignities suffered by loyal British subjects?" Uncle Reginald asked him. "Or did your concern over such matters cease with the resignation of Oregon to American interests?"

Mr. Douglas rose from his seat. "You will be very careful with your speech and manners in here, Sir Reginald," he said. "Am I perfectly clear?"

Uncle Reginald bowed. "My apologies to the Chief Factor. Of course all British matters are of grave concern to you. I should not have implied differently. I would have hoped, though, that you would have taken Sir Edward's side in this issue."

"Where is Sir Edward that he doesn't speak in his own behalf?" Mr. Douglas asked.

"That I cannot say," Uncle Reginald said.

"Then I can find no reason for you to argue with your niece," he said. "If she was there and you weren't, why would you doubt her?"

"Perhaps she feels the need to cover for Mr. Quincannon."

Owen started to speak, but I held his arm and stepped in front of him.

"You may be flesh of my flesh, Uncle Reginald," I said, "but you have no cause to bear insult against either myself or Mr. Quincannon. If you take such stock in Sir Edward's lies, perhaps you should consider your own inability to desire true satisfaction in this matter."

"True satisfaction in this matter, my dear niece, would be to face Mr. Quincannon in a duel."

"Are you that eager to die?" I asked.

"Sir Edward said he was of poor quality as either a hunter or a gentleman," Uncle Reginald said.

"Sir Edward is afraid to face him," I said.

Uncle Reginald laughed. "I find that very difficult to believe."

"Then I will ask the same question as the Chief Factor," I said. "Why isn't Sir Edward here for this discussion?"

Uncle Reginald glared at me and then at Owen. He turned on his heels and left the room.

"I know very little about this matter," Mr. Douglas said, "and I don't care to know any more. As for the whereabouts of Miss Lucy James, Dr. McLoughlin is correct. She's among the Chinook Indians, caring for the dying. One of my assistants will give you directions to the village."

Owen thanked the Chief Factor for his help and we prepared to leave right away. As we readied ourselves to board the coach, Uncle Reginald approached me and said, "Is it true? Were you the one who walked in on Avis while she was bedding someone else?"

"It was me," I said. "And that someone else was Edward Garr. I am sorry about the outcome but I don't believe that Uncle Walter could bear to live with the dishonor."

"But Sir Edward is an honorable man. Why would he lie about such a thing?"

"Uncle Reginald, you must admit that Sir Edward is not an honorable man. Otherwise, why would he be causing problems regarding the Oregon issue, in a matter that is already settled?"

"Perhaps he doesn't feel that the Crown acted in the best interest of its subjects here in this new territory," he said.

"That is a moot point," I said. "The Crown made the

decision and all British subjects are to abide by the law. Am I wrong?"

Under different circumstances, Uncle Reginald and I might have got along famously. But he had a deep disdain for anything American and he now saw me as the enemy.

"From my correspondence with my dear brother, Walter, I had always thought of you as an upstanding young woman who would make a good and dutiful wife. Perhaps you've changed."

"Perhaps it was never that way," I suggested.

"I would advise you not to look for Lucy James," he said. "You would be far better off leaving the territory immediately. I believe a ship comes into harbor in less than a week. Shall I book passage?"

"If you will excuse me, Uncle Reginald," I said, "I have pressing matters. If you wish to return to England yourself, that is your business. But, please, leave my business to me."

Gabriella's Journal

18 DECEMBER 1846, 2ND ENTRY

Owen and I paddled together. He might argue that I wasn't of any help, though. He has been trying his best to teach me the ways of the canoe and I haven't been learning all that fast. Or perhaps my mind was on Lucy James, who had given me birth. I must admit, I was having second thoughts about meeting her.

The day was open and the skies again filled with fowl coming and going from the river and its tributaries. We made our way past a family of sea otters frolicking in the water. They rolled onto their backs with their feet in the air and ate various forms of marine life they had pulled up from the bottom. I might have reached out and touched one of them.

We rowed still farther towards the village and began to see a number of graveyards. Huge piles of bones littered the hillsides and burial canoes lay resting on the rock islands that jutted up from the river.

"You don't have to go on," I said.

"What will I do? I didn't bring a fishing pole," Owen said. "Where you go, I go."

I thought about his statement for a moment. "Are you talking about just today, or every day?"

He cleared his throat and continued paddling. A short distance further, we heard the rush of a waterfall. Just ahead lay the mouth of a stream. The water around the canoe teemed with a late run of salmon. They were two and three feet long, pink-sided, swimming their way *en masse* up towards the distant falls. I could touch them easily and often reached into the current just to feel their slippery bodies.

We paddled upstream to a set of rapids, then began our ascent on foot up a hill along a well-used trail. The rush of pounding water grew louder and we could see the lower falls through an opening in the evergreens.

Owen stopped me and gave me a kiss. I blinked with surprise when he displayed a blue sapphire stone he had fashioned onto a makeshift wooden ring with pine pitch.

"You asked me back there if I always wanted to be with you," he said. "I truly do and I want you to marry me."

The water rushing past in the stream sounded nearly as loud as the pounding of my heart.

"What do you say?" he said anxiously.

"Yes," I told him. "Definitely, yes."

He slipped the ring on my finger and kissed me long and hard. Then he took the ring back off.

"I don't think it's too good of a ring," he said. "I wouldn't want you to lose the stone."

"How about if I just keep it in my pocket?" I asked.

We climbed ahead and soon reached a large opening in the trees. The falls were a series of drop-offs eight to ten feet in height that ran to a major fall of over twenty feet. The water was alive with salmon, forging their way through the water and jumping each of the falls, their tails pounding the water.

At the main falls stood a number of near-naked Indians with pierced noses and ears, and bowl-shaped haircuts. Their ornaments were seashells and finger bones. I don't know whether Owen didn't know about it or had simply forgotten to tell me, but the frontal lobes of their heads had been flattened.

"It's a sign of stature among their people," he told me, "so as to distinguish them from their slaves."

The men stood out over the falls on wooden scaffolds, wielding huge nets fashioned from wood and grass that had been secured to long poles. The ascending salmon often couldn't make the initial jump over the tallest fall, and in dropping backwards, were caught in the nets.

Women dressed in thatched cedar skirts and heavy moss blouses took the catch from the men, then skinned and gutted the fish. The banks were lined with drying salmon.

Younger male Indians stood elbow-to-elbow below the main falls and used spears and poles with hooks to snag fish and pull them to the bank.

Owen picked out whom he thought to be the leader, and having guessed correctly, made sign to him as best he could that we were friends of the White-headed Eagle and were looking for a white woman who helped with the sick.

The leader appointed one of the fishermen to lead us into the village. We could hear crying and wailing well before we got there and realized that had we not been escorted, we wouldn't have been allowed to enter and would probably have been killed.

Their lodges were dome-shaped and made of grass and bark. Unlike the Plains tribes, there were no hide shields on display and no scalp poles in the center of the village.

Three canoes were arranged side by side. Inside each was a corpse wrapped in blankets and arrayed with painted clothing, along with baskets of food and the deceased's own personal belongings. In one canoe I counted four bodies and Owen said he believed whomever had died was taking his slaves across with him, to see to his wishes in the Other Side Camp.

Villagers sat beating sticks against hollow logs while singing. Others screamed and tore at their hair, or cut it off, while slicing themselves with knives.

Our escort brought us to a lodge where three women sat outside fixing a meal. The woman in the center saw me and slowly rose to her feet.

She wore the same clothing as the Indian women, but was lighter-complected. She saw me and smiled. I felt as though I was looking into a mirror. But for her shorter hair, she could have been me aged a few years.

Tears formed in her eyes and she began to tremble.

"Gabriella?" she whispered. "Are you Gabriella Hall?"

I felt overjoyed and weak-kneed at the same time.

"Yes, I am," I confirmed. "Are you Lucy James?"

She nodded and opened her arms to me. I hugged her, feeling a completion to the mystery of the emptiness in my life, yet at the same time, I felt as if I was betraying the mother who had raised and loved me as her very own.

"I understand your feelings," Lucy said. "It must be hard for you."

"Having two mothers is not an everyday thing," I admitted.

"Please, spend some time with me," she said, "and at least get to know me."

We sat and talked, sharing bowls of dried salmon and roots. She told us that the sickness afflicting the tribe was measles, and that the virus had nearly run its course. She had been caring for various tribes for a number of years.

"I came to Fort Vancouver with my husband, who died in a hunting accident," Lucy said. "I decided to stay and complete what I believe to be my life's work."

She looked away, tears forming in her eyes, and said that she had felt guilty all of her life for having given me to the parents who raised me.

"I almost ran away with you in my arms," she said. "But I worried that they would send someone to find me. Where would I go? I was young and alone and had no means by which to travel."

She explained that my father had offered her substantial money and comfort any number of times before my birth, but that she had turned it down. One afternoon, as her mother lay dying, she decided she had nothing to lose.

"I sent a letter accepting the offer, and crossed the Irish Sea within the week," she said. "I almost backed away, but when I saw Mrs. Hall and the hope in her eyes, I knew that the Good Lord wouldn't damn me for going through with it."

I told her that I was glad she had finally accepted the arrangement and that she had written to say she wanted to meet me.

"I would have learned of your letter four years ago, had they told me about it," I said.

"I wondered if they had ever told you, or ever would," she said. "It's a crying shame that society has to be so difficult." She looked at Owen and said, "You don't look to me like a British lord."

I explained what had happened and we had a good laugh at how life provides numerous twists and turns that challenge our way of thinking. I then showed her the blue sapphire and said that Owen had proposed to me at the foot of the falls.

"This is indeed a special day," she said. "First, I find my daughter and then I gain a son."

We talked about her life and how it had changed with the coming of Americans and the claiming of Oregon. She said that it concerned her from the standpoint that the Indian people would soon discover their lives dramatically changed.

"They live in a simple manner and I've learned to do the same thing," she said. "I'm not worried about the Oregon issue because I live with the tribes, and they don't have land problems. When you don't worry about owning everything, the days run smooth and quiet."

"Surely you realize all that will change," I said. "The land around here will soon be developed."

"Yes, I suppose you're right," she admitted. "I don't want to think about that now."

She invited us to stay as long as we wished. I told her we would be glad to spend some time, and that we needed to return to the canoe to get our bags.

"I have something I want to show you," I said.

She brimmed with curiosity and insisted on coming with us. A number of armed men formed an escort and she explained that the people wouldn't allow her to go anywhere alone, as they revered her as holy and believed that in every village she visited, the sickness that might be there became afraid and left.

"I'm a medicine woman of sorts," she said.

We walked past the fishermen at the falls and down the trail. At the canoe, we discovered that Edward and Uncle Reginald were waiting for us, along with ten of Edward's men, who brought their guns to bear.

The Chinook men began singing war songs and Mother stopped them.

"Can this be dealt with peacefully?" she asked me.

"No, it can't," Edward said. He stepped forward and smiled coldly at me. "I've been waiting for you to reach Oregon."

"Why did you hide the letters from me?" I demanded.

"I didn't feel it necessary to tell you," he replied. "You never did learn that I am more qualified than you to decide the important issues in your life."

"Such as your affair with Avis?" I said.

He laughed. "Reginald has told me the lies you and Mr. Quincannon have been spreading about me."

I stared at him in disbelief. "Lies?"

"Yes, lies. Mr. Quincannon was bedding both you and Avis. Now I will settle this with him here and now. After all, I've been terribly dishonored."

"We will settle it," Owen said. "But not here, among the Chinook people."

"This is British soil," Edward said. "They are entitled to nothing. You and I will count off the paces. Now!"

"You had better listen to me," Owen said. "If there's bloodshed here, the Chinook people will act."

"They cannot stand up to rifles," Edward said.

"How many rifles do you have?" Owen nodded towards the large number of Chinook warriors who suddenly emerged from the trees armed with their bows. Mother whispered to me that she had sent one of the escort party back to the village for help. Had she given the command,

Edward and his men would have been filled with arrows.

"Yes," Owen said, "you will get your wish. But you are going to have to face me in front of witnesses now in an honorable match, something you need a lesson in."

Gabriella's Journal

19 DECEMBER 1846

The dawn came blustery and overcast, but not so cold that the wind bit strongly. Chief Factor Douglas would have nothing to do with the dueling arrangements but instead sent an assistant named Lowell Cribbs to document the proceedings.

A surgeon from the post accompanied Edward, along with Uncle Reginald. Lucy insisted on coming, but was forced to leave her Chinook escorts at the village. Owen and I helped her into the canoe and she said with sadness, "Peaceful mornings like this can never be fully enjoyed."

We rowed in two separate boats to a small island just upstream from the fort. The birds were singing, just as they had that April morning on Bloody Island out of St. Louis. The dueling site was level sand and gravel. The shore was lined with small birds searching the shallows for food.

Uncle Reginald kept staring at me as if he wished to talk. I approached him and we looked out over the shining river.

"Why do you feel so strongly in favor of Edward?" I asked.

"He has agreed to give me a good position within his

family back in England," he explained. "There is nothing left for me here. No one wants to soldier any longer."

"Why soldier when there is no need for dying?" I asked.

"That is the problem, my young niece," he said. "There is a need for dying."

"Uncle Walter always spoke so highly of you," I told him, "so I know you to be an honorable man. Why don't you go back to the fort and wait for this to be over?"

"I told Sir Edward I would act as his second, and I will do just that," he insisted. "Now please excuse me."

Mr. Cribbs spoke in a commanding voice and asked Edward not once, but twice, if he meant to go through with the duel.

"I shall have it no other way," Edward said.

"Very well, then, we will take care of the legalities first."

Mr. Cribbs insisted that Owen and Edward both sign a document releasing the Hudson's Bay Company and the British government from any affiliation with the encounter. Edward's red face reddened even more and he said, "I would think that the Crown would thank me for what I'm about to do."

"Great Britain is not at war with the United States," Mr. Cribbs said. "That fact seems constantly to escape you."

Edward slammed the pen against the parchment and handed them back to Mr. Cribbs. "Let's get on with it, then."

Mr. Cribbs called the arms bearers forward and Edward selected a pistol from a box of a matched pair. Uncle Reginald did the same.

Another arms bearer opened an identical box and offered Owen his choice.

"You pick first," he said to me.

"What is going on here?" Edward asked.

"I am acting as Mr. Quincannon's second," I explained. Edward stared at me. "You must be mad."

"Do you wish to call this off?" I asked.

"Never!"

I picked a pistol from the box. "Then keep your impressions to yourself."

I stepped back with Owen and watched him load the two pistols. I couldn't help but notice that his injured elbow had begun to bother him in the cold and damp.

"Call this off, Owen," I said. "Please."

"I can't," he said.

Mr. Cribbs began reading the instructions loudly. When he came to the part regarding distance, Owen interrupted him.

"I suggest we duel at twelve feet," he said.

"Are you serious?" Mr. Cribbs asked.

Owen was staring at Edward. "Most definitely."

Mr. Cribbs turned to Edward. "What say you, sir?"

"Twelve feet it is," Edward said.

The distance was paced and marks drawn in the dirt. I stood to one side, holding my pistol cocked and pointed down. Uncle Reginald faced me a short distance away, averting his gaze.

Owen and Edward took position with their pistols pointed downward and awaited the order to fire. Edward turned towards me, watching my hands.

"Gentlemen, are you ready?" Mr. Cribbs asked.

Owen and Edward both nodded. I cringed, awaiting the inevitable sounds of pistol blasts. Edward kept watching me, as if concerned that at any second I might raise the pistol towards him.

"Fire!" Mr. Cribbs yelled.

Edward had already begun to lift his pistol towards me and I raised mine and shot. Both Owen and Uncle Reginald fired at the same time. I felt a hot sensation along my side and noticed a red stain growing. I sank to my knees.

Owen and Lucy rushed over to me. Uncle Reginald was right behind them.

Lucy heaved a sigh of relief. "It grazed your ribs is all."

Uncle Reginald gently placed a hand on my head. There was a deep sadness in his eyes.

Owen helped me up. "Thank God," he said. "I could never stand to lose you."

He took me in his arms and held me tightly. I buried my face in his shoulder to escape the scene nearby. Edward had been hit three times and, against the surgeon's wishes, would not lie down. He staggered in circles, trying to speak from vocal cords shot to pieces. His left arm hung limp and a red blotch grew ever larger along his lower left side.

It occurred to me that all three of us had fired on Edward. Uncle Reginald later told me that he had finally realized the truth and knew that he must act as Edward's second to keep him from murdering me.

Edward continued to garble words and make violent movements with his hands.

"Has he gained his satisfaction?" Mr. Cribbs asked the surgeon.

Edward shook his head and made signs with his hands that he wished another duel to take place. The surgeon argued emphatically against it, trying again to get him to lie down. But Edward reached out with his good arm and pushed him away.

Mr. Cribbs turned to Owen. "What say you, Mr. Quincannon?"

"I would decline to fight, unless Sir Edward insists."

Edward gestured emphatically that he wished to proceed.

"Very well," Mr. Cribbs said. "If that is your wish."

The pistols were loaded again and Edward stared at me

bitterly. He held his good hand against his torn throat, blood bubbling through his fingers. He staggered over to take one of the weapons, but it slipped through his fingers to the ground.

He dropped to his knees and his throat made a strange gargling noise as he tried to vent his rage. Then he suddenly sagged as though the air had gone out of him and he fell sideways and lay still.

The surgeon checked his pulse and shook his head.

" 'Tis a sad end to a sad man," Mr. Cribbs said.

Quincannon's Journal

19 DECEMBER 1846

This morning Edward Garr was buried unceremoniously. I stood with Ella and looked out across the Columbia and wondered at the changes that have come to this land, and also at the many people who have come and gone, most of them lost to history.

No one will ever know that Edward Garr sought to stop the emigration into Oregon single-handedly. Many could believe that a British nobleman could be adamant against the movement, especially if he stood to lose his own land grant. But such was not the case here. This man simply had no idea how to alleviate his frustration regarding his own family and sought to gain notoriety as a defender of the British cause, even when the British cared no longer about the cause in Oregon.

I wonder also how many other similar circumstances have been lost in the mists of time. Last night Ella's mother was telling stories she had heard from the Chinook about horned men with hairy faces dressed in skins who came across the big waters in giant canoes with sails. Their shields were metal and their huge knives four times as long as any they had seen before. Some of these men stayed and some left, was how the story went. Those who stayed became major leaders and their bones eventually went into canoes forever lost in the swelling waters of eternity.

I don't know whether it was Ella or me, or Reginald Dodge who put the ball through Edward Garr's throat. It doesn't really matter; it's finished. But I suppose we'll talk about it any number of times in the future.

That future for Ella and me will be a grand one. I intend to act as her agent, touring with her in all the courts and castles we can find, showing her grand pieces of art to all the kings and queens and noblemen throughout Europe. She is so capable at what she does that her reputation will be built in no time.

Last night she presented me with the self-portrait I had asked her to paint. It is a work of genius.

Two ladies, exact twins, stand beside a plush carriage. One is dressed in a blue dress and hat, with dazzling blue dancing slippers. The other lady wears a white doeskin dress and knee-high moccasins.

Though certainly from two different worlds, the twins appear completely content with one another. Tied to the carriage are two pintos that look exactly alike and behind them rise the majestic Rocky Mountains.

"I want to live in the courts of Europe and perhaps meet with geographical and philosophical clubs, then come to the wilds of the American West," she told me. "We can have it both ways."

She presented me with another painting that I will always admire. Two men, both of whom look exactly like me, are standing with the two ladies. One of the men is dressed in finery, the other in buckskins. Both are holding the reins of a buckskin horse.

"We must keep these paintings in a very safe place," I said. "We can cache them in a remote cave . . ."

"No caves," she said with a laugh. "They will be very secure with my mother in Lancashire. She will be glad to meet you and hear your stories, I'm sure."

Ours will be a life no two people have ever lived before. In this age of men traveling and leaving their families at home, Ella and I will be an exception. We will see all the trails that we can see in as many lands as possible, and she will preserve them all forever in oils and watercolors.

And if by chance we should have children, they will travel with us and see what we see and learn what we learn. We will be able to afford the best of tutors for them; and if they promise to take the responsibility seriously, they might be able to have a terrier or two as pets.

Gabriella's Journal

29 DECEMBER 1846

We spent Christmas visiting in Oregon City. Dr. McLoughlin welcomed us and wished us the best for our future together. The news of our engagement had preceded our arrival and I guessed that some of his Indian friends had paid their annual visit for bags of holiday candy.

Lucy accompanied us to Oregon City, attired in one of my dresses. She seemed at ease and was pleased to meet some of our friends from the wagon train who had arrived for the festivities. We discovered Silas McCord and Guynema Rowe listening to carolers in the main square. They had come up from the Umpqua with the girls and the dogs to purchase supplies and Christmas presents. They were happy to hear that we would be married and told us to visit anytime we wished.

Pearl said that Rufus missed Owen something terrible and the little dog proved her right. He rose on his hind legs in front of Owen and woofed for attention. Then he sat down and lifted his nose, howling. Owen bent over and allowed Rufus to lick his ears—the little dog's way of greeting special friends.

Jake was equally affectionate, prancing around with a small stick. I petted both terriers and asked the girls how their dogs liked their new home.

"They're not quite used to all the rain yet," Pearl said. "But they're already chasing squirrels around the yard."

Katie sat on Owen's lap and gave him a quick kiss on the cheek.

"I'm glad you haven't gone to climb a mountain yet," she said.

Owen promised the two girls he would take them up a mountain someday, when they were older. It was difficult to say good-bye, but we promised to visit them the first chance we got.

We were married the day after Christmas beside the waterfall where the salmon jumped. Lucy helped with the arrangements and asked us to allow an old man who lived in isolation deep in the forest to preside over the ceremony.

She called him Old Man, but his full name meant Man with Eyes of Stone Who Hears the Birds Talk. His hair was long and white and his eyes blue. His skin was a pale red-brown and hung in leathery folds about his jowls and body. He spoke no English, but Mother said that one of his long-ago ancestors had come from another land and that the eye color had been hidden for many generations before emerging again with his birth.

Old Man had a pet raven that never flew, but always walked just in front of him. It was as if the old man was being led by the bird, or was possibly directing the bird. No one knows for certain.

Though Mother said he never spoke English, I'm not convinced that he doesn't know the language. Owen was talking to me about where we would spend our honeymoon and the next thing I knew Lucy was telling me that as part of his ceremony, Old Man is supposed to have the first night with me.

"He's just kidding," she assured me. "But he wanted me to tell you."

When I looked at him, his eyes were smiling. I said to him in English that he only got an hour, and his mouth twitched ever so slightly.

Owen chuckled. "He's probably reading your mind."

As Old Man and Mother laid out special plants for the ceremony, Owen told me about the few true medicine people he had known.

"They don't differentiate a person by race or color," he said. "They look into your soul. And they see you in a fraction of a second."

The raven came and stood in front of us while Mother and Old Man sang a number of songs. We both took sweat baths in different lodges—Owen with Old Man and I with my mother. Then Old Man had us each place a seashell necklace around the other's neck and raise our hands to the sky and to the earth, and then to the four directions, signifying the unity of all that is living within the sacred circle.

He finished by burning plants and saying special prayers, and told us in an ancient language that we were joined as two beams of light would blend together into one, and should we ever decide to part, it would rip our souls in half.

When the ceremony was finished, we feasted on smoked salmon and received a great many presents from well-wishers, including baskets and seashell adornments for me, and for Owen, knives with whalebone handles, and bows and arrows adorned with feathers and shells and equipped with bone-tipped heads.

At twilight, we were ceremoniously seated in a large canoe and pushed into the current, to be carried out into the ocean. The canoe was layered with bear and otter skins, and filled with water bags, baskets of roasted roots, and smoked fish. We drifted in the darkness while the Northern Lights swept right overhead, thin clouds of red and blue and white, like spirits dancing on the ocean breeze.

I reached up as if to touch them, as I had done back along the trail, and felt a calm I had never known before.

"It is a sign of good things to come for us," Owen said.

We held one another throughout the night and made love while the lights danced overhead. When dawn arrived, Owen took a paddle and began to row. I could see no land and asked him how he knew which way to go and he said that Old Man was telling him.

31 DECEMBER 1846

As I look out across the beautiful waters of the Columbia and think of the life that lies ahead of me, I know that it is connected to the power of those gracefully sweeping lights in the ocean sky. Owen has shared his many phantasmic dreams and I do believe they will all come to pass. He has so much confidence in my abilities that he can see only complete success for us.

There is a large English ship docked in the harbor, the *Isabella*, and we will be celebrating New Year's Eve on her decks. On the morrow, we will be off across the waters towards Liverpool, where we will begin our efforts to bring my paintings to the masses.

Owen will be doing his part, I am sure. I can't imagine anyone seated in a court or castle dining hall or gallery who won't be mesmerized by his stories of the vast American West. The vision of the enormous buffalo herds alone will be enough to make each listener intent.

He intends to have me unveil paintings of the landscapes and the Indian people we have met and known. Once the audience sees the image, he will tell the story behind it.

I cannot imagine that we won't do very well everywhere we go. I have already written Mother in England to let her know that I have found Lucy James and that everything is wonderful between us. I wanted Mother to know also that I hold nothing against her for the years of secrecy. It must have been very difficult to hold it in for so long.

I will be sorry to leave Lucy, my real mother, with

whom I have developed a very close and special bond. But she knows that I'll be back and with a great many stories for her. I've promised to set money aside for good causes and if she so desires, she can help me decide where to donate. She's so content living with the natives that there is little doubt that she will want to do anything else with her life.

I can understand how she feels. I will miss this paradise. I watch the sea fowl circle in great flocks overhead to alight on the great waters, and I watch the otters at play, and I cannot think of spending my time doing anything but relaxing on the shore.

But Owen will bring me back very soon. He will again take me into the mountains to dig roots and to view the skies above the peaks at dawn and sunset. And we'll come back here and take our honeymoon canoe into the calm waters at the mouth of the Columbia, and I'll once again reach up into the night sky and let those beautiful Northern Lights flow over my fingertips.